SHERRYL WOODS

STARLIT SECRETS

The Delacourt Scandal and
The Paternity Test

mira

mira™

Recycling programs for this product may not exist in your area.

ISBN-13: 978-0-7783-6953-0

Starlit Secrets

Copyright © 2024 by Harlequin Enterprises ULC

The Delacourt Scandal
First published in 2000. This edition published in 2024.
Copyright © 2000 by Sherryl Woods

The Paternity Test
First published in 1998. This edition published in 2024.
Copyright © 1998 by Sherryl Woods

For questions and comments about the quality of this book, please contact us at CustomerService@Harlequin.com.

TM is a trademark of Harlequin Enterprises ULC.

Mira
22 Adelaide St. West, 41st Floor
Toronto, Ontario M5H 4E3, Canada
www.Harlequin.com

Printed in U.S.A.

CONTENTS

THE DELACOURT SCANDAL

Prologue

"Bryce Delacourt is the most powerful, sanctimonious man in all of Texas, so, yes, if you can find a way to bring him down, by all means do it," Griffin Carpenter said, his wrinkled face an inscrutable mask. Only the telltale blaze of excitement in his black eyes indicated to Maddie Kent the intensity of his passion for this particular story.

No one knew why Carpenter had it in for the power brokers of Texas, but he'd made it his life's work to expose their foibles. In his late fifties now, he'd been described alternately as an ambitious crusader or a vengeful, mean-spirited man. Maddie didn't care which he was or what his reasons were. Those were the words she had been waiting most of her life to hear, the chance she'd worked her butt off to get.

The Delacourts had ruined her family, and now they were finally going to pay. If there was so much as a hint of a scandal in their past, so much as a whiff of illegalities in their business dealings at Delacourt Oil, she would find it. And she would expose them for the heartless, rotten human beings they were behind their facade of generosity and family loyalty and perfection.

Her own passion for the hunt had been a long time building. She had been ten when her father had come home one day to announce that he'd been fired, cast aside because of a simple mistake that anyone could have made. As he told it, it had been nothing more than an accounting error that should have meant nothing to someone with the Delacourt wealth.

But Bryce Delacourt was a hard man, and so Frank Kent found himself out of work without a reference. He would never work as an accountant again, at least not for a company of any size or respectability. Delacourt had seen to that.

The humiliation of it had broken the man Maddie had adored. For five years, his self-esteem in tatters, he had moved from one dead-end job to another, never earning more than minimum wage. His family had suffered far more due to his increasing depression than because of the lack of income. The warm, generous man who'd been involved in every aspect of his children's lives was gone, lost in lonely, self-imposed isolation and bitterness.

When Maddie was fifteen, her father committed suicide. He'd almost botched the attempt and had lain in a coma for two horrendous weeks before finally getting his wish and dying.

That final act of a sad and desperate man had all but destroyed the family, financially and emotionally. Maddie's mother had retreated into her own private hell, aided by alcohol. Her brothers had turned into street thugs to get what they wanted. Only Maddie had used that defining moment to strengthen her resolve to succeed. She had vowed at her father's grave that one day she would be in a position to make the Delacourts feel that same kind of pain.

Now, thanks to Griffin Carpenter, she had her chance. She didn't care why Carpenter hated Bryce Delacourt or any of the others who fell victim to his paper's venom. It was enough that the publisher's agenda matched her own. Most newspapers in the state were in awe of the Delacourt wealth and power, but Carpenter had his own resources and a pit bull's tenacity when it came to digging up dirt on the entrenched power brokers of the state.

Carpenter's Dallas-based tabloid, *Hard Truths,* was a wealthy Texan's worst nightmare. His reporters turned over rocks and crept through back alleys in search of scandal. More often than not, they found it, then took delight in sharing it with the public in the most colorful terms possible.

It was not the sort of journalism Maddie had trained for or respected. She'd attended one of the nation's best journalism schools, taken her fair share of courses in media ethics and responsibility. And she intended to follow all of those rules with absolute diligence—once she had written this one exposé....

For now, though, she was happy to be Carpenter's newest recruit, and she intended to be his best. In no time at all the Delacourts would be making headlines, and for once it wouldn't be on the society or business pages. She planned to make them the talk of Texas, until they understood humiliation as intimately as her father had.

She gazed across the wide mahogany expanse of

Griffin Carpenter's desk, straight into eyes glinting with anticipation.

"I won't let you down," she vowed to her boss.

Then she mentally whispered the same words to the father she had lost so long ago.

One

Tyler couldn't help noticing the woman sitting at the other end of the bar. She had been there for the past week. Petite, with auburn hair cut boyishly short, she had a sweet face with a very kissable mouth—innocence and the promise of sin combined. Tonight she was wearing a prim little white blouse and a bright red skirt that kept creeping up, revealing a very shapely thigh. More of that intriguing innocence-sin contradiction.

She was a plucky little thing, fending off passes with a few words and an engaging smile, nursing what appeared to be ginger ale. What she was doing here in the first place was beyond him. She wasn't looking for a man, that was clear enough. Nor did she drink. And yet here she was at O'Reilly's, night after night, same stool, same bland, disinterested expression, same polite brush-offs.

In times past Tyler would have taken that as a challenge. Harmless flirting with a beautiful woman was second nature to him, as it had been to his brothers.

Any one of the Delacourt males would have moved closer and satisfied his curiosity.

At the moment, though, Tyler just wasn't up to his usual casual banter.

He had way too much on his mind. His whole future, for instance.

Until a week ago he'd been out on a rig in the Gulf of Mexico off the Louisiana coast for three straight months, trying to forget the past, trying to lose himself in hard, physical, mind-numbing work. At the end of the day all he cared about was a cold beer, a rare steak and sleep. That was the way he wanted it, the way he *needed* his life to be—clear and uncomplicated.

Women were a definite complication. Family was both a blessing and a curse. He'd intended to steer clear of both for the foreseeable future.

Then the edict had come down that all Delacourts were required to be in Houston for his parents' fortieth anniversary bash. Even Trish, who never came back to Houston if she could avoid it, had been corralled into attending. Only his brother Michael had escaped, because he and Grace were away on their honeymoon.

There was nothing on earth Tyler hated more than being all dressed up in a fancy tux, unless it was being back in an office. In the past week he'd found himself in both these situations.

And if Bryce Delacourt had his way, Tyler would stay in Houston indefinitely. Judging from his father's offhand comments, Tyler had a hunch that this time it was going to be a whole lot harder to wrangle his way out of the Delacourt Oil corporate headquarters and back onto a rig. He envied Trish and Dylan their escapes to the peace and tranquility of Los Piños all the way across the state. They were back there now, out of their father's reach, while Tyler was still here, still very much under his thumb.

He took a sip of his beer and wondered if the time hadn't finally come to cut the family ties completely—professionally speaking, anyway. He wouldn't be the only one in the family to do it.

His oldest brother, Dylan, had been the first to shun the family business, infuriating their father by setting up shop as a private eye. Then Trish had managed to slip away to another city, have a baby and open her second bookstore—all before their father had caught up with her just in time to see her wed a rancher. Jeb had one foot in Dylan's business, which he'd moved to Los Piños after his marriage to a pediatrician there, and another at corporate headquarters, but he managed to stay out from under Bryce Delacourt's control most of the time.

Only Michael relished being at the helm of a multinational oil company and, ironically, their father couldn't seem to see that he was the only one really suited for the job. Usually Michael provided adequate cover for Tyler, but his current absence had reminded their father that he had one remaining son he could groom for the executive suite.

More than the others, Tyler hated the thought of disappointing his father, but he hated paperwork even more. He shuddered at the prospect of facing a lifetime of it. There were oil companies around the country—around the world, for that matter—that would be happy to hire someone with his lifelong history in the business, with his expertise and willingness to work endless hours, with his daring and fearless approach to oil exploration. Maybe it was time to check into some of them. Maybe it was time to stop worrying so much about being a dutiful Delacourt and worry more about being himself.

His thoughts dark, he barely glanced up when the woman from the other end of the bar slid onto the stool next to him. For once the prospect of an evening's flirtation didn't do a thing to lighten his mood. He just wanted to be left alone to wrestle with the past and with the decision that had to be made about the future.

"Hi," she said, leveling amber eyes straight at him until he finally met her gaze.

"Hi, yourself."

"I've seen you here before."

"Every night this week," he agreed, turning back to the beer he'd been nursing, hoping she would take the hint and go away.

"I thought you'd make a pass by now."

The offhand observation caught his attention. He regarded her with a wry look. "Did you now?"

"You're the only male in this place who hasn't." She made the claim with a surprising lack of conceit and just a hint of puzzlement.

Tyler regarded her with amusement. "Since you turned down every one of them, I figured I'd cut my losses and save myself the trouble."

"Then you were interested?"

"Any male with blood still pumping through his veins is interested in an attractive female."

Suddenly her expression brightened. "You think I'm attractive?"

He shook his head. "Don't be coy. Of course you are."

"*I* know that," she said with a touch of impatience. "I just wasn't sure if *you* did. I wasn't certain you'd even noticed me. You looked kind of lost, as if you were off in another world and not too happy about it. That's why I decided to break my rule."

"What rule is that?"

"I never, ever, talk to men I don't know, not without a proper introduction. I'm Maddie, by the way. Maddie Kent. It's Madison, technically, but whoever heard of a woman named that? I think it was a family name on my mother's side. She was convinced it could be traced back to James Madison, but I never saw any proof of it." She beamed at him. "Who are you?"

"Tyler," he said, deliberately leaving off his last name. Mention of "Delacourt" in this part of Texas tended to stir up all sorts of reactions that had more to do with his father or the family wealth than him. He'd learned to hedge his bets when he first met a woman, see if her reactions were genuine before he laid his full identity on her.

"Why are you here, Maddie?" he asked. He gestured toward the ginger ale. "It's obvious you're not a big drinker."

"I just got to town a couple of weeks ago and moved into this neighborhood. This seems like a nice place. It's definitely better than going back to an empty apartment."

Something about the comment stirred Tyler's suspicions. If she was here to stave off loneliness, then why not accept the attentions of one of the men who'd approached her? Why come here if she had such a hard-and-fast rule about not talking to strangers? And why zero in on the one man who hadn't made a pass at her?

Just because she liked a challenge? Or because she knew precisely who he was, after all?

"You've had quite a few admirers the last couple of days. Why have you rejected all of them?" he asked.

"I told you. I have a rule. Besides, they were looking for more than a little friendly conversation. You can tell, you know, at least if you're a woman."

Tyler definitely knew. On any other night of any other week, he might have been one of them, and chit-chat would have been the last thing on his mind. He enjoyed flirting, but the prospect of making the occasional conquest made it more interesting. It kept his mind off another woman, one who'd slipped out of his life when he'd least expected it and now was lost to him forever.

"So you came over here because I looked safe enough?" he asked.

"Exactly."

"Darlin', I wouldn't count on it. The only difference between those men and me is that I've got a lot more than sex on my mind these days."

She didn't bat an eye at that. "Tell me. I'm a good listener. Maybe I can help."

He studied her eager expression and wondered if an impartial outsider could offer a perspective on his life that he hadn't yet considered. The trouble was, he'd made it a rule not to share any of his deepest longings and ambitions with anyone—and especially not a woman. Not since Jen.

From the moment they'd met, he'd told Jennifer Grayson everything.

She'd led a tough life but had come through it with a surprisingly sweet and gentle nature. He'd given her his heart. Hell, he'd even gotten her pregnant and given her a baby, but she'd steadfastly refused his offer of marriage, wouldn't take a penny of support money for their daughter, wouldn't accept the gifts he'd sent. She'd insisted she could make it on her own, without any charity from some rich Texan whose family would only look down on her because she'd come from the wrong side of the tracks.

Talk about reverse snobbery. Jen had had it in spades. Nothing he'd said could persuade her that his offers were motivated by love not pity. He had admired her pride, even as it had exasperated him. He'd accepted her terms, because she'd given him no choice.

Jen and his baby girl, his precious Rachel, had lived in Baton Rouge, conveniently nearby whenever he had time off from his work on the Delacourt rigs in the Gulf of Mexico. Despite her refusal to marry him, Jen had been the best thing in his life.

Even so, he had never shared her existence with his family. She'd accused him of being ashamed of her, but the truth was that at first he'd just wanted something that was his alone, not part of the Delacourt dynasty, not subjected to media scrutiny. Jen had been his secret and his joy.

The time had come, though, after the baby was born, when he'd wanted his family to know everything, wanted them to get to know Jen, even if their relationship was unconventional. Six months ago, after endless arguments, he had finally persuaded her to come to Houston and meet his parents. He had held such high hopes for that trip. He'd been so sure that once she got over that hurdle, Jen would see that she could fit in, that she would be accepted just because he loved her.

In one last surge of stubborn pride, she had insisted on driving, rather than accompanying him in the company jet. He had agreed, to his everlasting regret. En route there had been an accident. The crash had occurred after midnight, and the police suspected Jen had fallen asleep at the wheel, though they would never know for sure. There were no other cars involved, and there had been no witnesses. Jen and Rachel had both died at the scene.

From that moment on Tyler had descended into his own personal hell of guilt and loneliness, made worse because he'd refused to share his torment with anyone. He'd considered the silent suffering to be his penance for pressing her to do something she hadn't really wanted to do.

That was another reason he didn't want to leave Louisiana. All of his memories of Jen and the baby were in Baton Rouge. And when they got to be too much for him, he needed the demanding work on the rig to exhaust him. The waking memories were difficult enough, but the nightmares about that crash were a thousand times worse. At home this last week he'd awakened every single night in a cold, drenching sweat, heart pounding, tears running unchecked down his cheeks.

His family knew something was terribly wrong, but he refused to talk about it. Michael had even made the trip to Baton Rouge to see him before his wedding to Grace. His brother had poked and prodded for two straight days, but Tyler hadn't been ready to reveal a whole part of his life he had kept secret for years. He still wasn't. Someday he would be able to talk about

Jen, but not yet, not even to the brother who knew him better than anyone on earth.

He sighed heavily.

"Hey, where'd you go?" Maddie asked, snapping him back to the present.

"Just thinking about someone I used to know," he admitted without meaning to.

Her eyes brightened with curiosity. "Were you in love with her?"

"I was."

"And she loved you?"

"She said she did."

"What happened?"

"Stuff," he said, because talking about the tragedy wouldn't change anything, and he'd already said more than he should have.

"You don't want to talk about it," she concluded.

"Brilliant deduction."

"Then tell me about yourself. What do you do, Tyler with no last name?"

So, he thought, she had caught the deliberate omission. "I work on an oil rig, or at least that's what I did last week. This week it's hard to say."

"Did you lose your job?" she asked, regarding him sympathetically.

"Not the way you mean." This was not a conversation he intended to have, not with a stranger, not tonight. "Look, Maddie Kent, it's been nice talking to you, but I've got to run." He tossed some bills on the bar. "That ought to take care of your drink. Welcome to Houston. Maybe I'll see you again sometime."

"Maybe so," she said cheerfully, showing neither surprise nor hurt that he was walking out on her.

Only after he was outside, sitting in his car and wondering what the heck he was going to do with himself for the rest of the evening, did he regret his impulsive decision. If nothing else, Maddie with the kissable lips might have provided a much-needed distraction from his dark thoughts. He thought of that blend of innocence and sex appeal and sighed. Then again, she might be nothing but trouble.

Maddie watched Tyler Delacourt walk out of the bar and barely concealed a little smile of satisfaction. She'd made progress tonight. She'd actually held a conversation of sorts with a Delacourt. A civil conversation, at that.

Based on all of her research, she had a feeling that of all of Bryce Delacourt's sons Tyler might be the one person who could get her into the bosom of the tight-knit family.

Finding him hadn't been all that difficult. His name and picture had popped up in old society-page items with great regularity. That had stopped a couple of years back, but in the meantime it had given her a starting point. Many of those items mentioned O'Reilly's as his favorite watering hole.

They also mentioned his reputation as an outrageous flirt. At one point one columnist had kept a running count of the number of women with whom he'd been spotted. Whatever his past habits, Maddie had seen no evidence that he was womanizing these days.

In fact, he'd looked so down, so totally alone, that she'd almost felt sorry for him. If he had been anyone other than a Delacourt, she wouldn't have let him get away without convincing him to spill his guts. Since he *was* a Delacourt, she had known she had to proceed with caution, not scare him off with her limitless curiosity.

She flipped open her cell phone and called Griffin Carpenter, as promised.

"I made contact tonight," she told him.

"With Delacourt?"

"No, with his son, Tyler. There's something going on with him."

"We're looking for something on Bryce, not his son."

"But if I can get Tyler to open up, to trust me enough to confide in me, I'm in. He'll pave the way with the rest of the family."

"That's your angle?" Griffin asked worriedly. "Maddie, watch yourself. Tyler's got a reputation with women. At least, he did before he started spending so much time out of town, working on that rig over in Louisiana. Forget about Tyler. Why not get a job at the company, something that'll give you access to their files?"

She wasn't about to explain that any, even the most superficial, background check by Delacourt Oil's personnel office would reveal her link to a man who'd once been fired. They'd never hire her.

"I like my way better. I can handle Tyler," she assured her boss. "I'll be in touch."

She put the cell phone back in her purse and thought about the man who'd just left. Thank heaven he wasn't her type. With his blond hair, dimpled smile and muscled build, he was too good-looking by far, too used to having women swoon at the sight of him, no doubt.

When she'd first seen him a few nights ago, she had

been surprised by his preference for jeans and chambray shirts, rather than fancy suits; for sturdy work boots, rather than expensive cowboy boots. He'd told her he worked on an oil rig, and he certainly looked as if he could handle hard work. In fact, she could imagine him out on a rig in the blazing sun, his chest bare, muscles rippling. The unexpected image left her mouth surprisingly dry.

Where had that come from? she wondered, not one bit pleased by the reaction.

"You need another drink?" the bartender asked.

Maddie nodded. When the ginger ale came, she drank it down in one long gulp, but it didn't seem to do much for her parched throat. This wasn't good, not good at all.

Repeat after me, she instructed herself. Tyler Delacourt is the son of the man who destroyed your father. Therefore, Tyler Delacourt is a despicable toad. Tyler Delacourt is pond scum.

Tyler Delacourt is the sexiest man I've ever met.

Maddie moaned at the traitorous thought. This assignment had just gotten a whole lot more complicated. Maybe she would be better off trying to slide her credentials past personnel and accepting some bland, innocuous job taking dictation at Delacourt Oil.

With a shudder she dismissed the idea. Tyler Delacourt was vulnerable.

She had seen it in his bleak expression. Her hormones had never been a problem before. She could certainly keep them in check now. She was too close to her goal to let anything—least of all a handsome Delacourt—get in her way.

Two

Tyler avoided O'Reilly's—and the very disconcerting Maddie—for the next few nights. In fact, he pretty much stayed in his apartment for a solid week, sorting through the options he had for the rest of his life. He ignored the phone, letting his answering machine take messages, most of which were from his increasingly impatient father. There was no getting away from the fact that the time had come to make a decision, and no matter which one he made, there was going to be hell to pay.

When he got a call from Daniel Corrigan, supervisor of operations on the rig and Tyler's boss, Tyler thought about ignoring it, too, but something in Daniel's voice as he left a curt message told him that he shouldn't. He snatched up the phone just as the older man was about to hang up.

"Daniel, what's up?"

"Good. You're there. Now the question is, when are you coming back here?"

"Why? Is there a problem?"

"That's what I want to know. I had a call from your

father this morning telling me not to expect you back. I wanted to hear it from you before I filled the position. I told him that, too. I figured if you'd decided to quit, you owed it to me to call yourself." He hesitated then added wryly, "It also occurred to me that you might not know about it."

It looked as if the matter was about to be snatched out of Tyler's hands, unless he took some decisive action. He muttered a harsh expletive under his breath, then assured Daniel, "I'll take care of it."

"That's not really answering my question now, is it, Tyler?"

"Look, I'm sorry you're caught in the middle on this. I'm trying to work it out. For now, though, don't fill that job, not until you hear from me."

"Anything I can do to help, like reminding you that you're the best man I've got on the job over here?"

Tyler couldn't help being pleased by the compliment. Daniel Corrigan was an incredibly demanding man, one of the best the company had, Tyler's father conceded, even though there was some bad blood between the two men.

Daniel had been with Delacourt Oil for most of his life. He was loyal to the company, but even more fiercely loyal to the men who risked their lives working the rigs. He'd tried a desk job briefly nearly thirty years earlier, but by grudging mutual agreement with Bryce Delacourt, he'd gone back to working the rigs. Bryce had never entirely forgiven Daniel for abandoning the corporate role he'd been offered. Tyler assumed that was the main source of the friction between them.

In addition, it was evident that his father didn't much like the bond that had formed years earlier between

Daniel and Tyler. The older man had taken Tyler under his wing when he'd first expressed an interest in learning the business literally from the ground up. Even though Bryce was no longer in any position to spend time in the oil fields with a curious young boy, he'd been resentful of turning the task over to another man. Stubborn, even as a kid, and sure of his own interests, Tyler had had to badger him into it.

Now, when Tyler didn't respond, Daniel sighed heavily. "I suppose this is none of my business, but is this mood you're obviously in really about work?"

"Of course it is," Tyler insisted, guessing where his boss might be headed.

"You sure of that? Or is it about Jen? I know that accident tore you up inside. You've been brooding about it for months now. Have you even told your family what happened?"

Tyler regretted ever telling his boss about Jen, but at the time he'd felt he had no choice. He'd had to give Daniel a way to reach him if he was unexpectedly needed on the rig. As a result Daniel had been the one who'd come into Baton Rouge personally to deliver the news when Tyler's father had suffered a heart attack a year ago. He'd also been the one to break the news about the accident. The police had found Daniel's office number in Jen's purse as an emergency means to contact Tyler. Despite all that, it didn't mean the man had a right to go picking at the scabs on Tyler's emotional wounds.

"Daniel—"

"You listen to me," his boss said sharply, ignoring the warning note in Tyler's voice. "What happened wasn't your fault."

"You don't know—"

"I know all I need to know," Daniel retorted gruffly. "I saw how much you loved that woman and your daughter. You gave them everything Jen would let you. I've watched you suffering ever since they died. Grieving's normal, but at some point you have to move on."

Tyler sighed. "Okay, you're right. It's just not easy."

"Of course it's not. If it were, it wouldn't say much about the love you two shared, now would it? My best advice? Get your sorry butt over here and get back to work."

"If it were up to me, that is *exactly* what I'd do."

"Who's it up to, if not you?"

"You know Dad," Tyler said wryly. "Michael's away, so he's staring around the corporate offices looking for a likely substitute. No matter how many times I explain it to him, he just doesn't get the fact that I hate the whole suit-and-tie routine."

"Wear blue jeans and an oil-stained T-shirt to the office," Daniel suggested. "Maybe then he'll get the picture."

"Maybe then he'll have another heart attack," Tyler countered, not entirely in jest. "You know how he feels about the Delacourt image."

"You can't live your life for your father," Daniel reminded him mildly. "I'm not trying to tell you what to do. I'm just saying it's your life, and when it's over, you're the one who'll have to live with any regrets. Personally, I figure the fewer I go out of here with, the better."

That philosophy held a lot of appeal for Tyler, too. "Don't fill that job just yet," he said again. "I promise I'll get back to you."

"Don't take too long. I'm getting too blasted old to be doing all the hard labor in your place."

Tyler laughed. Daniel Corrigan could outlift and outscramble any man working for him, Tyler included. "Let me know when you're ready to retire, old man. Maybe I'll apply for that cushy job of yours."

"Funny, kid. Very funny. I'll give you till the end of next week. Then I'm hiring somebody who hasn't got such a smart mouth."

"Whatever you say." His grin faded. "Thanks, Daniel. I owe you."

"You do indeed, and I intend to keep reminding you of it."

Tyler slowly replaced the receiver, then switched off the answering machine. Based on Daniel's news, the clock was definitely ticking. He'd better have a decision before morning, and the strength of will to defend it. He needed total quiet and solitude to think this through. That and a pot of industrial-strength coffee to clear the cobwebs out of his brain.

He was on his third cup of coffee and his twelfth *final* decision when he was startled by a quiet, but insistent knock on his door. He stared at the closed door, trying to imagine who might be on the other side. Nobody got past the doorman downstairs without Tyler's okay, not even family. And if his father had somehow managed it, there would have been nothing subtle about the knock. Bryce Delacourt would have been pounding on the wood to announce his displeasure with Tyler's refusal to take his calls.

Since there had been no call upstairs, whoever it was couldn't possibly know he was inside. Therefore, if he just ignored that incessant tapping, it would eventually stop. Or so he hoped.

Instead, he heard the scrape of a key in the lock, the

murmur of voices, then saw the knob slowly twist. He was on his feet in a heartbeat.

"What the hell?" he demanded, jerking the door the rest of the way open and dragging a very startled Maddie Kent with it. "You!"

He stared from her to the apologetic doorman. "Rodney, what is the meaning of this?"

"She said you hadn't been answering your phone. She said you'd been very upset and she was concerned about you. Since you hadn't said anything about leaving town again and I hadn't seen you for a couple of days myself, I figured it was worth checking out."

Tyler raked a hand through his hair. How could he blow a gasket over the man's very real concern? Rodney was a valuable building employee precisely because he cared about the condo owners and paid close attention to their security and well-being. The elderly owners considered him a friend.

Maddie was another story.

Tyler patted the doorman on his back. "It's okay, Rodney."

The man regarded him with genuine dismay. "It won't happen again, sir." He backed away. "Let me know if you need anything."

Other than peace and quiet, Tyler couldn't imagine what that might be.

Rodney disappeared on the elevator, leaving Maddie behind. "Mind telling me what you're doing here?" he asked.

"Your doorman pretty much summed it up. You haven't been at O'Reilly's. No one's seen you since the other night."

"So?"

"You weren't in the best mood," she said, as if that were somehow significant.

"And that would be your business because…?"

Her gaze clashed with his, not wavering by so much as the flicker of an eyelash. Those amber eyes glowed with warmth and concern. "I was worried, that's all."

To his amazement, she sounded as if she actually meant it. What had she thought might happen? "Maddie, I drop out of sight all the time. Usually I'm back out on some rig."

"But you're not there now, are you?" she pointed out reasonably.

"No, but…"

"So, something could have been wrong."

"But it's not."

"Thank goodness," she retorted fervently.

He regarded her with suspicion. "How did you know where to find me? I never even told you my last name."

"O'Reilly told me. He was worried, too."

Tyler laughed at that. Kevin O'Reilly rarely worried about his patrons unless their bar tabs weren't up-to-date. More likely, he'd just fallen for little Ms. Kent's innocent act of concern.

"He *was*," she claimed indignantly. "He told me exactly where to find you. Said you owed him one." A frown knit her brow. "I'm not sure what he meant by that."

Tyler knew. O'Reilly obviously thought he'd been doing Tyler a favor by delivering a sexy little package straight to his doorstep. "I'll have to speak to O'Reilly about minding his own business."

"He seems like a very nice man, very helpful."

"Yes, I suppose you would see it that way." He

sighed. "Well, now that you're here, I suppose you might as well come on in and have something to drink. I'm fresh out of ginger ale, though."

"Juice, water, whatever you have," she said agreeably. She was already wandering around the apartment, studying it with undisguised curiosity.

Tyler went into the kitchen, poured her a glass of soda, added ice, then returned to find her holding a family portrait, one taken at Christmas the year before. There was an odd expression on her face, one he couldn't quite interpret.

"Do you have a big family?" he asked.

She shook her head. "Just two brothers. Both my parents are dead."

"I'm sorry. Do you spend much time with your brothers?"

"Not really." She put the picture back very carefully.

There had been a few occasions when Tyler had regretted being part of such a large, tight-knit family, but seeing the sadness in Maddie's eyes, he realized once again just how lucky he really was. From time to time he and his siblings might aggravate the daylights out of each other, but they would go to the ends of the earth for each other.

And with the rest of them married and starting families of their own, the Delacourts were an impressive bunch when they all got together in one place as they had last year for the holidays. His father's heart attack had been a reminder to all of them how quickly things could change. They had vowed at the hospital never to let another holiday season pass without some sort of reunion. Last year Trish had managed to lure even their parents to Los Piños for a quiet, old-fashioned family celebration, rather than the Houston social whirl they preferred.

"That's too bad about you and your brothers," he told Maddie. "Did you have a falling out?"

"No. We just drifted apart. We don't have much in common anymore."

"I'm sorry," he said, helpless to think of anything more profound to say.

"You're very close to your family, aren't you? I can see it in the picture."

"We get along well enough—most of the time, anyway. Like all families, we have our ups and downs." After his illness, a mellower Bryce Delacourt had seemed to accept the decisions his children had made for their lives—all except Tyler, apparently.

Maddie curled up in an oversize chair facing him. "Tell me about them—I love hearing about big families. And yours is pretty much legendary here in Texas."

Since that particular cat was clearly out of the bag and she didn't seem overly impressed by it, Tyler gave her a brief rundown of the various Delacourts, right down to the most recently adopted grandchildren, Josh and Jamie, two brothers taken in by Grace and Michael, who were currently staying over on Trish's ranch in Los Piños while the newlyweds traveled on their honeymoon. Maddie listened raptly to every word he said, prodding him with questions every time he thought her curiosity must surely be satisfied.

"You have to be bored hearing all of this," he said at last. "It's like watching home movies of people you don't know or vacations you didn't share."

"No, really, I love it. Tell me more about your father. I've read about him, of course. What's he like?"

"He's stubborn, ambitious, dynamic and generally a pain in the butt," Tyler said honestly. "But we all love him just the same."

Suddenly she glanced at and then picked up a tiny framed picture of his daughter, the only one Tyler had. He froze as she studied it. Cursing the fact that he hadn't put it away as he usually did when company came over, he waited for the questions he sensed were about to come.

"Is this a niece or nephew?" she asked.

"No," he said tersely, then forced a smile. He restrained himself from snatching the picture out of her hands. Eventually she put it back in place, though her gaze kept straying back to it.

"Enough about my family," he said, when it seemed she was about to ask more questions. "Tell me more about yours. Were you very young when you lost your parents?"

"I was fifteen when my dad died," she said.

Tyler saw the pain behind her stoic expression, heard the sorrow in her voice. As irritating as he often found his father, he couldn't imagine losing him. Last year's heart attack, though mild, had scared all of them, reminding them that even the larger-than-life Bryce Delacourt was merely mortal.

"That must have been hard," he said sympathetically.

"It was."

Since she didn't seem inclined to say more, he asked, "And your mom?"

"My mother died just last year, but she was never really the same after my dad died."

Since both of them seemed to have valid reasons for not wanting to delve any more deeply into family history, Tyler changed the subject. "What do you do for a living, Maddie Kent?"

"I'm…" She turned away, then finally met his gaze. "I'm between jobs right now."

Tyler couldn't tell whether pride had put that embarrassed flush in her cheeks or whether it was because she was lying. He had spent enough time around women to sense when one wasn't being completely honest with him. And something was telling him now that Maddie Kent had been skirting the truth from the moment he'd met her.

"Is that why you came to Houston, to find work?"

She nodded. "I thought it might be easier in a big city, that there would be a lot of opportunities."

"The classifieds are definitely full of jobs. No nibbles yet?"

"Not yet, but I'm still hopeful," she said cheerfully.

"What kind of work are you looking for? I could check at Delacourt Oil. Maybe there's an opening there that would suit you."

An odd expression crossed her face, but Tyler couldn't quite interpret it. "I'm pretty flexible, actually, but I don't want you to go to any trouble. I'm sure I'll find something anyday now." There was a touch of stubborn, if admirable, pride in the lift of her chin.

"There's nothing wrong with getting a little help, Maddie. A lot of people find their jobs through networking. It's the way the corporate world works. Why do you think so many women fought to get into clubs that were open only to men? They knew that's where the men were finding out about job openings."

"Is that how you found your job?"

Tyler laughed for the first time in days. "No, I'm

afraid I got mine through nepotism, pure and simple. The truth is I'd have a hard time *not* working at Delacourt Oil."

"Then you work for your father?"

He met her bright gaze, tried to discern if there was something more than curiosity behind her questions. "Yes, unfortunately."

"On one of the company's rigs?"

"For the moment," he said tersely. "Could we talk about something else? The weather, maybe?"

"Your job's a sore point?"

"Oh, yeah," he said fervently.

"How come?"

"If you knew my father, you'd understand."

"Since I don't, why don't you explain it to me? I'm a good listener."

He was surprisingly tempted to do just that, to share all of the hopes and frustrations he'd been keeping bottled up inside since Jen's death. The mental comparison with Jen was enough to bring him up short.

"So you've said, but I've taken up enough of your time, Maddie." He stood up abruptly and looked pointedly toward the door.

Maddie didn't budge at first, but then her eyes widened. "Oh," she said softly. "You want me to go. I suppose I did burst in uninvited and disrupt your plans for the evening. I'm sorry."

Oddly enough, he realized that he didn't want her to leave, not really. And that made him more determined than ever to get her out the door. She asked too many questions. Sooner or later she would work the conversation back to that baby picture. Or to his father. Or to his job. None were topics he cared to explore just now.

Sooner or later he would have to kiss her just to shut her up. Just thinking about it made him feel disloyal to Jen's memory.

That was another thing that was worrisome about Ms. Maddie Kent. No other woman had been able to make him forget about Jen, not even for a second, but for a little while tonight he'd been aware only of the woman who'd bullied her way into his apartment simply because she was concerned about him. Somehow she had managed to banish some of his suspicions about her in the process. He'd been counting on that wariness to keep him from getting in too deep.

"Yeah," he said gruffly. "No offense, but I want you to go. It's getting late. Do you need a ride home? I can call a cab for you."

She shook her head. "My car's over by O'Reilly's. I can walk."

Tyler bit back an oath of pure frustration. "Not alone, not at this hour," he said. "I'll walk with you."

Her chin rose stubbornly. "It's a few blocks. I'll be perfectly safe."

"With me along, you will be," he agreed. "Got everything?"

She patted her purse. "Right here."

"Then let's go."

Outside, there was something about the heavy night air closing in around them that made Tyler feel as if they were still all alone. It was the kind of atmosphere that invited confidences. But instead, they walked in surprisingly companionable silence for a bit. Tyler hadn't realized Maddie could be so quiet for so long. Thrown off guard by it, he felt a sudden need to figure out what made this woman tick, to unravel the contradictions he'd sensed in her.

"Maddie, what really brought you to my place tonight?"

She regarded him with surprise. "I told you, I was concerned when you didn't show up at O'Reilly's."

"You have to admit it's unusual to take such an interest in a virtual stranger."

Her gaze met his. "Not for me."

"Then you make a habit of riding to the rescue of people you barely know?" The thought bothered him for some reason he couldn't quite explain. On some purely masculine level, he wanted to be different, which was absurd when not five minutes ago he'd feared getting any more deeply involved with her.

"Only the ones with potential," she teased lightly.

"Potential?"

"Of becoming friends."

Friends. The word echoed in his head, annoying him irrationally. Had he been misreading the signals that badly?

"Can you believe how hot and muggy it is?" she said, stealing the chance for him to question the limitation she seemed to be placing on their relationship. "It feels like rain. Maybe that will cool things off."

Because she seemed so determined to move to an impersonal, innocuous topic, Tyler deliberately gave the conversation a provocative turn.

"Some people think there's something sexy about a sultry night like this." His gaze locked with hers. "The weather gets you all hot and bothered. You start stripping off clothes till you're down to almost nothing."

Maddie swallowed hard, but she didn't look away. "Sounds…" Her voice trailed off.

"Tempting?" he inquired, amused by her sudden breathlessness, relieved that he hadn't lost his touch, after all.

She blinked away the hint of yearning in her eyes, seemed to struggle to regain her composure. "Disgustingly sweaty," she said tartly. She turned away, then stopped, looking relieved. "Here's my car."

"Well, good night, then. Drive carefully."

"I always do."

For some reason he didn't entirely understand, he impulsively captured her chin in his hand and brushed a light kiss across her lush mouth. Maybe it was just so he could catch one more glimpse of that startled flaring of heat in her eyes. He was amply rewarded for his efforts. She stared at him in openmouthed astonishment, but unfortunately that quick taste and her surprise didn't seem to be quite enough to satisfy him. Besides, her lips were soft as silk and sweet as sugar. What man could resist?

But even as he lowered his head to claim another kiss, she ducked away and slid into her car. The rejection might have stung if he hadn't noted the way her hands trembled ever so slightly before she clutched the steering wheel tightly.

"Good night," he said again, but the words were lost as she started the engine.

He watched her drive away. Then, instead of turning toward home, he headed for O'Reilly's, his throat suddenly parched. Rather than simplifying his life as he'd planned to tonight, he had a feeling he'd just made it a whole lot more complicated.

Three

This was going to be much more difficult than she'd anticipated, Maddie concluded as she drove slowly away, trying to calm her jittery nerves after that unexpected kiss. She should have seen it coming, should have steeled herself against it. After all, wasn't Tyler's easygoing flirtatiousness one of the very reasons she'd chosen him as the best Delacourt to approach?

However, her instantaneous reaction was a warning. She had to get a grip, find some way to avoid being alone with him on hot, sultry nights that held the promise of romance in the air. Otherwise this investigation of hers was going to get very dicey.

And, unfortunately, that wasn't the only potential problem she'd discovered tonight. She'd also realized that the man didn't trust her. Apparently she wasn't nearly as good at deception as she'd hoped to be. He'd watched her suspiciously from the instant she'd arrived on his doorstep, then deftly skirted many of her questions. Obviously, she was going to have to work harder to gain his trust.

Of course, the worst glitch of all, the most unexpected was the fact that she instinctively liked him.

Hormones were one thing, but actually relating to the man was something else entirely—and in some ways even more seductive and dangerous. Tyler was a funny, low-key kind of guy, surprisingly unpretentious for a man with the Delacourt wealth and standing in the community. Under other circumstances...

She caught herself before that particular thought could take shape. The circumstances were what they were. She couldn't let herself like Tyler, or any other Delacourt. If that meant reminding herself that they were the enemy a hundred times a day, then that was exactly what she had to do. She was up to her fiftieth reminder so far tonight, and the message apparently wasn't getting through.

Unfortunately, she was as certain as ever that Tyler was the key to getting what she needed. All of her preliminary research indicated that his brothers and his sister were leading exemplary lives. And since Tyler was the only remaining bachelor, he was the only one who was readily accessible to her. It had been easy enough to discover his usual routine, the places he tended to haunt. O'Reilly's was one, but there were more locations where she was certain she could bump into him "accidentally" to keep the contact alive.

After all, if there were skeletons in anyone's closet, Tyler would know.

Whether she could get him to reveal the information was something else entirely. Although he'd given a cursory sketch of the various family members willingly enough, he had definitely balked whenever she'd pressed for details. Was that natural reticence, protectiveness of their privacy...or something more? Were there secrets he was trying to guard?

During her first couple of years in journalism, Maddie had gotten used to being in an adversarial position with some of the people she interviewed. She was putting them on the spot, asking them about things they might not want their neighbors to read about over their morning coffee. She'd developed a technique for disarming them, straightforward honesty tinged with sympathy. She told them up-front that, like it or not, the story was going to appear in the paper, but she was giving them a chance to shape it in their favor by telling their side. It almost always worked.

She could hardly do that with Tyler. Unlike the everyday assignments she'd had for her first small daily newspaper, she had to work undercover on this one, get as much information as she could before approaching Bryce Delacourt armed with the facts that would bring him down or, at the very least, publicly humiliate him.

But as she'd learned tonight, the deception was definitely going to be trickier than she'd anticipated. It went against her natural penchant for the truth, which was what had brought her into journalism in the first place. But in this case she was convinced that the end justified the means. She tried not to dwell on the fact that the saying originated with Machiavelli, the princely advisor renowned for his duplicity.

Remember the goal, she reminded herself sternly. Retribution, revenge...whatever it was called, it was going to make a few uncomfortable weeks of staying in Tyler Delacourt's face—a few weeks of lying to him worthwhile.

When she reached the small but well-furnished apartment that Griffin Carpenter had arranged for her, she opened her purse and took out the tiny, voice-activated recorder. Flipping on the tape, she listened again to Tyler's description of his family. Despite herself, she was filled with an inexplicable envy. He had grown up surrounded by the kind of love, the kind of security, she and her brothers *should* have had, the kind Bryce Delacourt's arrogant, hard-hearted actions had cost them.

An image of the Delacourt family portrait, taken last Christmas, flashed in her head. She had been struck by how happy they'd looked. She'd almost been able to hear the sounds of teasing and laughter as the camera recorded the moment. And in the center of the group sat Bryce Delacourt, the subject of their devotion, the man they all looked up to.

What a contrast to her own holiday season last year. Her mother's funeral had been held the day after Thanksgiving. Maddie hadn't even been able to locate her brothers to notify them. She had stood all alone beside the grave, mourning the woman she had really lost years before.

That was the moment she had formulated her precise plans for bringing down the Delacourts. The rest of the holidays had passed in a blur. She had spent the intervening months looking at back issues of newspapers around the state trying to determine which one might be open to such an exposé.

Hard Truths, as distasteful as she found its tactics and reporting to be, had clearly been her best shot.

Remember the goal, she had reminded herself a dozen times as she had placed that first, fateful call to Griffin Carpenter to arrange an interview. It appeared she was going to have to repeat that refrain a lot before all was said and done.

When her tape of the conversation with Tyler ended, she began making notes of everything else she could recall about the evening, from the decor of his apartment to his sexily rumpled appearance. She tried not to linger too much over the latter because it kept bringing her back to the kiss, and that was definitely not a memory she wanted to encourage.

"Think, Maddie," she ordered herself sternly. "Did he say anything, anything at all that could be a lead?"

It was less what he'd said than what he *hadn't* said, she finally concluded, thinking of his curt responses to many of her questions. Then there was the fact that he'd clammed up about that baby picture. That was promising.

Who was it? she wondered. Not a niece or nephew. He'd said that much. Then why not just say it was a cousin or a friend's child or any of the other myriad innocent explanations he could have given? Why had he looked as if he'd wanted to snatch it out of her hands?

Could the child be his? He'd never been married, according to her research, but that didn't mean he hadn't fathered a child. An illegitimate Delacourt baby wasn't the scandal she'd been hoping for, but it would make for some great headlines just the same.

Even as the thought occurred to her, she winced. It wasn't Tyler Delacourt she wanted to bring down or embarrass. It was his father. The baby picture might be a lead, but if it turned out to be linked to Tyler, would she use it just because he and Bryce shared the same last name? She honestly didn't know.

And for one tiny moment she wasn't sure she liked what that said about her or this path she was heading down.

After nursing a single beer for an hour at O'Reilly's and giving the bar owner a good deal of grief about sending Maddie on her supposed mission of mercy,

Tyler eventually went home. To his surprise, the apartment felt a whole lot emptier. Had that brief visit by Maddie counteracted years of solitude here, made him yearn for the female companionship he'd lost after Jen's death? This apartment had always been a bachelor pad, a retreat. Even before he'd met Jen, he'd rarely brought a woman here, preferring to visit his dates at their homes. This place had been his sanctuary.

So why, suddenly, was he so restless in his own world? Was it because of the woman whose lips had been warm and yielding under his? Or was it simply because of the decision he'd been alternately wrestling with and avoiding for the past few days?

He was still holding the same internal debate in the morning. Because he'd tired of it, he grabbed up the newspaper and headed down the block to a restaurant that specialized in strong coffee and greasy food. Today he needed eggs, bacon and hash browns, not gourmet bran muffins or wholewheat pancakes. Maybe once he was fortified with a hearty breakfast, he'd be able to handle a meeting with his father. Maybe he'd even produce a compromise they could both live with.

At nine o'clock the place was still bustling with its own form of bluecollar power breakfast. The waitresses were sassy, the service quick. Tyler had a steaming plate of food in front of him before he could scan the frontpage headlines. He had company before he could taste the first forkful.

"Looks dangerous," Maddie observed, staring at the eggs swimming in butter and the strips of crisp bacon.

Tyler thought *she* looked a whole lot more dangerous in her snug-fitting tank top and thigh-skimming skirt.

Her hair looked as if she'd done little more than run her fingers through it. The effect was rumpled and sexy and had an effect on his pulse he didn't like one bit.

"What brings you to a place like this if you don't like the menu?" he asked.

"The coffee," she said at once. "It's lethal."

He grinned at that. "It is indeed." His gaze strayed over her formfitting outfit. "Going job hunting?"

She returned his gaze with an innocent expression. "You disapprove?"

"Darlin', I could never disapprove of anything that shows your assets to such advantage, but it might just be a tad underdressed for the average office."

"Maybe I'm not looking for an office job."

"What, then? Or should I ask? Vice squad maybe?"

She frowned at him. "You do disapprove."

Tyler wasn't sure why he was making such an issue of it. What Maddie wore was none of his business. Maybe it had something to do with the fact that every man's mouth had dropped open when she'd walked in. He'd instinctively wanted to wrap her in a blanket and bundle her off to someplace out of view.

No, he corrected, what he'd really wanted to do was pummel those men until they thought twice about staring, then take her somewhere private and strip away the scanty attire she *was* wearing. Bad ideas, both of them. "Just a little friendly job-hunting advice," he said mildly. "First impressions count, and this isn't freewheeling California or trendy New York. We're in Texas, darlin'."

"I'll keep that in mind."

To his surprise her eyes were bright with amusement as she sipped her coffee and watched him over the rim of the cup. He deliberately turned his attention to his food.

"So, what are your plans for the day?" she asked.

"As soon as I've eaten, I'm going to drop by the office."

"Really?" She did her own slow survey of his jeans and dark-blue Tshirt. "A little underdressed for the executive suite, aren't you?"

Tyler scowled. "Okay, touché. But unlike you, I already have a job, and I'm definitely well acquainted with the boss. I doubt he'll fire me."

Of course, as he'd told Daniel the day before, his father might very well grumble about his lack of attention to corporate image. Maybe that was why he'd deliberately chosen these particular clothes this morning, just to goad his father into remembering who he was: Tyler, not his clotheshorse brother Michael, who had standing appointments to have his suits custom tailored.

Maddie studied him, her expression thoughtful. "But you'd like him to, wouldn't you?"

Tyler was startled by the observation. "Like him to do what? Fire me?"

"Yes."

"Of course not."

"Are you sure about that?" she probed. "You never really got into what it was that had you so down, but I'm guessing from a couple of offhand remarks you made that it has something to do with work. You apparently love working on the rig, yet you're here. What's that all about?"

"Command performance," he said succinctly. "I'll be back in the Gulf of Mexico in no time."

"Really?"

One way or another, he would be, he decided right then. This constant push-pull for power between him and his father had to stop. Now was as good a time as any to make it happen.

"Really," he said very firmly.

"Why do I have the feeling that you just came to a decision about something?" she asked.

"Because I did," Tyler said, shoving his plate away and tossing down his napkin. He took one last swallow of coffee, then stood. "Thanks, Maddie Kent. Order something. Breakfast's on me."

"Why?"

He grinned. "Just because."

"You're a very enigmatic man, Tyler Delacourt."

"I certainly hope so." In fact, he'd always been the most tight-lipped of the Delacourts, the one who displayed a lot of flash and dazzle for the world but kept his innermost thoughts to himself.

Why, then, had Maddie Kent—a woman who'd known him for only a few days—been able to read him like a book? He had a feeling he'd better figure that out soon, before she zeroed in on things he'd never shared with anyone.

In the meantime he had his father to deal with. He arrived at Delacourt Oil twenty minutes later and went straight to his father's office.

"You sure you want to go in there?" his father's secretary asked. "You've been avoiding his calls. He is not amused."

"All the more reason to get this over with," Tyler said. "You might want to go to the coffee shop in case there's fallout from the explosion."

She winked at him. "I can take it. I've known the man since before you were born. He doesn't scare me."

"Then you're the only one."

Tyler drew in a deep breath and opened the door. His father was on the phone. He scowled at the interruption, but when he spotted Tyler, he muttered a curt goodbye to whoever was on the other end of the line.

"Where the devil have you been?" Bryce demanded.

"Home."

"Then why haven't you been answering your phone or returning my calls?"

"I think that should be obvious."

"Not to me. Explain it."

"I didn't want to have this conversation," Tyler said honestly. "I didn't want you to bulldoze right over me, the way you usually do."

"Since when have I ever been able to get you to do a blasted thing you didn't want to do?" his father said with a hint of exasperation. "There's not a one of my kids who pays a bit of attention to what I want. And you're the worst of all."

"Aren't you forgetting about Michael? He would walk through fire for you. He loves this company every bit as much as you do."

His father waved off the reminder. "Where is he now? We're in the middle of a critical negotiation."

"He's on his honeymoon. For once in his life, he put himself first. Surely you're not going to fault him for that?"

His father flushed guiltily. "No, of course not. He married a fine woman." His expression brightened ever so slightly. "And those two boys they've adopted, they're something. Could have been born Delacourts.

They'll be a part of this company someday. Michael will see to that."

"He probably will," Tyler agreed.

"A man works his whole life to create something to leave to his children and what happens? Mine turn right around and throw the opportunity out the door."

Tyler bit back a sigh. How many times had he heard this? A hundred?

More? "That's not how it is," he said mildly.

"You see Dylan anywhere around here? Or Trish?"

"No, but—"

"Jeb might as well not be here," his father complained. "He's taking on more and more private cases, instead of learning the ropes here at Delacourt. And that corporate spy case he pursued for us turned into a fiasco."

Tyler chuckled at his father's interpretation of that particular event. "Whose fault was that, Dad? There was no selling of Delacourt secrets. You set Jeb up because you wanted him to fall for Brianna."

"That's not the point."

"What is, then?"

"That not a one of you show any gratitude at all for what I've built for you."

"I repeat, Michael is here a thousand percent. Can't you be satisfied with that? It's no wonder he works himself to death. You take what he does for granted, and it's never enough."

"That's absurd."

Tyler leveled a look straight at his father. "Is it?"

"Okay, okay, you've made your point. You sound like your mother. She's always on my case about showing more appreciation for the job he does."

"It couldn't hurt."

"Well, once you're back here full-time, you'll pick up some of the slack, take a little of the pressure off Michael."

"I'm not coming back," Tyler responded, quietly but emphatically.

His father reacted as if he'd uttered blasphemy. "Why the hell not?"

Tyler gave a resigned sigh. "You know why not, Dad. How many times do we have to have this conversation? I tried to do it your way. I've worked in every department in this place. The job I love, the one I'm suited for, is on the rigs."

"That's Corrigan's influence talking," his father said impatiently. "I knew it was a mistake letting you go over there and work for him."

"This has nothing to do with Daniel."

"It has *everything* to do with him. If the man had an ounce of gratitude in him, he'd follow my wishes and send my son packing."

Tyler grinned ruefully. "Yeah, I heard you'd told him I wasn't coming back."

"And he couldn't wait to run to you, could he?"

"Gee, he seemed to think it might be my decision to make. Now there's a crazy notion, isn't it?"

"Don't get sarcastic with me, boy. I'm still your father."

"I know that."

"Then give me a little credit. I know what's best for you."

"No, Dad, you don't. You know what you want for me, not what I want."

"If it's money you're after…"

"Don't be absurd, Dad. This isn't about money. I know what you pay your top executives. It's more than I could make working eighty hours a week for Daniel, and that's saying something."

"Then I just don't get it."

"I like the physical work, the challenge, being outdoors. I'd suffocate being cooped up in here all day."

"Dammit, Tyler, working those rigs is dangerous. There was a time when I was learning the ropes that I did it, too. Came damned near to getting killed in a fire on one of them. Your mother would never forgive me if anything happened to you."

Tyler saw the ploy for exactly what it was, a pitiful attempt by his father to shift the blame for his own hardheadedness onto his wife by suggesting that she was the one who feared for Tyler's safety.

"Then I'll just have to see that nothing happens." He met his father's gaze evenly. "And if you want me to, I'll explain my decision to Mother. I'll assure her you did your absolute best to keep me right here in Houston."

For just an instant his father looked so thoroughly bewildered and defeated that Tyler almost relented. Then he stiffened his spine and his resolve. This was the way it had to be.

"Dad, this is for the best. Someday I'll be too old to work the rigs. If I'm lucky, there will be a nice desk job waiting for me then."

"Don't count on it."

Tyler matched his father's scowl. "Would you rather I went to another company?"

Red patches darkened his father's cheeks at the suggestion. "Maybe that would be for the best. It would get you away from the influence of that hooligan."

Tyler wasn't sure which of them was the most shocked by the response. "If that's the way you really feel—"

His father's anger dissolved. "Blast it all, Tyler, that's not what I want! You're a Delacourt. What would people think if you turned up working for one of our competitors?"

"That you and I had a falling out," Tyler said readily. "They wouldn't be off the mark, either."

"Well, I'm not going to be fodder for anyone's gossip. If you insist on risking your life, then you'll do it on one of my rigs. They've got the best safety record in the business—Corrigan's seen to that. The man costs me an arm and a leg with all his precautions."

"Do you begrudge him the money he spends so that you can boast about your safety record?"

"Of course not," his father retorted impatiently. "Do you have to twist everything I say?"

Tyler laughed. "Just imagine what I'd do if you had me underfoot every day."

Slowly a reluctant smile tugged at the corners of his father's mouth. "I suppose there is a positive side to this ridiculous decision of yours. At least we won't be butting heads on a regular basis."

"Just holidays and special occasions," Tyler suggested wryly.

"Better make it more often than that, or your mother will have my hide," his father countered.

It was as near as Bryce Delacourt was likely to come to an admission of affection, and Tyler found it oddly moving. "We definitely can't have that, can we?" he replied lightly. "Thanks for seeing it my way, Dad."

"You didn't give me much of a choice, did you? Go on, now, before Corrigan calls up and accuses me of stealing his best worker."

"If you don't mind, I think I'll stick around till the weekend, let Mother fuss over me a little. Daniel can manage without me a few more days."

"That'll make your mother happy," his father agreed. "To tell you the truth, I won't mind seeing you around the house a little more myself."

His words surprised Tyler. It was the closest he'd ever come to admitting that he missed one of his children. Instead he chose to grumble about their desertion of the family business. For the first time Tyler realized that what his father might mean but couldn't say, was that he hated the fact they'd drifted out of his life. Nor was he ever likely to admit that he might be the one who'd driven them away through his attempts to control them.

"Dad, you do know that we all love you, don't you?" Tyler said. "That hasn't changed just because we've chosen to go our own ways."

For a fleeting instant he thought he detected the sheen of unshed tears in his father's eyes, but before he could tell for sure, his father bent over the stack of paperwork on his desk.

"You be sure to stop by and see your mother," he said. "I've got work to do."

Tyler hesitated, wanting to say more but not knowing exactly how. He settled for pausing beside his father's desk long enough to give his shoulder a squeeze before leaving the office. As he closed the door behind him, he thought he heard Bryce sigh.

"You're still in one piece. Everything must have gone okay," his father's secretary said, surveying him intently.

Tyler nodded. "Surprisingly well," he told her.

So why was he leaving with the terrible sense that he had let his father down in some way he might never fully understand?

Four

A few hours after her morning encounter with Tyler, Maddie picked a sidewalk café in the same block as Delacourt Oil to have lunch. With any luck at all, perhaps Tyler would pass by and she could snag his attention. If not, maybe some Delacourt employees would sit at a nearby table and she would be able to overhear some juicy bit of corporate gossip. It was a long shot, but she had to admit she was losing patience with the snail's pace of her investigation. She'd been at it for two weeks, and had little to show for her efforts other than a vague feeling that Tyler had fathered an illegitimate child, something she would likely never use.

Used to the immediacy of daily reporting, Maddie concluded she was not cut out for the slow, tedious work of gathering material for an exposé. Nor was she certain just how long Griffin Carpenter would be willing to fund her fishing expedition. He hadn't said, and she didn't want to test him.

Hoping to come up with something—anything—she had spent most of the morning making calls to Baton Rouge trying to pick up any sort of lead on how Tyler spent his time there. She'd come up empty. The man didn't even have a listed phone number, and the Delacourt Oil offices had firmly declined even to confirm that he worked there. It looked as if she was going to have to go to Louisiana herself if she wanted to pursue that angle of the story. Maybe her time would have been better spent at the library going through old articles on Delacourt Oil in the Houston papers. She vowed to get busy at that first thing tomorrow—maybe even after lunch today if her plan to hook up with Tyler failed.

"Okay, who's responsible for that look on your face? Tell me and I'll beat them up for you."

Just the sound of that deep, slow-talking voice was enough to send goose bumps dancing down her spine. She glanced up into Tyler's twinkling blue eyes and felt another jolt of electricity. Even though his arrival was exactly what she'd hoped for, she obviously hadn't steeled herself against his thoroughly masculine effect on her.

"Thanks all the same, but I can fight my own battles," she retorted lightly, pleased that her voice was steady.

"Mind if I join you? Or would I be taking my life in my hands?"

She conducted a blatant survey of him from head to toe. "Oh, you look tough enough. I think you can probably take care of yourself. Have a seat and tell me what's put you in such a good mood. A couple of hours ago you looked as if you were heading off to war."

"In a manner of speaking I was. Battle's over. I won."

"Was there ever any doubt?"

"For a few minutes, there, it could have gone either way. Now let's get back to you. Any luck with the job hunt?"

"I spent the morning making calls," she said honestly. "No leads."

"Why don't you let me help you out? If you don't want to work for Delacourt, I know a lot of other people in this town."

"I'm sure you do, but I need to do this myself."

He nodded, his expression oddly irritated. "Pride's a funny thing, especially if you let your desire for independence overshadow common sense. It can cost you in unexpected ways."

She regarded him curiously. Had pride been an issue with him before? "Such as?" she prodded.

"Sometimes it keeps the people who care about you at arm's length at the very time when you need them the most."

"Has that happened to you?"

His expression clouded over. "In a way. Enough about pride, though. What's your game plan?"

Since her game plan was in a state of flux and had nothing to do with job hunting, she forced a brilliant smile. "I'm taking the afternoon off. How about you?"

"As it happens that's exactly my intention, as well." His gaze locked on hers. "So, Maddie Kent, want to do something impulsive?"

"Such as?"

"It's not impulsive if you have to know all the details ahead of time," he teased.

Her pulse promptly kicked into overdrive. It appeared that this lighthearted, victorious Tyler was even more dangerous than the brooding, vulnerable man she'd first met. No wonder he had a reputation. That smile of his could lure a woman into going against every sane, rational bit of advice she'd ever been given—to say nothing of severing the last fragile thread by which she was clinging to her ethics.

However, his mood played straight into her own agenda to worm her way into the heart of the Delacourt clan. "Name it. I'll go along."

"Come with me, then."

"I haven't even eaten."

"Don't worry, short stuff, you'll get to eat. In fact, I'll promise you the best seafood you've *ever* eaten, along with buttered corn on the cob and the perfect dessert for a steamy day like this."

"Lead me to it," she said.

He held out his hand, and after a second's hesitation she placed hers in it. The instant she did, she knew it was a mistake. His touch sent heat sizzling through her veins and set her every nerve to tingling.

Slow down, she warned herself. This was very thin ice, and given the temperature of her thoughts at the moment, it wouldn't take long to melt right through it.

"Where are we going?" she asked, then sighed when he frowned. "Sorry. Force of habit."

"You do ask a lot of questions."

"Can you think of a better way to get answers?"

"Well, just this once, stuff a sock in it. You'll get all your answers in due time."

He led her to a sporty, classic convertible from the sixties, its brilliant blue exterior the exact same shade as his eyes. She laughed when she saw it.

"And here I thought you'd have a rugged sports utility vehicle all covered in mud. Something practical and sturdy."

"I do. It's in Louisiana. This is the car I keep to impress the ladies." He regarded her with a grin. "Is it working?"

"It will if you let me drive."

"Not in a hundred million years," he said fervently. "I've worked like a fiend to restore this car. Nobody touches it but me."

"Then I'm not impressed."

He held open the passenger door. "Still coming?"

"Of course."

She realized within minutes that they were heading out of town and minutes after that, concluded that they were going to the beach. Still, she dutifully kept all of her guesses and her questions to herself and settled back against the soft, buttery leather to enjoy the ride.

When Tyler finally pulled to a stop in the driveway of a beachfront house, Maddie looked around with undisguised curiosity.

He chuckled at her struggle with restraint. "Okay, go ahead. You can ask."

"What?"

"I can see you're dying to know where we are."

"I know where we are," she retorted. "We're at the beach."

"At my family's house, to be precise." A boyish expression washed over his face. "It's been a while since I've been here."

She studied him intently, then concluded, "But you love it, don't you?"

"Every weathered shingle of it," he confirmed. "My brothers and I replaced those a few years back, after we bought it from our parents. My sister, Trish, says it's about the only work we ever did here. We tended to party a lot. Now the rest of them are married, so if there's any partying to be done, I guess it's up to me."

He held out his hand again. "Come on. I'll show you around."

He conducted the tour with evident pride, pointing out every change he and his brothers had made to the structure. The rooms were filled with sunlight and comfortable, worn furniture. The wood floors had been worn smooth by sandy feet. Ceiling fans, which he turned on as they went, kept a salty breeze stirring through the rooms. Finally he gestured toward a deck that faced the Gulf of Mexico.

"Have a seat and relax. I'll run to the store and pick up what we need for a feast."

The chaise lounge, deep in the shade, looked tempting. "Are you sure? I could come along and help."

"A polite, dutiful offer, but unnecessary. I've got it covered. If you want something to drink, there may be a few beers or soft drinks in the refrigerator—help yourself. And there are paperback novels scattered everywhere if you feel inclined to read."

"I'll be fine."

He studied her intently for a heartbeat, then grinned. "Thanks for coming with me, Maddie Kent."

Only after he'd walked away did she whisper, "Thanks for inviting me."

And for leaving her alone so she could snoop, she thought with some degree of guilt.

As distasteful as the thought was, the opportunity was too good to pass up. And so the minute she heard the sound of the car's engine begin to fade, Maddie began exploring.

Unfortunately, there didn't seem to be much to find,

she decided ruefully after completing her inspection of the second floor. The bedrooms were simply decorated. The drawers held an anonymous assortment of bathing suits, shorts and T-shirts. The closets were virtually empty except for the occasional pair of old sneakers and discarded socks. No secrets here, she concluded with regret. Just evidence of a houseful of bachelors who passed through whenever the mood suited them.

Back downstairs she found cupboards filled with playing cards and board games, stacks of CDs and old magazines, and the promised supply of dog-eared paperbacks. Far more enticing was the collection of old snapshots she found in a drawer. She took them with her to a chair and studied them with fascination.

The photos seemed to span at least ten years or more, beginning when Tyler was maybe twelve. She recognized his smile, as well as the fact that he was the smallest of the boys and the only one whose hair was the color of straw. She recalled various newspaper photographs of his parents, both of whom had darker coloring, more in keeping with that of his brothers and his sister.

None of the pictures appeared to be more recent than his college days.

Other than his sister, Trish, who was in the family photos, there didn't seem to be any women, not even as the boys grew into men. Whatever bachelor parties they threw, apparently no one wasted time taking snapshots.

Oddly, there didn't seem to be any pictures of their parents. Had Bryce Delacourt been the one behind the camera? Or had he and his wife not spent time here? She was still pondering the implications of that when she heard the purr of the car as it pulled into the driveway. Hastily she put the pictures back where she'd found them and walked outside just in time to see Tyler emerge from the car with an armload of groceries.

"Did you buy out the store?" she asked, chuckling at the amount of food he'd apparently bought for their supposedly simple meal.

"Once I got started, I couldn't seem to stop." His gaze settled on her face. "Maybe we'll have to stick around a few days so it won't go to waste."

Maddie's heart thumped unsteadily at the teasing suggestion. Staying here, alone with Tyler, was not an option. Alarm bells clanged from so many different directions, her head ached from the clamor.

"Let's stick to our late lunch, shall we?"

He regarded her with disappointment. "What's wrong, Maddie? No sense of adventure?"

"I'm as adventurous as the next person," she assured him. "But I'm also out of work. I need to keep looking for a job. I can't keep playing hooky."

"It's not hooky if you don't have a job to begin with," he reminded her as he carried the groceries inside and set them on the kitchen counter. "It's seizing the moment."

"Well, maybe you can afford to seize the moment, but I can't."

He paused while taking food from the bags to level a look at her. "If you're in a bind—"

"I'm not," she said hastily. "Not yet, anyway. I have some savings. I didn't just impulsively take off with nothing to fall back on. But it won't last forever."

"Well, if your situation changes, you can come to me. I want you to remember that," he said with apparent sincerity.

She stared at him in astonishment. "You hardly know me. Why would you be willing to loan me money?"

He shrugged. "Because I can."

She suspected he meant exactly that. She also had the feeling that he would make the same impulsive offer to anyone he ran across who offered up a convincing sob story.

"Tyler, you can't go around passing out money to everyone who seems down on his luck."

"Why not? What good is having money if you can't help other people?"

"It's not that," she said, frustrated by his inability to recognize the possibility that people might abuse his generosity.

"What then?"

"People will take advantage of you," she said, ignoring the fact that in her own way she, too, was doing exactly that, though not financially.

"I suppose. But I'd rather risk that than ignore someone who might really need a helping hand."

"Then give money to charities. Take a tax write-off."

"I do, but this isn't about getting a good deduction on my income taxes. It's about stepping up to the plate, even when there's nothing to be gained in return."

"Are you for real?" she asked, unable to imagine him as the offspring of the hard-hearted Bryce Delacourt. Who had taught him such a standard?

Surely not his father.

"You think there's something wrong with doing a good deed every now and then?" he asked, studying her.

"Of course not, but people like you can get taken to the cleaners by con artists."

He laughed. "I'd like to think I'm a better judge of character than that."

Maddie wasn't so sure. Take her, for example. She wasn't at all what she appeared, but he didn't seem to suspect it, not anymore, anyway.

Whatever suspicions he'd held when they'd first met seemed to have vanished. He seemed to be accepting her at face value now. He'd invited her here, hadn't he?

Was he truly beyond cynicism and suspicion where she was concerned? Or was she the one being deceived? Was this just his way of getting her to let down her guard so she'd slip up?

Maddie sighed. What a tangled web this was turning out to be.

"Why the sigh?"

"Just thinking about the fact that it must be nice not to be as distrusting and jaded as I am."

"Who made you that way?"

She wondered what he would say if she told him it had been his father.

Instead, she shrugged off the question. "Just life."

"You're way too young to sound so cynical."

"Twenty-six is not that young. I've lost both parents, and to all intents and purposes I've lost my brothers. That's enough to change your perspective on the world. *You* wouldn't know, though. You've apparently never lost anything or anyone important."

No sooner were the words out of her mouth than she realized her mistake. Even as Tyler's eyes became turbulent, his expression turned bleak. Before she could apologize for making such an assumption about his life, he whirled around and headed outside. The groceries lay forgotten on the countertop.

Maddie started to rush after him, then hesitated. Obviously she'd said something terribly wrong. She needed to give him a minute alone before she went after him and badgered him with questions he probably wouldn't want to answer.

She took her time and put the food away, then popped the tops on a couple of beers before venturing onto the deck.

Tyler was standing at the railing, staring out at the sparkling water. Something told her he wasn't just appreciating the scenery. In fact, his expression was filled with such sorrow it almost broke her heart. What memories had she unwittingly unleashed with her careless remark?

Without saying a word, she went to stand next to him and held out the cold drink. He accepted it without comment, without so much as a glance in her direction.

"I'm sorry," she said finally.

The apology was greeted by more silence.

"Tyler, I truly am sorry. I had no right to say such a thing."

"No," he said coldly. "You didn't. You know nothing about me, nothing at all about what I have or haven't lost."

"Then tell me," she pleaded. For once, the request had nothing to do with the story she was trying to piece together and everything to do with understanding this man who was turning out to be far more complex than she'd been led to believe by the media reports.

He shook his head. "No. It's not something I discuss. Not ever."

"Keeping that kind of pain bottled up inside can't be good for you," she said softly.

"Drop it, Maddie. I want to forget, not dissect it to death." He turned to her then, reaching for her as he did. "There's only one way I know to do that."

Before she could anticipate his intentions, his mouth covered hers in a hard, punishing kiss that had her senses ricocheting wildly and had her clinging to him. There was nothing gentle or tender, just fierce, primal need. She was gasping for breath by the time he pushed her away, his expression miserable.

"Now I'm the one who's sorry," he said, his gaze avoiding hers. "I had no right to do that."

"It's okay," she stammered, touching a finger to her still-tender lips. She had deserved some sort of retribution for her insensitivity, though a punishing kiss hadn't been what she expected. Worse, she had liked it. She had wanted more. No man had ever demanded so much of her with a mere kiss. The wild racing of her pulse was frightening yet exhilarating.

The fear, of course, stemmed from Tyler's identity, nothing more. On some level she had known he would never hurt her, never go beyond that dark and dangerous kiss unless she invited him to. The problem was, she couldn't feel this much with him, couldn't want so much, not from a Delacourt.

"Maybe we should go, though," she whispered, and this time her voice was unsteady.

Tyler dragged a hand across his face and muttered a soft curse under his breath. Then his gaze locked with hers.

"Maddie, I truly am sorry. What I did was unforgivable. If you want to go back, we will, but I promised you a seafood feast, and I'd very much like it if you'd stay and let me fix it for you."

"Are you sure?"

"I'm sure. In fact, I'm starving."

She offered him a tentative smile. "To tell you the truth, Tyler, so am I." She took a deep breath and came to a decision. "What can I do to help?"

"Stay out from underfoot," he suggested. "Great chefs need space. We can't have a beautiful woman diverting us from the task at hand."

Even though she knew she shouldn't be, she was pleased that he considered her a beautiful distraction. "Then by all means, let me make myself scarce. I want you to be entirely focused, if that means we'll get to eat sooner." She gestured toward the chaise. "I'll be right over there, tucked safely out of your way. Just don't forget all about me and eat everything yourself."

"Don't worry, Maddie. You're not exactly forgettable."

His words lingered after he'd gone inside. Despite all the warnings, the alarms, the stern lectures, she couldn't help replaying them, a smile on her lips.

She moaned softly. *You are in such big trouble, Madison Kent.*

When the blackened snapper was ready and the corn was dripping with melted butter, Tyler went outside to call Maddie. She was curled up where he'd left her, sound asleep. For a moment he stood where he was, studying her.

Though she'd admitted to being twenty-six, he couldn't help thinking that she looked like little more than a girl with her tousled hair and a face devoid of makeup, except for a hint of pink on her lips.

She might look like a sweet innocent, but she kissed

like a woman, with all the passion and intensity and hunger that could make a man forget all of his own rules. Though he'd set out to take greedily when he'd kissed her earlier, she had given all he asked and more. The responsiveness had shaken him more than a little. He could have taken her then and there, but it would have been a terrible mistake for both of them. He couldn't give her what she needed, couldn't be as open and honest as she deserved.

Even so, he'd started to feel things he hadn't felt in a very long time, things that went beyond sex and into the depths of emotions he'd vowed never to risk again. It was good that he was leaving soon for Baton Rouge.

Maddie stirred, drawing his attention back to bare legs and tempting curves.

"Bad idea," he muttered, tearing his gaze away. He took a few steps back, then said loudly, "Maddie, dinner's ready."

She came awake at once, bright-eyed and smiling. "Did you say something about dinner?"

He grinned at her eagerness. "It's on the table."

She bounded up and headed inside without sparing him a backward glance.

"I guess I know what your priorities are," he called after her.

She waited for him, grinning impudently. "It's important to set goals and stay focused."

"Is food your only goal?" he taunted.

For an instant a shadow seemed to pass over her face, but then the smile was back. "Hardly. Just the most immediate one." She looked over the table. "Oh, my, this looks heavenly. How did you learn to cook?"

"Self-taught. The rule in our house when it came to

fish was that whoever caught them had to clean and cook them. I didn't mind the catching or the cooking, but I hated the cleaning. Now I buy mine at the fish market, ready for the skillet."

"Isn't that cheating yourself of some male ritual or something?"

"I prefer to think of it as time saving."

"What about the corn?"

"No mystique to that. It doesn't take a lot to soak it and cook it on the grill. The grill is man's best friend, next to his dog, of course."

"Do you have a dog?"

"No, which is why I'm so fond of my grill."

The conversation stayed light and general during dinner and cleanup.

When the last dish was back in the cabinet, she turned to him. "Hey, I thought you promised me dessert."

"I did."

"Something perfect for a hot, sultry night, as I recall," she said, her expression bright with anticipation.

Tyler reached into the freezer and retrieved two Popsicles. "Lime or grape?"

"Shouldn't a gourmet meal end with sorbet at the very least?" she said, seizing the grape Popsicle, anyway.

"Same thing in more convenient form," he retorted, then watched as her mouth surrounded the icy treat. His body promptly hardened in response to the slow, provocative swirl of her tongue across the tip. What the hell had he been thinking? This was sheer torture. His own Popsicle melted in his hand. Only when he felt lime turning his hand sticky did he snap back to the present, abandoning the wicked direction of his thoughts.

"Something wrong?" Maddie inquired, eyes full of mischief.

"Damn thing melted on me," he retorted, heading for the sink to wash his hand.

Maybe while he was there he ought to take a little soap to his thoughts as well. Maddie Kent was getting under his skin in ways he hadn't anticipated.

Five

Maddie was playing with fire and she knew it. Even now, two days later, her face flamed when she thought of the way she'd taunted Tyler with that provocative little game with the grape Popsicle. What had she been thinking? Hadn't she warned herself only an hour or so before, that she was taking a huge risk with this man who was so critical to her investigation of his father?

Because she recognized the dangers, she had vowed on the ride back to Houston to limit her contact with Tyler to very public places and very innocuous situations. No more flirting with disaster.

No more flirting, period.

Fortunately he had mentioned that he'd be heading back to Louisiana in a few days. If she could stay out of his path, it would be for the best. She would find some other way to get the information she needed.

She had actually stuck to her guns for two whole days now. She'd spent them at the library, culling clip after clip about Bryce Delacourt from old newspapers. To her increasing annoyance, all of the stories were glowing testaments to his generosity and business acumen. If there were bodies buried in his past, the media offered no hints of it.

She made a list of every merger and acquisition mentioned, then resolved to contact the owners of the businesses to see if any of the deals had been shady or hostile. Perhaps the previous owners had been persuaded by Delacourt's wealth and power—or even threats—to remain silent at the time of the takeover. Perhaps the intervening months or years would have loosened their tongues.

Eventually she worked her way back to the year her father had committed suicide. As she scanned the issue in which his death was reported, her gaze was inevitably drawn time and again to the small headline buried among the other death notices, an insignificant mention of something that had been of life-altering importance to four people, and especially to one fifteen-year-old girl.

"Frank Kent died suddenly at his home…"

Tears stung Maddie's eyes as she read it again and again. She had forgotten the way it had been phrased. There had been no mention of suicide, no hint of the years of depression and anguish that had preceded it.

On the very same day in another part of the paper, there was a banner headline extolling Bryce Delacourt's donation to a local children's charity. The inequity of the coverage brought more tears welling up and stiffened her resolve. Maybe she could handle one more meeting with Tyler, after all.

It was late afternoon by the time Maddie finally left the library. For the first time in days she deliberately headed for O'Reilly's, convinced she had managed to harden her heart toward any Delacourt. She sat at the bar and ordered a ginger ale, then scanned the happy-hour crowd.

"Looking for someone?"

The seductively uttered words made her shiver. She glanced up into familiar, twinkling blue eyes. Her resolve took a hard hit to the solar plexus, but she managed a bright smile even as she reminded herself that this was exactly what she'd hoped for, another supposedly chance encounter.

"Fancy meeting you here," she said.

"Are you sure you didn't plan it?" Tyler teased.

Of course she had, but she wasn't about to admit it. "You're not the only man in here."

"Just the only one you've ever spoken to," he reminded her, sliding onto the stool next to hers and ordering a beer. "Where have you been?"

"Why? Did you miss me?" The flirtatious remark slipped out before she could control it.

"Desperately," he said lightly. "So what's the deal? Have you started a new job?"

Actually she'd been concentrating on the old one, but she could hardly share that little tidbit with him. "No. I've just been busy."

"Doing?"

"This and that."

"Are you being deliberately mysterious, Maddie Kent?"

"It's a woman's best weapon," she informed him.

"I didn't know we were at war."

"We're not. I was speaking generally." She grinned at him and ignored the alarm bells blaring in her head. Unfortunately, she was getting used to the sound. It didn't have the power to shake a little sense and re-straint into her as it once had.

"So, did you really miss me?" she asked again. "Tell the truth."

He matched her grin. "Nope. Too busy."

She tried not to feel deflated. "Doing what?"

"This and that."

She laughed. "Okay, touché."

"Have dinner with me. We can catch up."

"You make it sound as if we're long-lost friends who have years of separate lives to share."

"Sometimes even a couple of days can seem like a lifetime," he said, his tone serious while his eyes sparkled with amusement. "Besides, we just met. We have been apart for years. There's a lot to catch up on."

"You are an outrageous flirt, Tyler Delacourt. Any woman who takes you seriously needs to have her head examined."

"Then don't take me seriously," he advised. "Just dinner, a little conversation. Nothing dangerous in that, is there?"

If only he knew, she thought, even as she nodded an acceptance.

"Not here," he said, tossing some bills on the bar to pay for their drinks. "It's too noisy. There's a little Italian place around the corner that makes a lasagna that will bring tears to your eyes."

She laughed at that. "I almost never cry over my food. It ruins the flavor."

"Nothing could ruin this. Anna Maria deserves to be canonized for her lasagna."

As it turned out, he wasn't exaggerating. The huge square of lasagna was by far the best pasta Maddie had ever put in her mouth. She didn't have room for even half of it. Not that it went to waste—Tyler happily nabbed the remainder.

"Do you have a bottomless pit for a stomach or something?" she asked, moaning. Her own stomach felt stuffed.

"I'm not the one who filled up on garlic bread before the meal came," he retorted.

"It was too good to pass up." She'd also had some crazy idea that the garlic might ward off any amorous advances, something similar to its effect on vampires, perhaps.

She propped her chin on her hand and met his gaze. "How come you haven't gone back to work? Didn't you tell me you were planning to head back to Baton Rouge anyday?"

"I was, but something came up at the office, and Dad coaxed me into pitching in here until my brother Michael gets back from his honeymoon."

"When will that be?"

"It seems to change from day to day. I spoke to my brother just yesterday. He'd talked to Dad, who'd told him that I had everything under control. Michael was considering extending their trip for another week or ten days. Dad had already assured him that their kids are having a blast staying on the ranch with Trish."

"My, my, he is good, isn't he?"

"Who?"

"Your father. Sounds like he found a very clever tactic to get you to stick around indefinitely. Stir up a little crisis here, a little emergency there. Keep your brother conveniently out of town. Are you so sure you won that particular battle, after all?"

He appeared to take the suggestion in stride. "Dad's certainly devious enough to try something like that, but this was a real crisis. Believe me, I checked it out thoroughly just to be sure. As for Michael, he said he'd be on the next plane home if I gave him the word."

"Why didn't you, then?"

"How could I do it? Michael works too hard. We've badgered him for years about not taking any vacation time. In fact, we've pulled some very sneaky tricks to get him to take a little time off. So I'm willing to pitch in for a week or two if it gives him a much-deserved break. Who knows when he'll get around to taking another one, though Grace seems to be a good influence on him. She's fiercely determined to put some balance into his life."

Maddie looked at him in silence.

He shrugged. "Bottom line? I'm stuck here for a few days, and for once it wasn't something my father did deliberately to sabotage my plans to leave."

Maddie was surprised that he took her comment so seriously. "I was actually kidding. But you really don't trust your own father, do you?"

"No farther than I could throw him," he admitted candidly.

"Why not?" she asked, trying not to sound too eager. She could get a lot of mileage out of a rift in the family.

"Because when it comes to getting his way, he is a very sneaky man, especially where family's concerned. His heart's always in the right place, but you wouldn't believe some of the stunts he's pulled."

"Tell me."

Tyler shook his head. "Family secrets. You'll have to

ask Jeb and Trish and the others when you meet them. They love telling tales on Dad."

The thought of meeting other members of the Delacourt family filled her with more trepidation than she'd expected. If the rest of them were as kind and decent as Tyler, how would she ever bring herself to write a story that might wreck their lives?

"I doubt we'll meet," she said eventually.

Tyler's gaze locked on hers. He looked as if he were waging some sort of an internal struggle. Finally he said in a tone she couldn't quite interpret, "Oh, something tells me you will, Maddie Kent."

Tyler finally came to accept that Maddie was going to pop up whenever and wherever he least expected her. In fact, he was beginning to enjoy her unexpected appearances.

There was something about her that got to him. The woman had a million and one questions, but she listened attentively to each response in a way that was extremely flattering. No one except Jen had ever listened quite so closely to anything Tyler had to say.

Heaven knew his father didn't pay any attention. Even after they'd reached their agreement about Tyler's return to Baton Rouge, his father was still taking every opportunity to keep him in town. Maddie had been right about that. The crises did exist, but even with Michael away, his father could have handled most of them on his own. Tyler had given in and stayed, at least in part because doing so gave him a little more time to get to know the mysterious Maddie.

There was no doubt the woman fascinated him as no one had since Jen.

Despite her resilient, ever-cheerful, ever-perky demeanor, there was an unmistakable sorrow lurking in the depths of her eyes. That hint of vulnerability brought out all of his protective instincts.

Then, too, there was the disturbing memory of that bone-melting kiss on the deck at the beach. Even though he was ashamed of the way he'd taken advantage of her, he couldn't seem to forget how her mouth had felt under his, how her body had responded. He spent a lot of time fantasizing about how that night could have ended. One day, when the time was right, he expected to turn that fantasy into reality. Then he would discover once and for all if that moment had been a fluke.

The phone on his desk rang, shattering the tantalizing illusion. Just as well, he thought as he reached for the receiver.

"Yes?"

"Tyler, is that any way to answer the phone? I'm sure I taught you better manners."

He grinned at the scolding. "Hello, Mother. How are you?"

"I'd be considerably better if you would come to see me. You've been in town for weeks, and other than our anniversary party I've hardly seen you. Your father assured me you were going to stop by."

"I intended to, but you know how it is."

"I know exactly how it is. You're just like your brothers and your sister. You never come home unless I badger you into it, which is precisely why I'm calling."

"To badger me?"

"Yes. I want you here for Sunday dinner. Louise

Talbert's daughter, Mary Claire, is home for a visit. I'm going to invite her as well."

Tyler had a vivid memory of a child with thick glasses, limp brown braids, buckteeth and a disconcerting tendency to bite when she didn't get her way. "How old is she now?" he asked suspiciously.

"Twenty-two. She's in graduate school in finance. A brilliant woman. Your father and I are quite fond of her. I think the two of you would make a perfect match."

Tyler shuddered. A woman with a calculator for a brain? No way. "Not in this lifetime," he muttered.

"What was that?"

"I said that I'd rather pick out my own women, Mother."

"I haven't seen any evidence that you're doing that. Besides, if you met a nice woman here in Houston, you might be happier staying here."

He thought of Maddie. "Actually, I have met a nice woman here. I'll bring her to Sunday dinner."

"But what about Mary Claire?"

"That's up to you, but I'm bringing my own date."

His mother sighed heavily. "You were always a difficult child."

"Then I'm acting right in character, aren't I? I'll see you on Sunday," he promised, then added hopefully, "Unless you'd prefer I not come, after all."

"Don't be ridiculous. Be here at noon. We'll eat at one."

"As always," he murmured.

"I heard that. Routine is important, you know. Not that it was easy to manage, given your father's work habits, but I prided myself on trying to adhere to one for the sake of you children. Perhaps you should consider developing a routine."

"I have one that suits me just fine," he responded.

"Whatever. I just hope you'll find a way to include your family in it a little more frequently. I don't like you being so far away, and I truly don't approve of you doing such dangerous work. It's bad enough…" Her voice trailed off.

"What, Mother?"

"Nothing. I'll see you on Sunday," she said, and hung up abruptly.

Only after he was off the phone did Tyler realize that he'd promised to produce a date for Sunday and he had no earthly idea where to track Maddie down. If he showed up without her, he would never hear the end of it.

That was all the excuse he needed to flee the stifling atmosphere of the office and head for some of the places where he had run into Maddie. It was too late for lunch and not quite early enough for O'Reilly's, but that didn't stop him from checking out both the sidewalk café and the bar.

Once he was at O'Reilly's, he decided to stick around and hope Maddie would put in an appearance. He also vowed to find out how he could get in touch with her so he wouldn't have to go through this again. While chance encounters appealed to his take-what-comes nature, they were a damned nuisance at a time like this.

"Waiting for your friend again?" Kevin O'Reilly asked after bringing him an icy mug of beer.

Tyler nodded. "What do you know about her?"

"Less than you do, I imagine. Her name's Maddie.

She's new in town. Beyond that, not a thing. I don't pry into the lives of my customers."

"Since when?"

Kevin gave him an indignant look. "I never pry. People just tell me things. But Maddie hasn't told me anything much."

"Does she seem a little down on her luck to you?"

"Doesn't tip as if she is. Surprised me the first night she was in here. She's not what you would call a heavy drinker. Didn't order a bite of food, either, but she left a hefty tip just the same." He regarded Tyler with amusement. "Of course, now that you've started paying for the drinks, the tips aren't nearly as good."

"Watch it or I'll stiff you completely."

"You do and I'll introduce you to my bouncer."

"Seriously, Kevin, you're a good judge of human nature. What do you think of her?"

"Nice kid. A little nosy. Asks too blasted many questions." He shrugged. "That's about it."

"What kind of things was she asking you about?" Tyler asked, wondering if they'd gotten a similar third degree.

"Mostly about you," Kevin said at once.

"You mean after the night she and I met?"

Kevin hesitated, his expression thoughtful, then shook his head. "No, it was before. In fact, she asked me to point you out if you came in."

Tyler's heart sank. Their first meeting hadn't been a chance encounter at all. She had planned it. But why? What was she after? All of those initial suspicions he'd had about her—the ones he'd conveniently squelched—came roaring back.

But rather than warning him away, they simply

made him more determined than ever to figure out what Maddie Kent was all about. While taking her home to meet his parents was risky, it was also the ideal opportunity to gather more information. His mother knew how to ferret out every little detail about someone in the guise of friendly chitchat. She'd had years to hone her technique. Maddie's reticence wouldn't stand a chance against his mother's skill.

"Speak of the devil," Kevin said with a gesture toward the door.

Maddie hesitated just inside, probably to let her eyes adjust to the bar's dim interior. Then, as if she felt his gaze, she looked in Tyler's direction. A smile spread slowly across her face.

"Hey, you," she said, sliding onto the stool next to him. "You're here early."

"Looking for you, actually. You really have to tell me how I can get in touch with you without sitting on a barstool all afternoon. Kevin's worried I'm turning into a lush."

She laughed. "On one beer? I doubt that."

"How do you know I haven't had ten?"

"You never do," she said simply. "Now tell me why you were looking for me."

"I wanted to invite you to Sunday dinner with the folks."

For an instant her expression faltered. "Your parents?" she said. "You want me to meet your parents?"

"Sure. They don't bite. Are you game? Besides, I need cover. If you don't show up, Mother intends to matchmake. Her only consideration tends to be bloodlines, as if she were breeding a prize Thoroughbred."

"How did you explain me?"

"I just said I had my own woman, thank you very much."

"Then if I don't come, I make a liar out of you," she said, her expression thoughtful, but her eyes glinting with merriment.

"Something like that."

"Who's the alternative candidate?"

"As I remember her, she had bad teeth, bad hair and a nasty temper. Of course, she wasn't much more than twelve the last time I saw her."

"That type usually turns into a ravishing beauty. Are you sure you don't want to take a chance on her?"

"No way. It's you or a quick trip out of state."

"Then I'll come, by all means."

"You're a lifesaver."

"Which means you'll owe me one, right?"

"Absolutely. Anything you want."

She grinned. "I'll have to give that some real thought. I'm sure I can come up with something that will make you regret not going with the alternative."

"It'll never happen. I'll pick you up on Sunday at eleven-thirty. Where do you live?"

"Why don't I just meet you here? It's convenient for both of us."

Tyler regarded her curiously. "Is there some reason you don't want me to know where you live?"

"Of course not. This will just be easier. I'd better run now."

Her uneasiness only fueled his suspicions. "What's the rush?"

"I'm… I'm meeting friends."

"Really?" Last he'd heard, she didn't have any.

"From out of town," she said hurriedly, as if she'd read his mind. "They're just here for the one night."

He nodded. "Okay, then. Have fun."

She bolted from the bar. Tyler stared after her, bemused. She was lying through her teeth. But why?

Tyler was stilling trying to figure out Maddie's evasiveness when he pulled up outside of O'Reilly's on Sunday morning. To his surprise Maddie was standing by the curb waiting for him. He'd almost expected her not to turn up.

"I have to tell you this whole thing makes me nervous," she said as she slid into the car. "I mean these are *the* Delacourts."

Tyler chuckled. "I'm a Delacourt. Do I make you nervous?"

"More than you know," she retorted, then grinned, totally disarming him. "Just don't let it go to your head."

"Not much chance of that. How was your evening with your friends?"

She stared at him blankly. "What? Oh, those friends," she said as if there were so many that his question had confused her. "They're great. We had a wonderful time."

"Where'd you go?"

"My place. We ordered pizza, gabbed the night away. You know how women are when they haven't seen each other for a while."

"Did my name come up?"

"No," she said at once. "Why would it?"

He gave her a bland look, then echoed her earlier comment, "I know how women are. They love to talk about the men in their lives."

"You aren't… I mean it's not as if…"

"Isn't it really?"

Her gaze narrowed. "Tyler, what is it that you think we're doing?"

"Going to dinner with my parents at the moment."

"Beyond that?"

"Getting to know each other?" he suggested.

"Exactly. Not dating. Just getting to know each other," she said very firmly.

"I'm not sure I see the difference. Isn't the purpose of dating to get to know each other?"

"Yes, but…"

"But what?" he asked when she didn't finish the thought.

"Nothing." She fell silent.

Tyler let it go, because they were pulling into the long, curving drive to his parents' home. Out of the corner of his eye he tried to gauge Maddie's reaction to the impressive grounds and even more impressive home. She looked just a little stunned.

By the time they went inside, though, she had gathered her composure. She greeted his mother graciously, but to his surprise she stiffened ever so slightly when she was introduced to his father. There was an unreadable expression on her face, but it was gone in a heartbeat, replaced by a smile that was polite, if clearly strained.

The uncomfortable moment passed because his mother stepped in and took over, leading them into the library for a predinner drink and her usual inquisition. Maddie withstood all of the embarrassingly intimate questions with good grace and surprisingly few details.

About the best Tyler could say for the endless afternoon was that Maddie's presence kept the attention off him. For once, he and his father avoided verbal bloodshed. And his mother had apparently "uninvited" Mary Claire.

When the torturous dinner finally ended, Tyler couldn't wait to escape.

He made their excuses, claiming a prior commitment that clearly took Maddie by surprise, but she seized the opportunity to leave with an eagerness matching his, even if he didn't entirely understand her reasons.

Outside again, Tyler crawled in thankfully behind the wheel of his car, then turned to meet Maddie's gaze.

"I am so sorry," he said at once.

She laughed. "Your mother is really, really anxious to see you married, isn't she?"

"You have no idea."

"I'm not sure she found me up to her usual standards," Maddie said.

"You're female. You're available. You'll do," he said.

Then, because he'd been wanting to do it all afternoon, he drew Maddie to him and kissed her. Thoroughly. More gently than that other sizzling, memorable kiss, but this one turned out to be equally devastating.

At her stunned expression, he said lightly, "Just giving mother something to think about. She's bound to be watching out the window."

"Oh, sure," Maddie replied, still looking bemused. She swallowed hard, visibly fighting for composure.

They had been on the road for several minutes when she turned to him. "You know, I get the feeling you're her favorite child."

Tyler was startled by the observation. "Only because I was the only one there. Mother doesn't play favorites."

"No," Maddie insisted. "It was in her eyes when she looked at you. I can't quite describe it. It was as if she were looking at a memory. I know that sounds fanciful, but it's the only way I can explain it."

"You're imagining things."

She finally shrugged. "Maybe," she said, but she didn't sound convinced.

"What did you think of my father?" he asked, hoping he could prod her into revealing why she'd seemed so distant with him.

"He's a little intimidating."

"Really? He was on his best behavior today. He obviously liked you."

She regarded him with a startled expression. "He did? He hardly said two words to me."

"If he hadn't liked you, he would have made mother's crossexamination seem like a casual chat in the produce section at the market. Now *that* would have been intimidating."

"Men who wield their power like that make me sick," she said fiercely.

Tyler stared at her, startled by the intensity of her response. "Hey, what brought that on?"

"Sorry. It's just a sore point with me. It has nothing to do with your father," she added hastily.

Not for the first time Tyler realized he didn't believe her. How could he possibly be so fascinated by a woman, so attracted to her, when he knew with everything in him that she was lying through her teeth practically every time she opened her mouth?

He also knew he wouldn't rest until he got to the bottom of it, though his precise motivation for that was beginning to be a little murky.

Six

When Tyler suggested stopping by his place for a drink, Maddie threw caution to the winds and agreed eagerly. She wanted to take another look around, maybe get another chance to question him about that baby picture. She would just have to make sure there were no more kisses. That one in the driveway had come darned close to melting her into a puddle. She'd thought it wasn't possible to be any hotter than Houston in the summer, but apparently it was.

Upstairs in his apartment, Tyler flipped on one soft light, poured them each a drink—beer for him, ginger ale for her—then led the way to the small balcony with its incredible view of the Houston skyline. The setting was romantic, the glint in Tyler's eyes equally amorous. The fact that he'd stocked up on her drink of choice touched her. The yearning inside her was dangerous.

"Maybe we should go inside," she said when she felt her already weak resolve disintegrating.

"Any particular reason?"

"It's…umm…it's a little warm out here."

"There's a nice breeze, though," he said in an

amused way that indicated he knew perfectly well that the heat she was feeling had nothing to do with the weather.

"Maybe so, but I'm a big proponent of air-conditioning." Just to be sure he went along with her, she stepped back inside as she said it. Tyler followed.

Intending to keep some distance between them, she looked around for a chair, then realized that other than some small chairs that went with the dining room table, the only seating available was the large sofa and the far-too-intimate love seat. She opted for the sofa. When he chose the love seat, she breathed a sigh of relief.

"Are you nervous for some reason, Maddie?"

"Of course not. Why?"

"You seem a little jittery. I thought maybe you were thinking about that kiss in my folks' driveway. Like I said, it was no big deal, just a little something for my mother's benefit."

Maybe it wasn't a big deal to him, she thought with a touch of indignation. All the more reason to be sure there were no more. Apparently he went around dispensing kisses as casually as handshakes.

"It was nothing," she agreed. "I'd completely forgotten about it till you brought it up just now."

His eyes twinkled. "Had you?"

"Are you making fun of me?"

"I wouldn't put it that way. I'm just trying to get you to lighten up a little. You've been far too serious all day."

"I've had things on my mind."

"Such as?"

"Finding a job," she blurted, seizing on the most believable excuse she could think of.

"I've told you before, I can help with that. Or if you don't want me to make any contacts for you, I could loan you some cash till you're back on your feet."

She would sleep on the streets before she accepted a dime from a Delacourt. "That's very kind," she said stiffly. "But this is my problem."

He held up his hands. "Okay. I'm not going to give you another lecture on false pride. Just know that both offers are there if you decide you need anything."

Suddenly restless, Maddie stood up and began pacing, glancing idly at the photos as she moved about the room. Tyler watched her silently. When she came to the spot where the baby picture had been, he seemed to tense even as she realized it was missing. There was a faint mark in the dust on the tabletop confirming precisely where it had been.

"Something wrong?" he asked, his voice strained.

"Nothing," she said, reaching randomly for another picture. She grabbed a photograph of his parents that had evidently been taken many years earlier. "Your parents look very happy here."

"They were on their honeymoon. That was probably the last real vacation my dad took," he said with a laugh. "Maybe that's why he's encouraging Michael to stay away. Perhaps it's sentiment, rather than an attempt to keep me here."

"What happened to the other picture that was here?" she asked casually. "Did you move it?"

He met her gaze evenly. "Was there another picture there? I don't remember."

Should she push him on it? What did she have to lose? "Wasn't it a baby picture? You never did say who it was."

He stood up so abruptly, the movement threw her off balance, and she stumbled slightly but recovered quickly. She put her hand on his arm, felt the muscle jerk beneath her touch.

"Tyler?"

"Drop it, Maddie," he ordered, not meeting her gaze.

"But—"

"I said to drop it. Let's go. I'll walk you back to O'Reilly's so you can get your car."

She sighed heavily. It was clear she wasn't going to get a straight answer. What disturbed her even more, though, was that she couldn't quite decide if her disappointment was professional or personal. The line was getting more blurred all the time.

"Tyler, Tyler, Tyler, you've been holding out on us," his brother Jeb taunted on Monday morning. He strolled into Tyler's office, poured himself a cup of coffee, then planted himself on the corner of the desk as if he intended to linger awhile.

"Go away," Tyler snapped. He was in no mood to discuss Maddie, or much of anything else, for that matter.

"Is that any way to talk to your big brother?"

"In your case, yes. Go bother your wife."

"Brianna's away checking out some prospective drilling site that is going to make us all fabulously wealthy."

"And you're at loose ends? Go investigate something."

"I am."

"What?"

"Your love life. Fascinating stuff to hear Mother tell it. She liked your young woman, though she wasn't entirely sure she was—and I quote—one of *our* kind."

Tyler's gaze shot up. "She said that?"

"You know Mother, always concerned about the Delacourt image. She really had high hopes for you and Mary Claire."

"Blast it all, I told her that wasn't in the cards. The last thing I want is Mother choosing my dates for me."

"Which explains the unexpected arrival of Maddie," Jeb concluded. "Was she a decoy or someone you're really serious about, suitable or not?"

"Maddie is just… Maddie," Tyler responded, unable to find a designation that didn't make too much or too little of what he felt for the infuriating woman.

Her poking and prodding about that picture of his daughter had annoyed him so much that, after delivering her safely to her car the night before, he had vowed he would never see her again. He didn't need a woman around who was dedicated to reopening old wounds. Unfortunately, this morning he couldn't seem to get her out of his mind, though until Jeb's arrival he'd been making a valiant attempt.

Jeb studied him curiously. "And Maddie being 'just Maddie'—is that a good thing?"

"Hard to tell. We've just met."

Jeb settled on a corner of his desk. "Then tell me about her. Cute and perky was about all I got from Mother."

"Leave it to Mother to make that sound derogatory. Maddie *is* cute. She's also a perpetual optimist. And annoyingly mysterious. New in town. Looking for work. Beyond that I don't know a lot."

"How did you meet?"

"At O'Reilly's. She turned up there a couple of weeks ago. One night she introduced herself. We got to talking. I said good-night and that was that." He grinned. "Until she turned up on my doorstep with Rodney."

Jeb regarded him incredulously. "Your doorman?"

"Seems she was concerned because she hadn't seen me for a couple of nights. She managed to work the un-flappable Rodney into a frenzy until the two of them came sneaking up to check to see if I was dead or something."

"Oh, boy," Jeb murmured.

Tyler glowered at him. "What's that supposed to mean?"

"That was when you fell for her, wasn't it?"

"I haven't fallen for her. I'm intrigued, yes, but I'm also suspicious as hell."

"Why?" Jeb demanded. It was obvious that every investigative instinct had instantly gone on full alert.

"Because she dropped into my life out of nowhere. And there was something Kevin said, too," he admitted reluctantly. "She'd asked about me before we met."

"That's not so unusual. Maybe she'd been checking you out for a couple of nights and wanted to be sure you were available before she approached you."

Tyler shook his head. "Before that, before she'd set eyes on me."

"Uh-oh, I don't like the sound of that. She's after something, little brother. Want me to poke around a little, see what I can find out about her?"

"Absolutely not. If she's up to no good, I'll figure it out for myself."

"Look, Ty, I know you're a good judge of character, but that's when your hormones aren't involved."

"Who says my hormones are involved?" He sighed

heavily. "Never mind. It had to be Mother. I gather she saw the kiss."

Jeb grinned. "She did indeed. Made her toes curl, she said. She considered coming out and hosing you two off."

"She never said that."

"Not in those exact words, maybe," his brother agreed with a chuckle. "But she was definitely convinced that all her dreams for you and Mary Claire were going up in smoke, pun intended."

"Then I accomplished exactly what I set out to accomplish," Tyler said with relief. "I got Mother off my back."

"Not exactly."

He felt a little flicker of alarm. "Meaning?"

"She's wondering if you'll have a summer wedding or wait until the holidays."

"She isn't," Tyler protested.

"This is Mother we're talking about. She most definitely is." Jeb winked at him as he stood up. "If I were you, I'd go ahead and book the church and get it over with. Unless Maddie turns out to be an ax murderer, your goose is cooked, my friend."

"You don't have to sound so blasted happy about it."

"Hey, Dylan, Michael, Trish and I have been taking bets on when you'll get to the altar. Thanks to these recent revelations—which I have no intention of sharing with our siblings—my money's on August. Your Maddie strikes me as an impatient woman."

"She is not *my* Maddie. She is not *my* anything."

"Tell it to someone who'll believe you," Jeb taunted. "In the meantime, if you change your mind about checking out the bride-to-be, let me know. I don't have anything important on my plate right now."

"Maybe I'll pass the word on that to Dad. I'm sure he could think of something for you to do. Maybe a little stint in accounting. Hell, maybe you could just take over here, and I could get back to Louisiana and away from all the plotters and schemers in this family. And now that I think about it, does Mother have any idea that you're all placing bets on my future? She'll be praying for your sorry souls. You know how she feels about gambling. She had her fill of that back when Daddy was wildcatting to get his stake to start up Delacourt Oil. She considered *that* gambling enough to last a lifetime."

"Okay, okay, you've made your point. It's your life. You won't hear another peep out of me."

"I wish," Tyler muttered. "You are genetically incapable of keeping your nose out of other people's business."

"Just the Delacourt genes, bro. You have 'em, too. Maybe it's time you put 'em to use."

Maybe it was, Tyler thought, after Jeb was gone. Maybe it was time he tried to get a fix on just exactly what Ms. Maddie Kent was up to.

Unfortunately, when he went looking for her, she was nowhere to be found.

If the weather was steamy in Houston, it was downright oppressive in Baton Rouge. Maddie sat on a park bench and blotted ineffectively at the perspiration on her face. She could do nothing about the dampness trickling between her shoulder blades and down her back.

This whole trip, made impulsively after the disappearance of that baby picture and Tyler's reaction to her questions about it, was turning out to be as much of a bust as her earlier phone queries.

She'd tried every way she could think of to find out where Tyler lived when he was in Baton Rouge—utility companies, phone directories, real estate records. She'd butted up against tight-lipped bureaucrats at every turn. Even public records yielded nothing.

Now she was trying to work up the courage to go to the Delacourt Oil offices and see if she would have any better luck in person than she had when she'd called. Surely she could think of some believable ruse that would weaken their precious rules.

The risk, of course, was huge. There wasn't a doubt in her mind that someone would alert Tyler that a woman had been asking questions about him. He was a smart man. It wouldn't take him two seconds to conclude it was her. She doubted he would be happy about it.

Was it worth it? Was she likely to glean any significant information that could offset Tyler's usefulness as her entry into the Delacourt clan? She would never know the answer to that until she tried.

Maybe if she played the role of an old girlfriend trying to locate him just to say hi, no one would suspect anything. Old girlfriends probably popped up all the time in the life of a man as gorgeous as Tyler. Of course, that still didn't mean that no one would alert him about her search.

She sighed, then concluded that since she was here, she might as well go for broke. She checked her notes for the address, then headed toward the waterfront. She found the Delacourt offices in a converted warehouse that looked as if it had been around since the 1800s at least. Inside, however, the facilities were thoroughly modern and computerized. She wondered for a fleeting second if she was capable of breaking into the system, and if so, what corporate secrets she might discover.

Forget it, she told herself sharply. She was a reporter, not a thief. A file turning up right under her eyes was one thing. Hacking into a computer was quite another. She wanted to get information to nail Bryce Delacourt, not land in jail herself.

"Can I help you?" a woman in her early twenties asked with a friendly smile. Her Southern accent was as thick and slow as molasses.

"You surely can," Maddie said, falling comfortably into a similar speech pattern. "I am an old and very dear friend of Tyler Delacourt's, and I am wondering if you can help me locate him."

The woman's friendly expression wavered ever so slightly. "Sorry. I can't help you. It's against our policy to give out any information on employees."

"He does work out of this office, doesn't he? I could swear that's what his mama told me when I called there the other day. She said I'd find him in Baton Rouge, and since I was on my way over here, I thought we could catch up. It's been ages since we've seen each other."

"And I'm sure Tyler would love to see you," the woman said politely. "Unfortunately, he's in Houston at the moment. I'm surprised his mother didn't mention that."

"Oh, dear, maybe she didn't understand that I was already on my way."

At that moment a tall, broad-shouldered man in

jeans, work boots and a chambray shirt strolled out of an office. He gave a nod in Maddie's direction.

"Is there a problem, Gwen?"

"This woman's looking for Tyler."

He turned then and surveyed her more intently. "Is that so? Why did you want to see him?"

"We're old friends."

"And your name is?"

"Mary Claire," she said, seizing on the name of the woman Tyler had done all he could to avoid back in Houston.

"Well, now, Mary Claire, I'm real sorry, but I'm sure Gwen explained that Tyler's out of town."

"Do you know when he'll be back?"

"Now that's the million-dollar question. Soon, I hope."

"Maybe you could tell me something," she said, regarding the man hopefully. "Is he involved with anyone just now? I'd hate to make a fool of myself by trying to catch up with him if he's serious about someone. His mama said she didn't think he was."

The man's gaze narrowed suspiciously. "Mary Claire, I make it a rule around here not to discuss the personal lives of the people who work for me. Tyler's no exception, not even if the person who's asking is an *old friend*."

He said it in a way that told Maddie he wasn't buying a word of her routine. He gestured down the hall. "Why don't you come with me for a minute, though?"

"Really, I should just run along. I've already taken up far too much of your time."

"No, please, I insist," the man said in a way that suggested he wouldn't be pleased by a refusal.

With a sigh, Maddie followed him into his office. "Have a seat," he said politely.

When she was perched on the edge of a chair, he stood next to his desk towering over her. It was an intimidating tactic and, unfortunately, it was having the desired effect. Maddie wanted the floor to open up and swallow her. Obviously, she was not cut out to be a brazen liar.

"Why don't you tell me what this is really about, Mary Claire?" He gave her a penetrating look. "If that is your real name."

"Okay, Mr....?"

"Corrigan. Daniel Corrigan."

"Here it is," she said, making it up as she went along and sticking at least in the same ballpark as the truth. "I really am a friend of Tyler's. And I really do need to see him. I got the runaround when I called, so I decided to stop by and try my luck in person."

"Here's the best I can do. I'll give him a message and let him decide if he wants to speak to you." He picked up a pad of paper and handed it to her. "You can write the information yourself and I'll see that he gets it."

Maddie accepted the paper, jotted down a phony telephone number, then signed it Mary Claire. Daniel Corrigan looked it over, then reached for his phone. Her stomach plummeted.

"What are you doing?"

"Calling Tyler."

"Now?"

"I figure if you went to all this trouble, it must be important, right?"

"It's not that important," she stressed. "It can wait till he gets back from wherever he is."

"Will you still be in town then?"

"Probably not."

He smiled. "Then there's no time like the present."

As he began to dial, Maddie silently called herself a series of nonflattering names, beginning with fool and ending with idiot.

"Tyler," Corrigan said, his voice booming. "I've got a pretty little lady sitting right here in my office who says she's looking for you."

Maddie cringed.

"Her name? She says it's Mary Claire," he said in a way that clearly conveyed his doubts. He handed the phone to Maddie. "He's all yours."

"Thank you," she mouthed silently, then said a cheery hello.

"Maddie?"

There was no mistaking the shock in Tyler's voice or the fact that he'd recognized hers. Why bother denying it? "That's right," she admitted reluctantly.

"What the hell are you doing in Baton Rouge? And why did you tell Daniel you were Mary Claire?"

She sighed. "It's a long story."

"Well, why don't you sit tight?" he said, making it an order, not a suggestion. "I'll be there in a few hours, and you can explain it to me."

"There's no need for you to go to all that trouble."

"Oh, yes, there is," he said fiercely. "Let me talk to Daniel again."

Reluctantly she passed the phone back to the man whose gaze had never once left her face. He listened to whatever Tyler had to say, then nodded.

"Not a problem," he said eventually. "She'll be right here when you get here." His gaze locked with hers. "You can count on that."

Seven

Tyler fought to control his temper all the way to Baton Rouge, then finally gave up and allowed it full rein.

What the devil was Maddie up to? Why was she poking around in his life, pretending to be someone else? Was this feminine interest in him that had run amok? A fatal attraction, as it were? Or something far more sinister, some sort of tangled plot she'd dreamed up to get to his parents through him? All of his early suspicions returned in spades, but none of the scenarios he came up with fit what he knew about Maddie.

Then, again, what did he *really* know about her? Not much, except that she was all but impossible to resist. She was sexy and smart and mysterious.

And devious, he reminded himself. Best not to forget that.

He sighed heavily. Why was it that the first woman to get to him since Jen had to be up to something? Why couldn't she have been exactly what she appeared to be—friendly, sweet and innocent?

Maybe she was. Maybe this was all some huge misunderstanding.

Maybe she'd asked perfectly innocuous questions and the highly protective Daniel had overreacted. Which, of course, didn't explain what the heck she was doing in Baton Rouge in the first place or why she had flat-out lied about her identity.

Whatever the truth, Tyler was in a rotten mood by the time he finally stormed into the Delacourt Oil suite of offices long past closing hour.

"Where is she?" he demanded, cutting off the receptionist in midgreeting. "And what are you doing here so late?"

"Daniel asked me to stay. And your friend is in Daniel's office."

"He's with her?"

She nodded. "You know Daniel. Where you're concerned, he gets his back up if he thinks for a second that someone's out to hurt you. He hasn't let her out of his sight. Except when she went to the ladies' room, of course. He sent me with her then. I imagine that was why he wanted me around, in case something of a delicate nature came up."

She regarded him worriedly. "Should I call the cops or something? I'd hate to do it, because I kind of liked her. I don't know what she's really after, of course, but she seems like a nice person."

"No need to call the cops just yet. Not until I've had time to strangle her," he said, only partly in jest.

He drew in a deep breath, then opened the door to Daniel's office. His boss was sitting behind his desk, chair tilted back, feet propped up. The casualness of his pose was belied by the glint in his eyes. His gaze was pinned on the woman seated on the edge of a chair across from him. At the sound of the door, two pairs of eyes shot to Tyler. There was relief in Daniel's, but Maddie's filled with something he interpreted as resignation.

"Thanks, Daniel. You can take off now. I'll handle Ms. Kent."

His boss regarded him uneasily. "Maybe I should stick around until we know what she's up to."

Tyler shook his head. "Not necessary." He allowed himself a slight smile. "I assume you frisked her to see if she was armed."

Daniel stared. "Armed? Are you serious?"

"No. It was a bad joke. I think Ms. Kent's weapons are of the less deadly variety," he said, his gaze locked with hers. She turned pale at the taunt.

As Daniel left, Tyler pulled a chair away from the conference table at the far end of the room, turned it around and straddled it, facing Maddie. She jerked slightly when the door clicked closed behind Daniel. Under Tyler's relentless scrutiny she swallowed hard, but she didn't look away. He had to admire her for that. She was a gutsy little thing.

"So, Maddie, what's up?"

"I can explain," she began.

"I certainly hope so, because from where I'm sitting this doesn't look good. In fact, if I were a suspicious man, I would think you were up to no good."

Color flamed in her cheeks, but her gaze remained steady. "I like you, Tyler. I really do."

"You have a funny way of treating someone you supposedly like."

"I know it must seem that way, but I can tell that something's happened to you in the past, something to make you extremely cautious when it comes to women.

I thought if I could figure out what that was, I could help you get past it."

She spoke with utter sincerity, but he almost laughed at the pathetic explanation. "You're a psychologist, then?"

"No, but I—"

He shook his head. "Try again."

"It's the truth. I just wanted to know about your past."

"You could have asked me."

Her gaze clashed with his then. "Would you have told me? I don't think so. Every time I came close to asking about something that hit on a raw nerve, you clammed up."

"That should have been enough to convince you to leave it alone, then."

"Maybe so, but I couldn't."

"Why?"

"I told you—because I like you."

Again he listened for a false note, but he didn't hear it. At the same time he couldn't bring himself to trust a word she was saying. There was more to this than she'd confessed. Women didn't take off to dig around in a man's past just because he wasn't forthcoming about it. They nagged until they got at the truth or they gave up in frustration and moved on to someone easier to get along with.

What if he simply told her? What would happen then? Would she be satisfied? Or would she use the information in some way that hadn't occurred to him? And why did her dishonesty seem to matter to him so much? Why not write her off and move on to some less complicated relationship himself?

One glance into her beautiful, vulnerable eyes gave him the answer to that. He wanted her. Maybe even needed her, if he was ever going to get Jen out of his head.

Reaching an impulsive decision, he stood up abruptly. "Let's go."

She didn't budge. "Go where?"

"You want answers. I'm going to give them to you, but we're doing it my way. I just hope to hell we can both live with the truth once it's out in the open."

Maddie reluctantly followed Tyler out into the oppressive night air. Rather than feeling exhilarated that she was about to learn whatever secrets had been tormenting him, all she could think about was the bleak expression on his face when he'd promised to tell her everything.

How could she do this to him? What kind of person was she turning into? Was her revenge worth the kind of pain she was inflicting on a man who had been nothing but kind to her?

He needs to get it out, she told herself staunchly. It would be good for him to talk about it—whatever "it" was. Just because she was the sounding board didn't mean she had to use whatever he told her to hurt him. That decision was down the road. Maybe it was one she would never have to make. It was Bryce Delacourt's secrets she was really after, not Tyler's, which made her presence in Baton Rouge all the more difficult to explain. Maybe she had been driven to come here precisely for the reason she had given him, because she'd grown to care for him and wanted to understand him in a way that his having a secret hadn't allowed. It was a troubling possibility.

Tyler ushered her into his car, then headed through downtown to a neighborhood of small, cookie-cutter houses. When he pulled into a driveway, she stared around at the unkempt yard, the bedraggled garden that had suffered from neglect. For once in her life she had no idea what to say, what question to ask. She simply stared at him and waited for an explanation.

He hadn't moved since he cut the engine. His hands rested on the steering wheel—clutched it, really—and sweat broke out on his brow.

Maddie regarded him miserably as the depth of his anguish finally sank in. Stirring up things to get Bryce Delacourt had been one thing when it had been nothing more than an abstract concept of getting even. Now, face-to-face with his son's heartache, she was awash with regrets. She knew this kind of pain. She had lived it. Right now she was no longer a journalist after a story. She was a woman, aching for a man whose pain she had caused.

She reached over and touched his arm. "Tyler, we can forget this. I'm sorry. I had no right."

He shook his head. "No, we're here now." He shuddered. "It's the first time I've been back."

"You lived here?"

"For a time."

"Alone?"

"No." His voice was barely more than a shattered whisper. "This was her house, Jen's."

Maddie felt something cold settle into the region of her heart. "Was she your wife?"

"No, though not for lack of asking on my part. She

was everything else, though—lover, friend…" He drew in a deep breath. "The mother of my little girl."

"The baby in the picture," Maddie said with sudden, horrified certainty. "Oh, Tyler, what happened?"

For a minute, then two, he didn't say a word. He just sat there staring ahead, dazed, lost in the past.

"Tyler," she prodded gently.

"They were killed in an accident," he began slowly. "I'd finally convinced Jen to come to Houston to meet my family, but they never got there."

"Oh, Tyler," she whispered, her eyes stinging with unshed tears. "I'm so sorry."

"If only I hadn't insisted," he said in a voice laced with guilt and sorrow. "I should never have forced the issue. She didn't want to come. She was so sure they would disapprove of her and us. Nothing I said could convince her otherwise. I think she decided to come as much to prove me wrong as anything."

"When did it happen?"

"Six months ago." His gaze shifted back to the house. "Let's go inside."

Maddie didn't want to go inside. She didn't want to see the home where he'd been happy. She didn't want to be there when he dealt with the memories of a woman he'd obviously loved very deeply. This was an intensely private moment.

And she was jealous, wildly, bitterly jealous of a woman who was dead. Wasn't this exactly what she deserved for poking her nose in where it didn't belong?

"Tyler, are you sure? Maybe it's better to let it be."

"It's taken me six months to come here. I'm going in," he said with finality.

Like it or not, she couldn't let him face it alone. "Then, I'm coming with you."

As they neared the front door, Maddie got a closer look at the garden that had obviously once blazed with color. Clearly it had been tended with love.

Tyler put the key into the lock, then turned the handle. Inside, he flipped a switch, and a light came on in a tiny foyer. The living room was on the right. A hallway straight ahead apparently led to the bedrooms. Tyler stood right where he was, frozen in place. Maddie put a hand on his arm.

"Are you okay?" she asked.

"I'll survive," he said, sounding surprised. He walked into the living room and turned on a lamp that cast soft light over a worn sofa and scarred tables.

"She wouldn't let me replace anything," he said defensively. "This house was her pride and joy. She'd had nothing as a kid and was so excited to finally have a place of her own. She put her whole heart into this house."

Maddie compared it to the home in which Tyler had grown up and had to wonder how he had felt when he had first stepped inside here. Bright paint was a startling contrast to the subdued elegance of the wallpaper in his parents' mansion. Junk store castoffs, though polished lovingly, were no comparison to the Delacourt antiques.

Yet this had been a home. There was no mistaking it. Everywhere there were framed snapshots of Tyler, of that same baby who had aroused Maddie's curiosity and of a lovely young woman with the slender elegance of a dancer and huge brown eyes that shone with love. A glass filled with long-dead wildflowers sat atop a small table in what must have been a dining area. Beyond it, the ancient appliances in the kitchen still sparkled from the loving attention of a woman who took pride in her surroundings.

Tyler walked from room to room, his expression stoic, his shoulders rigid with tension.

A knock on the front door startled them both. Before they could move, an elderly woman opened the door and called out.

"Tyler, is that you?"

A smile broke across his face as he went to meet her, Maddie trailing behind. "Mrs. Andrews." He swept her up in a hug that had her laughing.

"Put me down, young man, before I take a ruler to your knuckles."

"You know they don't let teachers rap their students' hands anymore for misbehaving."

"Which is why it's just as well that I retired twenty years ago," she said.

She rested a hand against his cheek. "How are you? We've missed seeing you."

"I've missed you, too," he said. "But I couldn't come back. Thank you for looking after the place for me."

"I haven't done much. The yard's a disaster. I can't tend flowers the way your Jen could. The house needs to be lived in. Are you coming back? Is that why you're here?"

"No," he said at once.

"Have you left Baton Rouge for good, then?"

"No. I've been working on the rig, staying closer to the job."

"You should be here, Tyler. Jen would have wanted that." Her gaze settled on Maddie then. "Forgive me, my dear. I didn't see you over there in the shadows. My eyesight's not what it used to be. I'm Martha Andrews. I live next door."

"This is Maddie Kent," Tyler said.

"I'm very pleased to meet you," Maddie told the older woman, who was clearly in her eighties, though she appeared to have the energy of someone much younger.

"I'm glad to see you're moving on with your life," Mrs. Andrews told Tyler. "We're not meant to go through life alone."

"He's not…" Maddie began.

"I'm not…" Tyler said at the same time.

Mrs. Andrews chuckled. "Awfully quick to protest, aren't you both? Well, whatever the case, it's nice to see you here again. Tyler, you let me know if there's anything you need. I made your Jen a promise, you know."

He regarded her with surprise. "You did? What sort of promise?"

"She always asked me to look out for you."

"Why would she do that?" he asked.

"Why, because she loved you, of course."

"But why would she think she wouldn't be around to do it herself?"

Mrs. Andrews seemed startled by the question. "Now that you mention it, it does seem an odd thing to say at her age. It seems to me, though, that so many things had gone wrong in her young life and she was so happy with you that she never expected it to last. I used to scold her about that. It was clear to anyone who saw the two of you how deeply you loved her. I was so relieved when she finally agreed to meet your family. I thought that might be the beginning of the future you both deserved."

"But if she hadn't—"

"Don't you think like that," she said sternly, cutting him off in midsentence. "The accident was a terrible thing, but the Lord has His reasons for what He does. We just have to accept that."

Tyler sighed. "Your faith is stronger than mine. I can't find any reason for a woman like Jen and a precious baby girl to die."

"His reason will come to you in time," she said gently, then smiled at Maddie. "Perhaps it already has." She stood on tiptoe to kiss Tyler's cheek. "Good night, dear. God bless."

"Good night, Mrs. Andrews," he said softly, staring after her.

When she had gone, he turned slowly to meet Maddie's gaze. "Could she be right?"

"About?"

"You and me. That I had to lose Jen so I would be ready when you came along."

"Absolutely not," she said at once. Her plotting for revenge against Bryce Delacourt could hardly be part of some divine plan. It was merely a very human act, and it was that, not God, that had brought her into Tyler's life. "I'm with you. I don't think I understand anything that costs a very young woman and an innocent child their lives."

He seemed startled by her vehemence, but he nodded. "Yeah, you're right." His expression filled with sorrow, he took one last look around, then flipped off lights. "Let's get out of here."

Only after they were in the car did Maddie ask, "Will you ever live here again?"

"I honestly don't know. But I haven't been able to bring myself to sell it."

"Then the house is yours? You paid for it?"

"Oh, no," he said with a rueful laugh. "Jen bought it and paid the mortgage while she was alive. She wouldn't take a dime from me, not ever. But because of the baby, she had made a will leaving everything she had to be held in trust for our daughter. I'm the executor. Since there are no other heirs, it's up to me to decide what to do with it. I've paid off the mortgage and I take care of the taxes, so there's no rush. Maybe one day, when it doesn't hurt so much, I'll go back there."

"It's not exactly what you're used to."

"You mean compared to my parents' house or my condo?" She nodded. "Or the beach house."

"No," he agreed. "It's nothing like those places. But I was happier in this house than I've ever been in my life."

Maddie had to swallow hard around the lump in her throat. How could she—how could any woman—compete with that? And why did she suddenly want to so desperately?

"Your Jen was a very lucky woman," she said quietly.

Clearly taken aback, he stared at her. "How can you say that?"

"Because she was loved so very much. That's the greatest gift a man can give a woman, and you gave that to her. It's the intensity of the passion that matters, not the longevity."

"If that's the standard, then I was the lucky one," he protested. "Because she brought me nothing but joy."

Maddie couldn't help contrasting that to her own goal. What would he say months from now of the woman who was destined to bring nothing but anguish into his life? And how would she live with herself once she'd done it?

She glanced over at Tyler. "Thank you for telling me about her and about your little girl."

"I should probably be the one thanking you for forcing me to face this," he said. He reached over and touched a hand to her cheek. His expression registered surprise. "You're crying. What's wrong, Maddie?"

"Nothing," she insisted. She was just crying for what was…and for what would never be.

Eight

Tyler still wasn't thoroughly convinced that Maddie had been honest with him about her reason for being in Baton Rouge, but he couldn't help being grateful to her for more or less forcing him to face the past. Maybe he'd just been waiting for someone to come along who could.

He felt an amazing sense of relief now that he'd been back to the house he and Jen had shared. Seeing Mrs. Andrews again had given him solace, as well. She had been like a grandmother to Jen. If she could forgive him for his part in that fateful trip, then he knew he had to learn to forgive himself. Though he was far from there yet, he was beginning to believe it was possible.

Because he'd been too wired to sleep, he and Maddie had driven back to Houston that same night. To his continued frustration, she insisted that he leave her in front of O'Reilly's when they got to town.

As he pulled to a stop in front of the bar, he studied her with a narrowed gaze. "Maddie, what's with the secrecy about where you live? I know you're not working, so you're probably watching every penny.

I'm sure you had to choose some place where the rent was low. You know I'm not a snob, so it can't be that you're ashamed of it."

"I'd just rather leave things as they are," she said.

Because he was too exhausted to argue, he gave in. "We'll discuss this over dinner," he warned her.

"In that case, maybe it would be better if we didn't have dinner," she said wryly.

"I'll be here at six," he said with determined finality. "If you're not here, I will find you. You can count on it." He brushed a thumb across her bottom lip and felt her tremble slightly at the touch. "If I can't find you on my own, I have two brothers who are investigators. Believe me, you are no match for them."

The reference to Dylan and Jeb seemed to make her uneasy for some reason, but it served its purpose. She nodded agreement.

"Six o'clock," she said.

"I'll look forward to it."

"You will?" she said, clearly surprised.

Tyler chuckled at her expression. "Why do you find that so astonishing, Maddie?"

"Because I've caused you a lot of trouble. You had to take off and come all the way to Baton Rouge. I've poked my nose into things that were none of my business, stirred up a lot of painful memories."

He was silent as she paused.

She shrugged. "Worse, I honestly can't promise I won't do it again. Asking questions is second nature to me."

Now that his only secret was out in the open—with her, anyway—Tyler had nothing more to hide. "You can ask me anything you want to, as long as I can reserve the right not to answer."

She nodded solemnly. "Deal."

She held out her hand to shake on it. Tyler ignored it and leaned closer to press a kiss to her lips. He fought the temptation to linger and savor the sensations that the simplest touch stirred in him.

"What was that for?" she asked.

"Our deal was too important for anything less than a kiss to seal it."

"Kisses have a way of getting us in trouble," she reminded him.

He grinned. "Then we'll just have to practice until they're no longer any danger."

Maddie responded with a low chuckle. "I don't see that happening, Tyler. Not in this lifetime."

"What? The practicing?"

"No, making them less dangerous."

He regarded her evenly. "You may be right about that, darlin'. You definitely may be right about that."

In fact, that was only one of the reasons why he couldn't bring himself to cut her out of his life, even now that he knew she was capable of lying straight to his face. Whatever her real reason for that journey to Baton Rouge, she was still the most intriguing woman he'd met in ages. He simply had to remember to keep his guard up at all times and learn to slip in a few clever questions of his own. One of these days he was going to discover exactly what made Maddie Kent tick. He just had to be darn sure he didn't risk his heart in the process.

Maddie expected to spend the rest of the day sleeping. She was emotionally and physically exhausted after the trip to Louisiana. Unfortunately, nightmares plagued her. In them her father seemed to be taunting her for her failure to get back at his old nemesis. And there was always Tyler, watching her with an expression of deep sorrow on his face.

She awoke shaking, filled with an awareness that no matter what she did she was going to let one of them down, leave one of them bitterly disappointed in her.

Since she couldn't sleep, she decided to go back to the library and conduct more research. Scanning clippings didn't require the concentration she didn't have. It was a mindless if necessary task, perfect for a rainy afternoon. And it would keep her occupied until she had to meet Tyler.

She had stopped the last time when she had found her father's death notice. Today she began working back from that date, methodically looking for any mention of Delacourt Oil, no matter how brief, no matter how seemingly innocuous. A pattern was bound to emerge sooner or later. She just had to find enough pieces of the puzzle.

It was five-thirty when she reached the edition published a few days after her father's firing and five years before his death. There on the business page was a blaring headline: DELACOURT OIL ROCKED BY EMBEZZLEMENT SCANDAL. A subhead declared: Trusted Accountant Involved.

For a minute, she was unable to bring herself to read beyond those damning words. She knew with everything in her what would come next. She knew that accountant would be her father.

But…*embezzlement?* It couldn't be. It had to be a terrible lie. Her family had never had a lot of money.

They had barely made ends meet. If her father had stolen from Bryce Delacourt, where had the money gone?

She forced herself to read on, to try to absorb every damning word of the accusations against Frank Kent, a man who had been with Delacourt practically from the beginning, according to a quotation from Bryce himself.

"I am deeply saddened by this," he said. "I considered Frank a friend as well as a valuable asset to this company, but I could no longer ignore the evidence that was right before my eyes. A hundred thousand dollars is missing."

Maddie gasped. A hundred thousand dollars? It was absurd. It was crazy. Her father had never had that kind of money. Never! No wonder he had gone into such a depression when he had lost his job. To be accused of a crime like this must have been devastating, especially when he hadn't had the resources to fight it, to clear his name. No wonder her mother had refused to go out in public, had stopped seeing her friends. She had been humiliated by the lies. Naturally neither of them had wanted their children to know the kind of libelous claims being made about their father.

Maddie's indignation mounted. It fed the rage that had festered for years. She was glad to see precisely what had driven her father over the brink. It fueled her determination to clear his name and to get revenge. No man, not even the powerful Bryce Delacourt, should be allowed to slander an honest man in this way and get away with it.

Despite her anger, a niggling doubt taunted her. Bryce Delacourt wasn't stupid. Nor were the editors of the newspaper. Would any of them have risked a suit if the charges weren't true? If they didn't have hard evidence?

Maybe Delacourt was arrogant enough to believe that he could say what he wanted with impunity, but no responsible journalist would do the same. She noted the byline on the article, jotted it in her notebook. She would find Lawrence Timmons and see just who his sources had been, demand to know what evidence had been provided.

Even though it was bound to make her late for her dinner with Tyler, she checked the phone book and found a number for a Lawrence Timmons.

Hands shaking, she fumbled for coins for the pay phone and dialed. When a man answered, it was all she could do not to slam the receiver back in the cradle.

"Mr. Timmons?"

"Yes. Who is this? If it's a telephone solicitation, I can tell you right now I'm not interested," he said in a scratchy, irritable voice.

"It's not," she said hurriedly. "I'm looking for some information, and I was hoping you might be able to help me."

"Go on."

He still sounded wary, but at least he was willing to listen. "Were you a reporter for a Houston paper about sixteen years ago?" she asked.

"I was."

"Would you mind talking to me about a story you covered back then?" she asked, praying he was like other journalists and had a steel trap for a mind when it came to stories he'd covered.

"Why would you be interested in something that far back? Who are you?"

"My name is Maddie and I'm looking for some answers to an old puzzle."

"An old puzzle, is it? Well, I can't swear I'll recall the details, but I can try," he said, sounding a little more open. "Which story is it?"

"I'd rather not get into it on the phone. Could we meet? Maybe for coffee or for breakfast tomorrow? This is extremely important to me."

"I suppose. I usually have breakfast at a little restaurant around the corner from my place. You could come by." He gave her the name of the place and the address, then added, "I'm not as much of an early bird as I used to be before I retired, but I'm usually there by nine."

"I'll see you in the morning, then."

"What's your name, young lady?"

"Maddie, sir. Thank you for agreeing to see me. You'll never know how much it means."

"I'll look forward to meeting you, Maddie. I hope I'll be able to help you."

She hung up slowly, heart pounding. She had a source. An honest-to-goodness source who could tell her exactly what happened years ago. She had deliberately avoided mentioning her last name because she wanted Lawrence Timmons to give her an uncensored version of things, something he might be reluctant to do if he realized her connection to that story.

Hopefully he wouldn't press her for the name in the morning. Though, in his place, if she had his reporting background, she might, she acknowledged to herself.

She was still reeling from her discoveries when she finally reached O'Reilly's a half hour later than she'd promised to be there. She saw the look of relief that swept over Tyler's face when she walked in and wondered if he would be so glad to see her if he knew that she was very close to nailing his father as a liar.

"You're late," he said lightly.

"I overslept," she said easily, proud of herself for not allowing any of the emotions she was feeling into her voice.

"Really? You don't look all that rested."

She forced a smile. "Now that's what every woman wants to hear."

"Even exhausted, you're still more beautiful than most women," he said.

She laughed at that. "Better, but you won't win me over with audacious flattery."

His expression sobered. "What *will* win you over, Maddie?"

The truth, she almost blurted, but bit her tongue. It was doubtful that Tyler knew the truth. He hadn't been much more than a child himself when all of this happened. Would he recall the scandal? If she asked and he did, would he remember the name of the man at the center of it? She didn't dare chance it. If he recalled that the accountant was Frank Kent, it wouldn't take much for him to guess that she was Kent's daughter, for him to speculate about what she was really doing in Houston.

"It's hard to say," she said evasively, then added more truthfully, "I've been so worried about work for so long now that I haven't given any thought at all to a relationship."

His gaze locked with hers, made her toes curl. "Maybe it's time you did," he said.

"Maybe so," she agreed. Just not with him. Never with him, she thought sadly.

"My mother was asking about you today," he said.

"Oh?"

"She's been leaping to all sorts of wild conclusions ever since our visit."

"How wild?"

He grinned. "Wild enough. She made me promise to bring you by again."

"Perhaps I could schedule a lunch with her sometime," Maddie suggested. If she could see Helen Delacourt alone, perhaps she could dig for some answers from her without arousing suspicion.

"She'd love that," Tyler said. "Just let me warn you that she might insist on taking you to pick out china."

"Why on earth would she do that?" she asked, worried that she was beginning to grasp the sort of wild speculation in which his mother had been engaging.

"Like I said, the speculation has gotten pretty out of hand."

"What have you done to set her straight?"

"Not a lot," he admitted.

"Why?"

"For the moment it's actually keeping her off my back about my social life. But if you're not up to her thousand-and-one questions, I'd steer clear of her, if I were you, unless you have me around to provide cover."

Maddie chuckled. She had a feeling his reasoning was pretty self-serving. "I think I can handle your mother. After all, there's nothing to tell, so she won't get the wrong idea from me. In fact, I can set her straight and tell her I wouldn't have you on a bet. She'd probably pick up the phone and call—who was it, now? Mary Claire?—before I got out the front door."

Tyler regarded her with indignation. "You would do that?"

"In a heartbeat."

"Then you're not the least bit interested in me?"

"Not a bit."

"Is that so?" he said, his tone registering disbelief.

"Yep."

"I could make you change your mind."

Maddie realized then that she'd made the terrible mistake of uttering what amounted to a challenge. "But why would you try? Just for the fun of it?"

Eyes twinkling with mischief, he nodded. "It would be fun."

"But then what, Tyler? You're not over Jen. I'm not in the market for any kind of commitment. It would be a disaster."

"Not necessarily. Maybe we're both more ready than we realize. I know I haven't been able to get you out of my mind."

"That's very flattering…"

"I didn't say it to flatter you. I said it because it's true."

Somewhere deep inside, Maddie felt her resolve begin to crack. Under other circumstances she would play the game, see where it led. But not under these. She couldn't—for Tyler's sake and her own.

"What's new on the job front?" he asked, throwing her off-kilter with the change of subject.

She thought of the article she'd discovered. "I think I may have a lead," she said.

His gaze searched hers intently. "Why don't you sound happier about that?"

"It's not exactly what I was hoping for," she admitted, skirting as closely as possible to the truth.

"Then forget about it. You'll find what you're looking for. And if it takes longer than you were counting on—"

"Don't go there again, Tyler. I won't take money from you."

He held up his hands. "Okay, okay, I've gotten the message."

"I doubt that. You've just accepted that you're wasting your time tonight. Tomorrow's a whole new ball game."

He grinned. "You know me so well already."

"I know your type," she agreed. "Pushy, arrogant, determined."

He laughed. "Exactly the kind of man you love," he said.

"Hardly."

"Why else would you be here?"

"Because you threatened to hunt me down like an animal," she suggested lightly.

He winced. "That sounds so…"

"Rotten?" she supplied.

"Extreme," he countered. "I merely wanted you to know that I wouldn't give up easily."

She regarded him curiously. "What would it take to make you give up?"

"Discovering that that little trip you took to Baton Rouge wasn't the only deception you've pulled with me," he said readily.

Maddie felt her heart begin to hammer in her chest. Now she knew that it would be only a matter of time before Tyler walked out of her life. She'd been deceiving him from the moment they'd met, and he wouldn't forgive her for it.

Even though she'd known from the beginning that he could be nothing more than a means to an end, hearing him state so flatly that he would cut her out of his life for lying to him saddened her.

"Hey," he said. "Why so sad? You look as if you're about to lose your best friend."

Not yet, she thought. But it wouldn't be long. She just had to postpone the inevitable for a little longer, until she could get closer to his parents, dig a little deeper for Delacourt secrets.

"I hope not," she said softly. "Friends are hard to come by."

"I hope you consider me one of yours," he said.

That was the trouble. She did. In the end would this exposé she was planning cost her more than she gained? Would it cost her the friendship and respect of a man she was coming to care for a great deal?

At that modest house in Baton Rouge, she had seen the kind of man Tyler Delacourt was, the powerful emotions of which he was capable.

Would her determination to avenge her father's death cost her a chance at a deep and abiding love most women spent a lifetime praying to find?

Because the answer to that was too disconcerting to contemplate, she forced a smile. "I thought you promised me dinner. I'm starved."

"Let's go to my place," he suggested. "I'll cook."

"You cook? More than that fish you prepared at the beach?"

"I'm so good, you'll swear I must have been a chef in another life," he declared.

"Then by all means, let's go to your place."

When they walked into the lobby a few minutes later, Rodney greeted her with a grin. "Nice to see you again, Ms. Kent."

"You, too," she said, then nodded toward Tyler. "This time you won't have to help me break in."

"That's very good, miss." He held open the door to the elevator for them. "Have a nice evening."

Just as the door was about to close, he grabbed it and held it open. "Oh, Mr. Delacourt, I almost forgot. Your brother was here. If he comes back shall I send him up or tell him you're not in?"

"Jeb?" he asked.

"Yes, sir. He says he's at loose ends since his wife is still out of town. He had their daughter with him. I believe they were going to have ice cream, then stop back. Miss Emma said he'd promised her a hot-fudge sundae."

Tyler laughed. "I wonder if Brianna knows how he spoils that child when she's away."

"I imagine not, sir, but it would be hard to resist giving Miss Emma anything she wants."

"Isn't that the truth? The girl is an angel." He glanced at Maddie. "What do you say? Are you up to another Delacourt inquisition? Jeb has an insatiable curiosity, and he's been prepped by Mother. You'll love Emma, though. She's had a very tough time of it, but she's a remarkable child."

The thought of withstanding an investigator's scrutiny, no matter how well intentioned it might be, made her tremble, but she couldn't think of a single gracious way to say no.

"By all means, let them come up."

"You heard the lady, Rodney."

"Yes, sir. Shall I ring first?"

"No need."

As the elevator doors slid closed, Tyler met her gaze with an amused grin. "You're a brave woman, Maddie."

"Oh?"

"If you've got a secret, Jeb will worm it out of you, so I advise you to be on your guard."

"No problem," she said. She had already planned on doing exactly that.

"Does that mean you have no secrets, or that you're prepared to withstand any inquisition?"

"Do you honestly think I'd tell you that?" she said lightly. "It might be all the incentive you need to get your brother to bring out the rubber hoses and water torture."

"Oh, I think his techniques are more subtle than that. When he starts mining for secrets, you won't even see it coming."

Maddie doubted that. She was pretty sure she'd recognize a sneak attack the instant it was launched. After all, she was pretty darn good at them herself.

Nine

Tyler wasn't nearly as relaxed as Maddie appeared to be when the doorbell rang an hour later announcing Jeb's arrival. He knew what his brother was capable of. Maybe Emma's presence would keep him on his best behavior.

"You were mighty late getting home tonight," Jeb said when he came through the door, slowing his pace to accommodate Emma's halting gait. "The munchkin and I were going to buy you ice cream."

Tyler knew the precise moment when Jeb caught sight of Maddie, because a glint of anticipation lit in his eyes. For once Rodney had been discreet. The doorman apparently hadn't said a word to Jeb about Tyler's company.

"You must be Maddie," he said at once. "I'm Jeb, the handsome one. And this is Emma, my princess."

Maddie smiled and held out a hand to Jeb's stepdaughter. "I'm very happy to meet you, Emma."

Jeb turned to Tyler. "She didn't say she was happy to meet me. What have you been telling her?" he asked with feigned indignation.

"Just the truth, big brother."

"Don't listen to a word he says," Jeb advised. "I'm innocent of all charges."

Maddie grinned. "I suppose that remains to be seen."

Emma listened attentively to the exchange, then turned to Tyler, obviously bored by the grown-ups' conversation. "Uncle Tyler, can I go play with your video games? Jeb promised."

"Oh, he did, did he? He always did like to give away my toys. Go on, darlin'. If you want to get your socks beat off, call me."

Emma laughed delightedly. "It'll never happen. You're pitiful."

"And you're entirely too smart."

"Mama says a woman can never be too smart," Emma said primly.

"Not when dealing with a Delacourt, that's for sure," Maddie agreed.

"Hey," Tyler and Jeb protested in unison.

Emma and Maddie shared a grin.

"Maybe you should come play with me," Emma suggested to Maddie. "I'll bet you're really good at video games."

"Maybe I will, if these two get too obnoxious. But the truth is, I've never played a video game."

"See you in a few minutes," Emma said confidently. "I can teach you everything you need to know."

Jeb regarded her with a wounded expression. "I think my little angel just insulted us."

"She did. It hasn't taken her long to get to know you, has it?" Tyler watched as Emma hobbled off, amazed by her fierce determination to overcome the injuries that had threatened her ability to ever walk again. Then he turned to Maddie. "Emma is Brianna's little girl and Jeb's stepdaughter. She was in an accident a couple of years ago. She's just learning to walk again."

"Forget walking. She's running me ragged," Jeb said. "She gets stronger every day, thank goodness."

Tyler watched his brother as he deliberately turned his attention to Maddie.

"So, Maddie Kent, tell me all about yourself. When's the wedding?"

"Very funny," Tyler said. "I told you Mother got that all wrong."

"You told me," Jeb agreed. "Have you told her?"

Tyler shook his head. "Not a chance. It's serving my purposes. But Maddie's threatening to tell her." He gave an exaggerated shudder. "Which is fine by me as long as I'm not close by for the explosion."

"How exactly did he maneuver you into doing his dirty work?" Jeb asked, his expression incredulous as he stared at Maddie.

"I wasn't maneuvered. I volunteered. Somebody has to set her straight," she said, shooting a pointed look in Tyler's direction.

"Brave woman," Jeb declared.

"That's what I told her when she agreed to let you come up here tonight," Tyler said.

"You warned her I'd ask all sorts of impertinent, personal questions?"

"Absolutely," Tyler said.

"Well, that certainly spoils all the fun," Jeb said. "I guess I'll have to wait to catch you off guard, Maddie."

"I'll look forward to it," she said with a laugh.

Tyler was startled by Jeb's apparent decision to back off. "Giving up so soon?" he inquired.

"How can I trip her up when you've warned her what I'm up to?" Jeb countered.

"Forewarned is forearmed," Maddie agreed.

Despite the light response, Tyler thought he detected a hint of relief in her expression. Were there secrets she was afraid that Jeb might ferret out? It was the second time that night that she'd hinted at as much, but he hoped to heaven he was wrong. He wanted very badly to believe that Maddie Kent was the woman who could bring something that had been missing back into his life.

Maddie breathed a sigh of relief when she got back to her apartment that night. She had a feeling she had indeed dodged a bullet with Jeb Delacourt. He was an amiable scoundrel on the surface, but she'd seen the intelligence in his eyes, the concern for his brother's well-being. It was the same sort of protectiveness she'd seen in Tyler's gaze when he looked at her. These were men who took seriously their commitment to look out for anyone about whom they cared.

She had also seen the love and tenderness Jeb had displayed toward his stepdaughter. It was obvious that Emma adored him. Maddie had known then that he had a soft spot, even though she had recognized that it wouldn't be wise to count on it when it came to her. She had a hunch Jeb would show no mercy if he thought she was about to hurt his younger brother.

As if to remind her that that was exactly what was likely to happen, she spotted the blinking light on the telephone answering machine. Only one person knew this number. She hit the play button. There were three messages, all from Griffin Carpenter, just as she'd anticipated. He sounded increasingly impatient as he demanded updates.

Even though it was late, Maddie called him back. It didn't surprise her that he answered on the first ring.

"It's about time you called. What the devil has been going on over there? I expected news by now."

"I'm getting close," she said. "I have an interview in the morning that could break things wide-open."

"Tell me," he demanded eagerly.

"I'll call you afterward," she promised. "Let me see if it pans out."

"Don't put me off, young lady. I'm spending a bundle on this. I think I have a right to know what's going on."

"Of course you do. I'll be in touch before noon."

"See that you are," he barked, then slammed down the phone.

His curt attitude was a wake-up call. She needed to remember that she might be on a personal vendetta, but Carpenter had his own agenda and his own way of doing things. The normal rules didn't apply. If she didn't produce something that would satisfy him, he could easily yank her financial resources and her forum for any exposé. Though no deadline had ever been discussed, it was apparent that hers was fast approaching. He was clearly anxious to get something about Bryce Delacourt into print.

She had that looming deadline on her mind when she arrived at the designated restaurant precisely at nine the next morning eager for her interview with the retired business writer for the Houston paper.

"Table for one?" the hostess asked.

"Actually I'm meeting someone, Lawrence Timmons. Is he here?"

The woman frowned. "Now that you mention it, no. He's usually here by now. I hope he's okay. He hasn't been feeling up to snuff lately. We worry about him. Too many years of smoking have taken their toll. His lungs are a mess. Why not have a seat. He could turn up yet."

"Thanks, I will," Maddie said, swallowing her disappointment. What if his failure to show up had nothing to do with feeling poorly?

What if he'd regretted agreeing to meet with her? What if Bryce Delacourt had gotten to him?

Slow down, she warned herself. Not even she believed that Delacourt was a murderer, not in that way. She might blame him for her father's death, but he hadn't pulled the trigger on that gun.

She waited until ten o'clock before finally accepting that Lawrence Timmons wasn't going to show up. She had his address from the phone book, and he'd said it was in the neighborhood. Maybe the hostess could direct her to it.

"You gonna see if he's home?" she asked after she'd given Maddie very precise directions. "Good. Let us know if there's anything he needs, okay? We think of him as family. He doesn't have anyone else. We try to look out for him, at least as much as he'll let us."

"I will," Maddie promised.

She walked the three blocks to his address in a small development of town houses. The grounds were well kept, but the homes were showing their age. There was a car parked in front of Timmons's place. She went up the sidewalk and knocked on the door.

An elderly man who had the rigid bearing of an ex-soldier opened the door and regarded her with a sigh. "I figured you'd turn up here sooner or later. You're Maddie?"

"Yes."

His gaze was sharp as he studied her. "Maddie Kent, I imagine."

The statement, made with absolute confidence, threw her, but it was proof that his reporter's instincts were still sharp. "How did you know?" she asked.

"I pulled my notes and the clippings I had from the time period you mentioned. It didn't take much to tie you to the story I did about Frank Kent. Your name was in my notes, even though I didn't use it in the article." He gestured inside. "Now that you're here, you might as well come in."

"Thank you."

Maddie preceded him into a tidy living room furnished with so much chintz it made her dizzy. Timmons caught her expression and gave a hoarse chuckle.

"My wife loved flowers," he explained. "Didn't matter to her if they were in the garden, in paintings, on dishes or on the upholstery. Believe it or not, I've toned it down some since she passed on, but it didn't seem to make sense to get rid of perfectly good furniture just because it's too fussy for my taste."

Maddie smiled. "I imagine this would seem cozy in the English countryside."

"Which is exactly where she came from," he said. "Always said the flowers could make her forget it was a rainy day. She made a great pot of tea, too. She managed to make a convert of me. Haven't had coffee in years. I have some Earl Grey I just brewed if you'd like a cup."

"If it's no trouble," she said.

"None at all. Have a seat. I'll bring it in."

While he was gone, Maddie noticed the file folders that had been jammed with yellowed newspaper clippings and narrow notebooks that would fit in a reporter's pocket. The folders and notebooks had been neatly dated. All of those on the table were from the year her father had been fired from Delacourt Oil.

When Timmons returned, he handed her a cup of tea, then set sugar, lemon and cream on the table next to her. He was wheezing slightly from the exertion and sank heavily into an easy chair opposite her.

"I imagine you want to talk about your father."

Confronted with all those folders, presumably packed with facts, she swallowed hard but nodded. "Until yesterday I had no idea he had been charged with embezzlement. I can't believe it. It had to be a lie. We never had any money, certainly not a hundred thousand dollars, which is what your story said was missing."

"All I know is that Bryce Delacourt didn't make that charge lightly. I interviewed him in person. He was tormented by it. He had considered your father his friend, as well as an employee."

"What evidence did he have?"

"Check stubs, altered deposits, padded bills, that sort of thing."

"And my father was the only one who could have been responsible? Surely there were other people in the department."

"Only one at the time, a young woman."

"Couldn't she have been the one?"

"I checked that out thoroughly myself. She was a numbers cruncher, nothing more. She didn't have the same access to the accounts that your father did. Remember, this was the early days of Delacourt Oil. It was a small operation. Computers were still to come. There wasn't a doubt in my mind after my investigation that Delacourt had the evidence to back up the charge. Whether your father would have been convicted is anyone's guess."

"Because he died before a trial," she said slowly.

"No, because Delacourt worked out an arrangement with him. Your father vowed to make restitution."

"How?" she asked, shocked. "He was barely earning minimum wage. It would have taken forever."

"I don't think that was a consideration for Delacourt."

"Because he just wanted to watch him suffer," Maddie said angrily.

Timmons looked shocked by her conclusion. "Absolutely not. It was because he didn't want him to go to jail. He knew he had a wife and children. He thought you had suffered enough."

Maddie refused to believe that. If Bryce Delacourt had been so concerned about their suffering, he would have found some way to help them, she thought angrily. He would have kept her father on the job so he could earn a decent enough living to make restitution.

Even as she reached her own conclusion, a part of her could see that she was being irrational. If her father was guilty of embezzlement, Delacourt could hardly have kept him on.

If. That was the key word. She still didn't believe a

word of this preposterous accusation. Timmons, however, clearly did, so questioning him any further would be a waste of her time.

"Do you remember the name of the woman who worked in the department?"

"Not offhand, but I'm sure it's in my notes," he said. "Give me a minute."

He flipped through several notebooks before stopping at a page. "Pamela Davis, that's it. In her early twenties, then, so she might still be working there."

"Thank you so much," Maddie said.

"I'm sorry I couldn't tell you what you wanted to hear. It's a sad thing when a parent a child has idolized turns out to have had feet of clay. I'm sure your parents thought they were doing the right thing by keeping the truth of what happened from you."

"Yes," she agreed. She just didn't happen to believe that her father was one of those parents who wasn't as honest as she'd believed him to be.

Especially since not even a single dime of that stolen money had ever turned up at their home.

An hour later she was back at her apartment and on the phone to the personnel office at Delacourt Oil.

"I am trying to contact a woman I was told works for your company or did at some time in the past," she told the receptionist who answered the phone. "Could you help me with that information?"

"You'll need to speak to a supervisor. One moment, please." Maddie waited.

"Hello, this is Mrs. Lockhorn. May I help you?"

"Yes." She repeated her question.

"Normally we don't give out information on our employees, past or present," she said.

Maddie reached for a credible excuse and came up with one that she'd heard usually worked. "I'm working for a lawyer handling the estate of a relative. This woman has inherited quite a bit of money. I'm sure she'd want to know about it. Couldn't you at least tell me if she is still employed there?"

Mrs. Lockhorn hesitated, clearly torn by the promise of large sums of money for someone she might know. "Tell me the name," she said finally. "I'll see what I can do."

"Pamela Davis. I believe at one point she might have been in the accounting department."

There was a soft gasp on the other end of the line. "Oh, dear, how terribly sad. Ms. Davis died about a year ago. She had cancer. It was a terrible pity. She was head of the accounting department at the time."

Maddie bit back her disappointment, murmured the appropriately sympathetic comments, then asked, "Is there anyone who could tell me a little more about her? Did she have a family?"

"No, she was unmarried at the time she died. I know because we handled all of the arrangements for her funeral. Mr. Delacourt insisted. He was quite fond of her. She had been with the company for a good many years."

Maddie immediately seized on the offhand remark. Was there a story there? Was that why her father had taken the fall, because Bryce Delacourt had wanted to protect a woman of whom he was "fond"? Was that the real reason he had never filed formal charges against her father, because he knew that Frank Kent was innocent?

"Really?" she said. "She and Mr. Delacourt were close?"

"Oh, dear, I didn't mean to imply anything," Mrs. Lockhorn said, sounding genuinely appalled by Maddie's interpretation. "She was an attractive woman, but I'm certain they were nothing more than employer and employee. Mr. Delacourt would never cross that sort of line, not in this day and age of sexual harassment suits around every corner."

Maddie let it drop. Such suits had probably been less prevalent back when any relationship between the two might have begun. Besides, there was always the possibility that both had been consenting partners. She knew one person who could tell her that, perhaps without even realizing she was being asked for such a personal revelation about her marriage: Helen Delacourt. Maddie resolved to schedule that lunch with her within the next few days.

"Thank you, Mrs. Lockhorn. You've been very helpful," she said and hung up.

Maybe more helpful than she'd ever intended to be.

That night when she met Tyler at O'Reilly's, she was feeling more optimistic than she had in days. She'd even managed to communicate that to Griffin without giving him specifics. Maybe that upbeat feeling was why Tyler managed to catch her completely off guard.

"I've been thinking," he began slowly, as they sat in a booth in a darkened back corner of the bar eating thick, juicy hamburgers.

"Should I be worried?"

"Funny."

"Okay, what have you been thinking?" she asked with more suitable solemnity.

"You still haven't found work, have you?"

"No, but I had two very promising leads today. Something should pan out very soon."

"That's great. Tell me."

"Not just yet. I don't want to jinx them. So what was your idea?"

Blue eyes regarded her evenly. "I think you should move in with me."

Maddie felt the burger slide from her fingers. Fortunately it landed on her plate. "Excuse me? Where did that come from?"

"Come on, Maddie," he said, leaning toward her, his expression earnest "Think about it. It makes perfect sense. In another week or so, I should be heading back to Baton Rouge anyway. You'd have the place to yourself, rent-free, until you're back on your feet."

She didn't like the way her heart fell at that reminder. She warned herself to stay focused on the fact that getting any closer to Tyler—longterm or short-term—was a very bad idea.

"I can't do that," she blurted at once.

"Why on earth not? If you're not ready for us to have a relationship, that's okay. I understand. Well, maybe I don't understand, but I can accept it. Not that I'd turn it down if you were interested in something more, but there is a guest room. We could keep it strictly platonic."

Maddie had serious doubts about that. Tyler was a very virile man. She was already having trouble keeping her attraction to him in check.

Proximity would be a very dangerous risk. And even worse than the physical closeness was the possibility that their emotional bond, already strong, would deepen.

"It's not that," she said, at a loss to explain what it was. She could hardly tell him that she had already let him get too close, that she was in danger of losing whatever shred of objectivity she might have for the exposé she was trying to piece together.

"Just think about it. You don't have money to throw around, and I'm not crazy about the fact that you won't even tell me where you live. It can't be safe."

"It is," she assured him. If only he knew just how pricey the apartment was that Griffin had rented for her. "It's right in this neighborhood."

"Parts of this area are better than others," he countered. "It's in transition, Maddie. You know that." He reached across the table to touch her cheek. "Maddie, I don't want anything to happen to you. I couldn't bear to lose someone else I care about."

She understood how devastated he'd been by losing Jen and their child. That he even considered her to be half as important in his life was amazing. Under other circumstances... She sighed. How many times would she come back to those unfortunate words?

"Nothing is going to happen to me," she insisted, resting her hand over his. "I promise. I am very careful whenever I go out. The neighbors look out for me, too. It's not as if I came here from a small town. I'm used to a big city, Tyler. I know how to protect myself."

From everything except him, anyway.

He frowned. "I'd feel more confident about that if you were at my place," he said stubbornly.

"I'll think about it," she said finally, though she had no intention of doing any such thing.

* * *

Despite her intentions, though, the thought was never far from her mind in the coming days. In fact, she thought about little else. A part of her desperately wanted to accept. A part of her even wished she had never started this blasted investigation, because in the end, no matter what she turned up, it was going to ruin her relationship with Tyler forever. She had deceived him from the beginning, and eventually, like it or not, she would betray him. How could either of them live with that?

In the end, though, after butting up against another dead end in trying to get information on Pamela Davis and Bryce Delacourt without having to go to Tyler's mother, she concluded that none of that mattered. She managed to convince herself that moving in would be a smart way to keep him and the rest of the Delacourts under constant surveillance. It would also give his mother even more reason to trust her. It would fuel her already wild speculation about Tyler's plans for a future with Maddie, maybe cause her to drop her guard with Maddie when they eventually got together.

With that as her avowed motive, Maddie was able to reassure herself that she hadn't yet lost her focus. She even managed to convince herself that she could keep her hormones on a tight rein.

Within days she knew it had been the right decision. As they grew closer, Tyler spoke more freely of Jen and the baby he had lost. He talked about his family, giving her insights that would one day be invaluable when she sat at her computer and wrote the story that brought Bryce Delacourt down.

Just thinking about that day sickened her, though.

She couldn't help wondering if she'd have the stomach for it when the time came. Already she knew that she would never print a word about Tyler and his illegitimate baby. That was Tyler's private pain, and it had nothing at all to do with Bryce Delacourt.

Realistically, though, Maddie knew that when the headlines about his father broke, her reticence about Jen and the baby would bring Tyler scant comfort. He would hate her, anyway, and that prospect was getting harder and harder for her to bear.

Ten

"Maddie, what's wrong?" Tyler asked, regarding her with concern as they settled in for the evening after meeting for a drink at O'Reilly's.

Tonight they'd gone on to their favorite Italian restaurant for lasagna, but Maddie hadn't been able to work up much enthusiasm for her meal. Now she was equally listless, and she could tell Tyler was becoming increasingly puzzled by her behavior.

"Nothing," she insisted. "Just a long day."

"None of those job leads have panned out yet?"

She shook her head. It was far worse than that, though she couldn't explain to Tyler. When Griffin Carpenter had discovered that she'd left the apartment he'd rented and moved in with Tyler, he had blown a gasket.

None of her excuses had satisfied him.

"You've fallen for him, haven't you?" he'd demanded. "I knew that was going to happen the minute you told me you planned to use him to get close to the family."

She hadn't been able to deny it, not with the vehemence that might have satisfied him. "My feelings for Tyler aren't important," she'd said. "I'm here to do a job and I will do it. I am every bit as highly motivated as you are."

"Why is that?" Carpenter had asked suspiciously. "You never said why this story is so important to you."

"And you've never told me why you want Bryce Delacourt brought down, either," she pointed out.

"I own this publication," he all but shouted. "My reasons don't matter."

Maddie had forced herself to remain calm. "Any more than mine do. We're both after hard facts, right?"

"Right," he conceded with obvious reluctance.

"Then leave it to me how I get them."

"As long as you don't do anything illegal," he agreed. "I expect more frequent updates, Maddie. I won't be kept in the dark on this."

"You'll have them," she had promised.

Which meant that now she had to make that call to Helen Delacourt, the one she'd been putting off, the one she would rather eat dirt than make.

"Come here," Tyler commanded softly, gesturing to a spot on the sofa in front of him. "Sit."

Because she was too tired to argue, she did as he asked. His hands settled on her shoulders and began to massage away the tension.

His touch felt heavenly. If she closed her eyes and shut off all the alarm systems she'd put into place when she'd moved in, she could almost pretend that she could have a lifetime of this, coming home to a man who would treat her with such tenderness. When his lips touched her brow, she sighed deeply.

"Maddie, you're driving me crazy," he whispered in a choked voice.

No man had ever said that to her before. She probably wouldn't have believed it if they had. With Tyler, though, she knew it was true, because he was driving her just as crazy. The chemistry between them was as volatile as it was…wrong.

His fingers skimmed lightly up her neck, leaving a trail of fire in their wake. Her senses went on a five-alarm alert. When his hands stilled and his mouth covered hers, it was as if a blaze had consumed every single alarm, silencing them and leaving her prey to the uncontrolled heat.

Her mouth opened and his tongue invaded. Within seconds dark, sweet swirls of desire curled through her. Her brain shut down and her senses came alive. Right and wrong flew out the window. All that mattered was here and now and this man whose touch was electrifying.

He broke the kiss only long enough to come around the sofa, scoop her into his arms, then settle onto the sofa himself with her in his lap. There was no mistaking the fact that he was as turned on as she was. The hard bulge of his arousal pressed into her hip.

For what seemed an eternity, he seemed to be satisfied with the devastating kisses alone. Maddie wanted more. She wanted his hands on her sensitive breasts. She wanted his touch between her legs where moist heat was already gathering ahead of a storm of more intense sensations.

When his hand slid under her shirt and grazed bare skin, she jolted at the pleasure of it. Her nipples puckered. By the time he began playing with each sensitive bud, that touch alone was enough to shatter her.

"Let it go," he murmured against her lips as wave after wave washed over her.

"I can't… I've never… Oh, Tyler." The last came on a gasp of surprise as she came apart in his arms.

But it wasn't enough. Not nearly enough. She wanted him to share this with her. She wanted to know the feel of holding him deep inside, wanted to experience a climax that rocked them both simultaneously.

"The bedroom," she whispered urgently. His gaze searched hers. "Are you sure?"

"I'm sure," she said, because anything less, any hint of uncertainty, would have brought his sense of honor into play.

They made it to his bed in awkward, almost laughable fashion, half-dressed by the time they got there, clothes strewn behind them. The urgency hadn't been lessened by the trip. Maddie's hands were everywhere, exploring, studying, savoring, even as she delighted in his gasps of pleasure, his protests as he told her she would cost him his control.

"That's the idea," she said. Neither of them could take the time for second thoughts, not now when they were so close to having it all, to knowing everything about the delight they were capable of sharing.

"Now," she pleaded. "Love me now."

Tyler knelt above her, his gaze steady. Slowly, his eyes never leaving her face, he entered her, stretched her, filled her. She gasped with the wonder of it, even as his strokes intensified, even as her body pulsed around his, demanding more and more of her…of him.

Then the world seemed to spin wildly out of control as the tension shattered in wicked, rippling aftershocks.

Nothing so magnificent had ever happened to her before. She doubted it ever would again. She touched his jaw in wonder.

"I never imagined it could be like this," she said.

"I don't think it's supposed to be," he teased.

"Oh?"

"Otherwise we'd never, ever stop doing it."

"Okay by me," she said, pushing aside the regrets that were already trying to crowd out the joy.

"Talk to me when I've recovered," he suggested.

"When will that be?" she asked, even as her touch stirred him to arousal.

He laughed. "Apparently a whole lot sooner than I imagined."

It was hours later before exhaustion overtook both of them and sent them into a deep, dreamless sleep. Maddie's last waking thought was that she needed to remember this tiny glimpse she'd had of heaven, because hell couldn't possibly be far away.

Tyler knew there were things that Maddie was still keeping from him. For the life of him, though, he couldn't get a handle on what they might be. She ran hot and cold. She would melt in his arms one minute, then freeze him out the next, as she seemed to be doing this morning after a night of electrifying lovemaking.

She had scooted out of bed before dawn, slipped in and out of the shower before he could even consider joining her, and now she was standing at the kitchen counter, barefoot, but otherwise fully dressed, eating a bowl of cereal as if she had no more than five minutes to spare.

As she bolted down her food, he stood there unobserved, regarding her with amusement and exasperation. "In a hurry?" he inquired mildly.

Her gaze shot up guiltily. "I didn't know you were awake."

"Were you hoping to avoid me for some reason?"

Her expression faltered, but then her chin lifted defiantly. "Of course not."

"Maddie, do we need to talk about what happened last night?"

"I hope not."

"No regrets, then?"

Her hesitation was enough of an answer.

"Apparently there are," he concluded with a sinking sensation in the pit of his stomach. "Want to tell me why?"

Ignoring the question, she turned and rinsed her bowl, then set it with careful deliberation on the counter. "No time," she said.

He caught her wrist before she'd taken two steps toward the door. "Maddie, what's going on?"

"Nothing. I'm late."

"For?"

"An interview, what else?"

"At seven a.m.?"

"It's a breakfast interview."

"Then why did you just eat?"

She turned and stared at the cereal bowl as if it had somehow betrayed her. "Because..." She swallowed hard. "Because I'm usually too nervous to eat during an interview."

He sighed. "Yeah, I'm sure that's it," he said, releasing her. "I hope everything goes okay."

For a moment she looked lost and alone, more vulnerable than he'd ever seen her. Responding to that, rather than his own frustration with her evasions, he kissed her gently. "Just something to put a little color in your cheeks. Good luck, Maddie."

"Thanks."

She flew through the door as if she feared he might change his mind and come after her. He heard the front door click quietly closed seconds later.

"What are you up to, Maddie? Who are you really?"

One thing for sure, she was the most complicated, thoroughly enigmatic woman he'd ever known. And even though he didn't entirely trust her, he realized that he was beginning to fall in love with her. He found the prospect terrifying, especially with all of those unanswered questions.

He finally concluded that he needed answers before he allowed himself to get in any deeper. He could have turned to either Jeb or Dylan for help, since investigating was right up their alley, but bringing in a professional felt too much like a betrayal. There were a few things he could do himself.

He began by going back to talk to Kevin O'Reilly, who was out in front of his bar sweeping the sidewalk.

"You're here early," Kevin said. "I don't start serving for a couple of hours yet."

"I came for information, not a drink."

"About?"

"Maddie Kent. Do you know anything at all about her?"

"Hey, you're the one living with her. Isn't that a

question you should have asked before you invited her to move in?"

"I didn't come by for a morality lecture, just for a little background information."

"Sorry. I can't help you."

"Any idea where she lived when she first got here?"

Kevin stopped sweeping, his expression thoughtful. "Come to think of it, she said she lived in the neighborhood. She said she'd just moved to town."

"That's all she told me, too."

"Well, there aren't a lot of choices. This area's still in transition. There's a very pricey building in the next block."

"Which is where she lives now with me," Tyler reminded him.

"Oh, yeah. Okay, there's an older building that's being gentrified, but prices in there are skyrocketing. There are a few older tear-downs that will go as soon as some developer realizes what a gold mine this area is going to be. Most of those are vacant and condemned."

He snapped his fingers. "Wait a minute. There's a boarding house two blocks up. A woman named Kate Porter runs it. Keeps it clean, but I can't say much else for it. It might be just right for somebody new in town who's trying to save while looking for a job. Kate looks out for her tenants."

That had to be it, Tyler concluded. "Thanks, Kevin."

"Tell Kate I said hello. Let her know I have a beer on tap for her if she helps you out."

Tyler laughed. "I'll do that."

Unfortunately, Kate Porter had never heard of Maddie Kent. She suggested a few other small places nearby where someone could rent a room or an apartment cheaply, but after hours of going door to door, Tyler hadn't found a single soul who knew Maddie Kent or anyone fitting her description. It was the single most frustrating day he'd ever spent in his life.

It was topped off by a call from his mother, cheerfully announcing that she and Maddie were having lunch. What the hell was that about? he wondered. It only added to his awareness that he didn't understand Maddie Kent at all.

When he waited for Maddie that evening at O'Reilly's, he was in no mood to hear any more of her lies. He intended to get to the bottom of her tight-lipped secrecy once and for all, even if he didn't like the answers.

But Maddie never showed up.

Maddie knew that time was running out. Even if Griffin Carpenter hadn't been pressuring her, what had happened the night before between her and Tyler would have been warning enough. She couldn't let that happen again. It had been too magical, too perfect. If she allowed a relationship to continue, to deepen, she would lose her nerve. She would do everything to hold on to Tyler, instead of trying to seek justice for her father. For the first time in her life, her loyalties were divided.

She had had to get out of the apartment first thing in the morning, because lingering was too dangerous. She wanted to stay in Tyler's arms too badly. The frustration in his voice, the sparks of anger in his eyes, had almost destroyed her, but there had been no other way. If it was this difficult now to lie to him, what would it be like for her when she betrayed him and printed an exposé of his father?

It was midmorning before she found a pay phone and forced herself to make the long-delayed call to Helen Delacourt. This was a make-or-break meeting. If Mrs. Delacourt couldn't tell her what she needed to know, then she would have to confront Bryce Delacourt directly. It was not a position she wanted to be in, not without more facts than she had at her disposal now.

"I would absolutely love to have lunch with you," Mrs. Delacourt said at once. "I'm looking forward to getting to know you better, since you are clearly so important to my son."

"Tyler and I are just..." She hesitated, at a loss to describe what they were.

"Don't tell me you're just friends, my dear. I know better. I could see the sparks flying when you were here and you'd only just met. That sort of spontaneous chemistry is as rare as it is wonderful."

Maddie couldn't argue with her about that. She would give anything to be able to hold on to it...anything except the justice she sought for her father.

"I've been worried about my son for some time now," Mrs. Delacourt said, snagging Maddie's attention.

"Why?"

"He's seemed terribly sad to me, but of course he won't talk about whatever's bothering him. Typical of a man, don't you think? They suffer in silence or expect us to guess what's wrong with them. At any rate, there was a sparkle back in Tyler's eyes when he brought you here."

"Please don't make too much of that," Maddie said, feeling miserable at getting this woman's hopes up when she knew she would only dash them at some point in the very near future.

"We'll discuss it some more over lunch. Perhaps whatever reservations you're feeling I can put to rest. Believe me, when it comes to Tyler, I can't say enough good things."

Once more Maddie sensed a special bond between Mrs. Delacourt and Tyler. She sighed, dreading what was to come. Even so, she made arrangements to meet Tyler's mother at her country club at noon. With any luck by midafternoon she would know if Bryce Delacourt had been involved in a relationship with Pamela Davis and if that could be why he had accused her father of embezzlement, to cover up the acts of his lover.

The country club dining room was tastefully furnished in the style of an English tea room. The atmosphere was cozy, perfect for sharing confidences. Or so Maddie hoped.

She and Mrs. Delacourt sat across from each other, sipping iced tea and eating chicken Caesar salads, making small talk. The food was delicious, but Maddie was having a hard time swallowing.

"I am so delighted to have this chance to get to know you better," Helen Delacourt said again. She was dressed in a smart designer suit in a deep blue that perfectly matched her eyes. "I spoke to Tyler earlier. He seemed surprised that we were meeting."

"I didn't mention it to him," Maddie admitted. "I called on impulse."

"Well, I am so glad you did. Tell me about yourself, Maddie. How long have you been in Houston?"

"Just a few weeks."

"You work?"

"I have a lead on a job now."

"Well, good, I hope you get it, if that's what you want. Though, of course, once you and Tyler are married, you certainly wouldn't have to work unless you wanted to."

Maddie felt lower than pond scum for deceiving Tyler's mother about their plans. Worse, she was about to turn this woman's private life into a public spectacle. Bryce Delacourt might deserve such a fate, but Tyler's gracious mother didn't. Then she thought of her own family's anguish, of her mother's descent into lonely isolation. Those memories made it easier to harden her heart.

"I hear you've moved in," Mrs. Delacourt said casually.

"That's just temporary," Maddie said, embarrassed that she knew.

Mrs. Delacourt laughed. "I'm not shocked, if that's what you're thinking, though I do hope it's a prelude of things to come."

"What things?" Maddie asked, afraid that she already knew.

"A wedding, of course. Perhaps later this summer?"

"I don't think so, but perhaps you should discuss that with Tyler," Maddie said. "To be perfectly honest, I don't know what to make of your son."

Helen Delacourt looked genuinely perplexed by the comment. "How can that be? Tyler has always been a very straightforward man, at least until recently."

Maddie knew exactly what that was about, but it wasn't up to her to enlighten Mrs. Delacourt about Tyler's loss. She shrugged the comment off, then used the topic to slide toward her goal of discussing the

Delacourts' marriage. "Perhaps it's just me. I don't have a lot of experience with relationships. I haven't had the time."

"No past loves?"

She shrugged. "None of importance."

"Well, you couldn't do better than my son. Tyler is a unique man," she said, clearly prepared for an enthusiastic hard sell of her son. "He has a mind of his own, much to his father's dismay, but then all of our children do. They blame that on their father, but the truth is, I am capable of my share of stubbornness when something matters to me. Seeing Tyler settled down is one of those things that matters."

Unfortunately, Maddie knew that all too well. She decided the time had come to get into a sensitive area. She just prayed she had the finesse to carry it off without arousing suspicion.

"You've had a long and happy marriage," she said to the older woman. "That's so rare these days. How have you managed it?"

When her question drew an evasive look, Maddie sensed that she was, in fact, onto something. Perhaps it was no more than uneasiness at discussing something so personal with a virtual stranger.

"I'm sorry," she said sympathetically. "Have I said something I shouldn't have?"

"Of course not," Helen Delacourt said with a rare display of testiness. "All marriages have their ups and down, I suppose. Mine no more than others. If you're committed to the marriage, you work things through."

"Surely it was never anything serious?"

"I'm not sure what you mean by serious. Even little annoyances can take on a life of their own unless they're nipped in the bud."

"I suppose I was thinking more of the really big things that can happen, a genuine betrayal, for instance. I can't imagine what I'd do if my husband cheated on me."

A faraway look came into the older woman's eyes, then she blinked and it was gone. "I suppose that would depend."

"On?"

"How important the marriage was to you," she said at once. "Betrayal can knock the wind right out of you, but if your family matters at all, you pick yourself up and make peace with it. You put your family first before your own feelings. That requires tremendous strength, but in the end it's well worth it."

Was that what she had done? Maddie wondered. Found a way to make peace with her husband's affair?

"Then you never thought of separating?" she asked, then covered quickly for her insensitive bluntness. "I'm sorry, that's far too personal. I have no right to ask. I have this terrible habit of poking my nose into other people's business. If your husband cheated on you, I'm sure it's all in the past."

Mrs. Delacourt turned absolutely ashen. "Why would you even say such a thing?" she demanded indignantly.

"I'm sorry," Maddie said again. "It was rude of me. It's just that I'd heard… Well, I should know better than to listen to gossip."

"Yes, you certainly should. My husband is the most honorable man I know. He would certainly never dream of cheating on me," Mrs. Delacourt told her with surprising vehemence. She put her napkin on the table with trembling fingers, then stood. "I really think I'd better go. Suddenly I'm not feeling well. We'll do this another time."

"Of course," Maddie said, furious with herself for not easing into the topic more subtly. Now she had scared the woman off. She doubted she would ever get another chance to ask such probing questions. She was a little taken aback by the fierce denial that Bryce Delacourt had ever had an affair, but what else was his wife supposed to say? Following the protesting-too-much philosophy, wasn't such a firm declaration tantamount to an admission?

She regarded Mrs. Delacourt worriedly, a reaction she didn't have to feign. "You look pale. Shall I come with you?"

"No, you stay," Tyler's mother said politely. "Enjoy your lunch, dear."

Back straight, Helen Delacourt strode from the dining room, nodding politely to her friends, a mask of composure firmly in place. Maddie could only guess at the torment she must be suffering as she relived painful memories.

Memories that Maddie had deliberately resurrected, she thought guiltily.

She felt like the sleaziest of tabloid journalists, a media Peeping Tom, seeking headlines at the expense of another's peace of mind.

What kind of woman was she? Maddie wondered despondently as she pushed the remainder of her salad away. What kind of person had she become? Even for the sake of avenging her father, how could she prey on a woman who'd been willing to welcome her as a daughter-in-law? How could she betray a man like

Tyler, a man whom she could love with very little effort at all?

Would Mrs. Delacourt tell Tyler about her uncomfortable meeting with Maddie? If so, Maddie had no doubt that he would be furious. He might even kick her out in a justifiable rage. Maybe that would be for the best, she told herself.

But if it was, why did she feel as lost and alone now as she had when her beloved father had died?

Eleven

It was nearly midnight when Tyler called Dylan. He'd grown tired of waiting up for Maddie, and he needed to do something constructive to get the answers he wanted. On his own, all he'd accomplished was to stir up more questions. Her failure to turn up at O'Reilly's—which had become their nightly haunt— unsettled him. And the fact that she still wasn't home aroused in him an uneasy mix of anger and panic.

Had something happened to her? Or had she run out on him? And what the devil had she been doing with his mother? It might not have surprised him to learn that his mother had arranged to see Maddie, but Helen had made it clear that their lunch was at Maddie's instigation.

Was Maddie off on another fishing expedition, as she had been in Baton Rouge? By now didn't she already know everything there was to know about him? Or did she have some other agenda he couldn't imagine?

"I need you to run a check on somebody for me," he told Dylan before he had a chance to reconsider.

Even though his brother had obviously been asleep before the phone had rung, Dylan sounded wide-awake at once.

"Name?" he asked with brisk professionalism.

That was what Tyler liked about his oldest brother. Dylan didn't waste a lot of time asking the kind of questions Tyler didn't want to answer. Dylan simply knew Tyler wouldn't come to him unless it was important.

"Maddie Kent," he said with obvious reluctance.

"*Your* Maddie?" There was no mistaking the shock in Dylan's voice. "I thought…"

Tyler sighed. "I know what you thought. I'm sure you've gotten an earful lately from Mother and Jeb and who knows who else, but I'm not sure she's mine," he said wearily. "To be honest, after today I'm not sure who she is at all."

"What happened today?" Dylan asked, beginning what was bound to be a litany of questions, now that he knew this involved a woman Tyler cared about. Professionalism had clearly given way to brotherly concern. It was pretty pointless to try to evade the questions.

Resigned to satisfying his brother's ingrained curiosity, Tyler filled Dylan in on what he'd learned earlier when he'd searched the entire neighborhood where she'd claimed to live and come up with not one soul who'd ever heard of Maddie Kent.

"I see," Dylan said when he'd finished. "Tyler, are you sure you want to do this? Shouldn't you talk to her first? Ask her what the hell is going on?"

"I would if I could, but she's disappeared. Besides, what's to keep her from telling me another pack of lies?"

"Are you so sure they *are* lies? Maybe she did live in that neighborhood, just not on the blocks you covered. Maybe she kept a very low profile. That area's not the best, even though you claim it's going to boom anyday now. Maybe she didn't want to get to know her neighbors."

"Dylan, I covered a lot of blocks. Besides, she was always very careful never to let me pick her up at home. You have to admit that that in itself is suspicious. She had a million excuses, but I think the truth is that she didn't live anywhere near O'Reilly's."

"Why would she lie about something like that?"

"I wish I knew. To throw me off, maybe…keep me from finding out more about her. For all I know, Maddie Kent isn't even her real name."

"Are you thinking that she deliberately set you up in some way, that she came to O'Reilly's specifically to meet you?"

"It's crossed my mind."

"It's possible, I suppose," Dylan said thoughtfully. "You are one of the most eligible bachelors around and—though I certainly can't see it—I have it on good authority that you're handsome as sin."

Tyler chuckled. "Don't sound so disgruntled. Kelsey picked you, anyway." He paused, then added, "Of course, maybe that was because she hadn't met me yet."

"Leave my wife out of this. It's our baby sister who thinks you're good-looking, and she's prejudiced. As for Maddie, she wouldn't be the first woman to try to snag a wealthy man by making it a point to put herself in his path."

"True, but I honestly don't think it's my money she's

after. She's been having a tough time financially, but she wouldn't take a dime from me."

"But in refusing, she stirred all your protective tendencies and, *bam,* now she's living with you."

"It was a platonic arrangement," Tyler said defensively. "Because she was in a bind. It was all my idea."

"It *was* platonic?"

"It's changed," he said tightly. "Just stop with all the analysis and do this for me, okay?"

"Whatever you say. It's your call. I'll get on it first thing tomorrow. If she gets home, talk to her. Meantime, if you change your mind, call me back."

"I won't change my mind," Tyler said firmly. "I'm not sure of much these days, but I am sure of that. Just do whatever you have to do."

He sighed heavily as he hung up. That was it, then. He was having a woman he cared about investigated. What did that say about the future potential of the relationship? How much trust could they possibly have if he felt driven to have his brother go digging around in Maddie's life? Would trust ever be possible once she learned what he'd done?

At least a dozen times he told himself to call Dylan in the morning and tell him to forget it. At least a dozen more times he reassured himself that he had no choice. He had to know the truth about Maddie, even if he didn't like what he discovered.

If his tumultuous thoughts hadn't been enough to keep him awake, Maddie's absence from his bed would have been. Her scent was everywhere. Finally, driven by pure frustration, he got up and changed the sheets, then settled back down, but sleep continued to elude him.

He stilled when he finally heard the front door ease

open, then debated going to confront her. When he heard her quietly go into the room across the hall and close the door, he decided to wait until morning when they'd both be rested. Tempers tended to flare out of control when people were exhausted.

When the phone rang just after dawn, Tyler assumed it was Dylan.

Instead, it was his father, and he was spitting mad.

"Who the hell is this woman you've been seeing?" he demanded before Tyler had managed much more than a groggy hello. "What's she up to?"

"Dad?"

"Of course it's me. Now answer my questions."

"Maybe we'd better start over. Are you talking about Maddie? What's she done?"

"Are you seeing any other woman?" his father retorted sarcastically. "Of course that's who I'm talking about. As for what she's done, that's what I'm asking you."

"I haven't spoken to her since yesterday morning," Tyler said.

"What do you mean you haven't spoken to her? I thought she was living there."

"She is, but she got in after I'd gone to bed. What is it you think she's done?"

"I'm telling you I don't know, but she's got your mother over here sobbing her eyes out. She's been up half the night. If she keeps it up much longer, she's going to make herself sick. I don't know what the hell is going on, but I don't like it, son. I don't like it one bit. Nobody messes with your mother and gets away with it."

"If she was this upset after she saw Maddie, why didn't you call me sooner?"

"Because your mother told me not to. She insisted she needed time to think. Think about what, I ask you?"

Tyler didn't like the sound of this. It was one thing for his mother to work herself into a state. It was quite another for his father—the king of calm—to panic like this. More was going on here than his father had said.

"I'll be right there," Tyler said. "Don't worry, Dad. I'll get to the bottom of this. I'll see what I can find out from Maddie before I leave here."

He pulled on his clothes and headed for the door. To his surprise Maddie met him in the hall, looking groggy and more desirable than he wanted her to.

"Come with me," he said tersely, hauling her toward the kitchen. He put on a pot of coffee as she sat at the table and watched him warily.

"Is something wrong?" she asked finally.

"What was your first clue? The phone call at the crack of dawn or my mood?"

"Tyler, if there's a problem, just spit it out. Who called?"

"My father."

Was it his imagination or did her complexion turn pale? "Oh? Is everything okay over there?"

"Apparently not. It seems my mother has been upset ever since she saw you yesterday afternoon. You wouldn't have any idea why, would you?"

He poured them both a cup of steaming, strong coffee, then sat across from her. "Well?"

Her gazed clashed with his. "I don't think I like your implication or your tone."

"Well, there's a whole lot right now that I don't like, but let's stick to this for the moment. What went on between you and my mother?"

She stared at him silently, and for the longest time he wasn't sure she was going to respond. Finally she said defensively, "I met her at the country club. We had lunch. She said she wasn't feeling well and she left. End of story."

"Did you happen to chat about anything that might have disturbed her?"

"Tyler, what did she say? Did she blame me for upsetting her?"

"No, but my father seems to have pieced that theory together from the timing of her hysteria and from what she *has* said."

"I'm sorry. I like your mother, and I really am sorry if I did or said something that made her uncomfortable. It wasn't intentional."

Tyler listened for a false note, but he didn't hear one. She seemed to be sincere. "I want to believe that," he said.

Hurt registered in her eyes. "But you don't," she replied, her tone flat.

"How can I? My father doesn't tend to overreact, and he's practically bouncing off walls. My mother's been crying for hours. I'm just looking for answers."

"Well, I don't have any."

"Dammit, Maddie, you were the last person she saw. I'll ask you again, what did you talk about? Be specific."

"You and me. Marriage. That sort of thing."

"Did you tell her that you and I were just friends, that there was no wedding on the horizon?" he asked, wondering if that would have been enough to set his mother off. She hated to have her plans thwarted.

"I told her she'd have to discuss anything like that with you."

"You did say you talked about marriage, though?"

"Just in general. What it takes to make a good one, that sort of thing."

There was nothing in that to set off hysteria, at least not that Tyler could see. This wasn't getting him anywhere, and it was evident from Maddie's tight-lipped expression that she didn't intend to reveal anything more.

"I'd better get over there."

"Would you like me to come? I'd like to help if I can."

Tyler shook his head. "I don't think that would be such a good idea, not until I get to the bottom of this."

"Tyler, I really am sorry," she said, looking at him with apparent regret.

He put his empty coffee cup into the sink and automatically filled it with water. Then he slowly turned back to Maddie. "Are you absolutely certain you don't know what this is about?"

"Even if I did, it wouldn't be my place to tell you," she said.

He stared, trying to interpret her response. "What the hell does that mean?"

She returned his gaze, defiance mixed in with obvious misery. "Just go."

He made it as far as the door before he turned back one last time. "If you and I are going to have any sort of a future, it would be better if you told me everything, rather than make me drag it out of my mother."

But Maddie just shook her head. "I can't. It's not up to me," she repeated.

There it was again, that same vague hint that more had gone on than what she'd admitted to thus far. "What isn't up to you? Blast it all, Maddie, what did the two of you get into at lunch? Did you fight?"

"No."

"What then?"

"Please, Tyler, just go. She obviously needs you."

Since that was exactly what his father had said, he knew he couldn't stick around and try to get the truth out of Maddie. Clearly she didn't intend to say another word.

"I'll be back," he said in a tone that could only be interpreted as a warning. He had the uneasy sense, though, that Maddie might not be there when he returned.

The quiet click of the front door sent a shudder through Maddie. She pulled her knees up to her chin and stretched her oversize T-shirt over her legs.

"What have I done?" she murmured. Obviously she had opened up a hornet's nest in the Delacourt household. What confused her, though, was that Bryce Delacourt didn't seem to understand why his wife was so distraught. Surely if Maddie had ripped the scab off the wound of his old affair, Helen Delacourt would have lashed out at him about it.

Was he genuinely at a loss over his wife's distress? Had Maddie somehow gotten it wrong about the affair? Tyler's mother hadn't actually confirmed that there had been an affair, not in those precise words, though

Maddie couldn't see any other way to interpret either what she did say or her reactions.

"She denied it," she reminded herself aloud. "In no uncertain terms."

Was it possible that Maddie really had gotten it all wrong? If so, then why was Mrs. Delacourt so distraught now?

Maddie would have given anything to go with Tyler just to see Bryce Delacourt squirming. It would have been the perfect opportunity to get every last piece of evidence she needed to publicly humiliate him. But she hadn't been able to bring herself to force the issue when Tyler had refused to let her come along. And the truth was that she wasn't sure she could stomach it if her presence brought Helen Delacourt any more pain.

When the phone rang a few minutes later, she grabbed it, hoping it was Tyler with an update. Instead, an unfamiliar man's voice said, "Maddie?"

"Yes."

"This is Dylan. Tyler's oldest brother."

"Oh, hello."

"Is my brother there?"

"No, he had to go out."

"At this hour?"

"Your father called and asked him to come over."

"Why? It wasn't his heart again, was it?"

"No, I believe your mother was feeling a little under the weather," she said, proud of the innocuous way she managed to make the early-morning visit sound. "Shall I have Tyler call you when he gets back?"

"No, I'll catch up with him over at our parents' place."

"Okay, then."

"Wait, Maddie. I'm glad I have you on the line."

Her heart began to thud dully. Dylan didn't sound nearly as jovial as Jeb. In fact, she thought she heard something almost dire in his voice.

Wasn't he the hard-core investigator? Was he suspicious of her for some reason?

"Why?" she asked bluntly.

"I have a question for you."

"Sure."

"Why haven't you told my brother that you're a reporter?"

Oh, God, she thought miserably. Not this. The truth couldn't come out like this. Dylan couldn't be the one to tell Tyler.

"Why would you think that?"

He gave a dry chuckle. "Give it up, sweet cakes. I'm on to you. I know that you've worked for half a dozen small papers all around the state. I know that you quit the last one about six weeks ago. Wasn't that when you showed up in Houston?"

"I came here looking for work," she conceded.

"Really? My information suggests that you already have a job, a very lucrative job working for the sleaze of Texas journalism, Griffin Carpenter."

"Who told you that?"

"It doesn't matter."

Maddie swallowed hard against the wave of panic crawling up the back of her throat. She should have known her ties to the tabloid couldn't be kept quiet forever, not the way gossip spread among journalists. "Have you been investigating me, Mr. Delacourt? Is that the Delacourt way of welcoming someone new into the family?"

"I think you're missing the point," he said mildly.

"Which is?"

"What do you want with my family? My gut tells me it's not marriage you're looking for at all. So, a word of warning. If you hurt Tyler, if you hurt any member of my family, you will answer to me. Believe me, Ms. Kent, your career in journalism will be short-lived, at least in Texas. You'll never work for a legitimate newspaper again."

"An interesting threat," she said before she could stop herself. "So typical of a Delacourt. I see the bullying trait is alive and well in the next generation."

Breathing hard, she slammed the phone down before he could reply. Then she burst into tears. It seemed she was to share the same fate as her father, thanks to a Delacourt. Out of work in her field, doomed to a life of working for second-best weeklies in nowhere towns. Dylan Delacourt *could* see that it happened, too. She had heard it in his voice.

"Stop it," she ordered herself, brushing impatiently at her tears. "You knew this could happen when you made the decision to work for Griffin Carpenter, when you set out to bring Bryce Delacourt down."

She had told herself it would be worth it, if she could just get even with Delacourt for his deliberate destruction of her father. She had enough facts and theories now to do it, or at least to make his life damned uncomfortable. All she needed was an hour of his time, maybe less, to watch his reactions when she laid it all out for him, every stinking rotten thing he had done when he'd destroyed her father to save his girlfriend's neck. And she had to arrange it now, because once Tyler knew the truth, her access was going to blow up in her face.

She didn't want to confront Bryce Delacourt at the house, not with his wife already upset and with Tyler on the scene. She would have to go to his office, bluff her way in.

It wouldn't be easy, not with him already furious with her for her part in his wife's emotional crisis, but she could do it. She had slipped past tougher security than anything Delacourt Oil had. She had her ties to Tyler on her side, at least for the next couple of hours.

She hurried through a shower, pulled on her best, most daunting power suit, tucked a tape recorder into her purse and headed for her car. She would pick up the rest of her things later, if Tyler hadn't had her banned from the premises by then. She would find some way to try to apologize to him, some way to explain that she had had to do what she'd done for her father's sake. Surely he would understand her need for justice, even if he could never forgive her.

When she reached Delacourt Oil, she had no difficulty reaching the executive suite, but the secretary there shook her head when she asked to see Bryce.

"I realize I don't have an appointment," Maddie said, trying to cajole her into making an exception. "I wouldn't even be here if it weren't extremely important that I speak to him. Couldn't you at least see if he's got five minutes to spare?"

"It's not that I won't help you," the woman said. "I can't. Mr. Delacourt isn't in."

"I'll wait, then."

"I'm not expecting him today."

That was a wrinkle Maddie hadn't anticipated. The man was a well-known workaholic. She hadn't expected that even his wife's distress would keep him at home for long. She'd envisioned him bolting the second Tyler arrived to relieve him.

"You're not expecting him today? When is he due back?" she asked.

"I'm not sure. When he called, he said that he was planning to take his wife on an extended vacation and that he would be in touch later with the details."

"He's left town?"

"I doubt they're on their way just yet. You might try to catch him at home if you have the number there."

"I do," Maddie said.

There was just one problem. With Tyler likely to be smack in the middle of whatever was going on over there, did she dare use it?

Twelve

Tyler found his mother—usually the calmest, coolest woman on the planet—every bit as distraught as his father had described. She was curled up in bed hugging a pillow and sobbing as if her life were over.

"According to the housekeeper, she's been like this ever since she came home from having lunch with Maddie yesterday," his father said, drawing him back into the hallway. "She won't talk to me. She'll barely even look at me. Did you ask Maddie what happened at lunch?"

"I asked, but it was like talking to a wall. She all but confessed that something had gone on between them, but she refused to give me a clue. She said it wasn't up to her, whatever that means."

"What do you know about that woman?"

"Apparently not nearly enough," Tyler said with a resigned sigh.

He knew that she made his pulse race. He knew that she fascinated him.

He knew that his gut told him she was a decent woman, but his gut had been wrong before. He decided not to mention that even before his father's call he had already asked Dylan to check into her background. In a few hours at most, he should know more.

"Tyler?" His mother's voice was weak and hoarse from crying. "Is that you?"

"Go on," his father said. "See if you can get her calmed down. I'm certainly not having any luck."

As Tyler approached the bed, his mother reached for his hand, then gazed up at her husband who had followed him into the room. "Bryce, leave us alone for a moment, please. Tyler and I need to talk. There's something I have to tell him."

Sudden understanding flared in his father's eyes, followed quickly by obvious alarm. "No, you can't mean…"

"Bryce, please," she begged, her face haggard. "I have to."

"Sweet heaven, is that what this is all about? That woman knows…?"

"Perhaps she knows everything," Helen said dully. "Or at least enough."

"But how?"

"I have no idea, but Tyler has to be told."

Mystified, Tyler looked from his mother's pale, tear-streaked face to his father's shaken expression. "Will somebody please tell me what's going on? What is it that Maddie knows that I don't?"

"I'll explain," his mother promised him, then looked at her husband. "I have to do it, Bryce."

"Yes," he said wearily. "I suppose you do."

He leaned down and gave his wife a kiss. "Everything will be okay, Helen. We'll make it okay."

She caught his hand in hers. "I love you."

A sad smile crossed his father's face. "And I you, my dear. I always have."

As his father left the room, Tyler thought he detected the sheen of unshed tears in his eyes, but of course, that couldn't be. Bryce Delacourt was the strongest man he knew.

"Mom, what's going on?" Tyler asked when they were alone. "Is Dad right? Is Maddie responsible for upsetting you like this?"

"Come," she said. "Sit here beside me. And yes, in a way, Maddie is the reason that we're having this talk."

"What does that mean?"

"Darling, please don't rush me. I have to explain this in my own way."

Tyler bit back an impatient curse and resigned himself to a wait. His mother had always been able to embroider the simplest tale into a complex plot. It had made for wonderful bedtime stories when he'd been young, but now he could only regret the tendency.

"You already know that Maddie asked me to join her for lunch yesterday."

"Yes."

"I thought she merely wanted to get to know me better since I'm your mother, but it was clear from the outset that it was more than that. She was asking questions, a lot of questions."

"About?"

"Tyler," she scolded. "No interruptions."

"Sorry."

"Now that I think back on it, I'm not sure how much she actually knew or how much she was guessing, but I knew it was time. I suppose I always knew this day would come, but as the years passed, I thought maybe there would be no need."

"No need to do what? Mother, you're not making any sense. You're talking in circles."

"Patience, darling. I know it's not a trait the Delacourt men embrace easily, but it's one you should learn."

"So you've mentioned on more than one occasion," Tyler said wryly.

"Where was I?"

"You were about to tell me whatever it is that Maddie either knows or has guessed, but that I am completely in the dark about."

"Don't be snide, Tyler. I am going to tell you everything in my own way."

Tyler felt a knot form in his stomach. "Everything?" he repeated. He didn't like the sound of that. It implied there were terrible secrets that had been kept from him.

His mother clung to his hand. Her own was icy. "Years ago," she began slowly, then faltered and reached for a glass of water on her bedside table. Only after she had taken a sip did she go on.

"Years ago your father and I were having problems, as many young couples do," she said, her expression sad. "Marriage requires a lot of adjustments, and ours was no different. He was building up the company. I was feeling neglected, as if I were less important to him than some hole in the ground."

Tyler grinned at her dismissal of the exploration for oil as little more than digging in the dirt, but he managed to keep silent.

"It's not so unusual, really," she said. "In fact, it probably happens more than any of us would like to admit."

Knowing his father's all-consuming obsession with

Delacourt Oil even now, Tyler could easily imagine what it must have been like back then.

"What happened, Mother?"

She closed her eyes for a moment, as if gathering strength, then faced him squarely. "I turned to another man."

Tyler rocked back on his heels and stared. His mother? An affair? He might have believed it of his father, but *her?* She was the most devoted wife he knew. Besides, what business was it of his? Why was she telling him such a thing? And why now?

She reached out and brushed his hair away from his face. A half smile touched her lips as she said gently, "That man was your father."

Tyler heard the words, but he couldn't seem to make sense of them. Bryce Delacourt wasn't his father? How could that be? His whole life he had been treated as a Delacourt. He thought of Dylan, Jeb and Michael as his brothers, of Trish as his sister. How could that be a lie?

And yet it explained so much. Why he looked different. Why he had always felt a little like an outsider. Why he instinctively tried harder to be like Bryce Delacourt. Why his mother did treat him differently. She had been protective, as if she needed to shield him in some way. Now he understood why. She had been trying to ensure that he felt like the others, that he never felt excluded or different, but of course her behavior had had the opposite effect.

"Does Dad…?" He nearly choked on the word. "Bryce?"

His mother reacted angrily to his faltering inability to decide what to call the man he'd grown up thinking of as his father. "He is your father in every way that counts," she said fiercely. "I won't have you start thinking of him in any other way, Tyler."

He accepted the rebuke with a nod. "Does he know?"

"He's known from the beginning and he's long since forgiven me. In fact, you saw his reaction earlier. It was as if he'd almost forgotten completely that we shared this secret. If anything, our marriage became stronger because he accepted you from the first day he set eyes on you. I loved him so much for that. Please, please, don't let what I'm telling you ruin the relationship you have. I had to tell you now. I was so afraid Maddie was getting close to the truth."

"But how is that possible? Why would she even care?"

"I don't know, but it made me realize I couldn't risk her being the one to tell you. This had to come from me. I had to be the one to make you understand that Bryce is your father. He's earned the right to be."

A million and one questions raced through his brain. He asked the first ones that came to mind. "But my real father? Who is he? Do I know him? Have I ever even seen him? Does he know?"

Tears welled up in her eyes then. "Please, Tyler, don't do this."

He hardened his heart against the tears. "Please, Mother, I have to know it all. I can't settle for half the truth."

The tears continued to roll down her cheeks unchecked. "Yes," she said wearily, "I suppose not. It's only right that it all come out. Then there will be nothing anyone can use against us."

For an instant he was distracted. "Why would anyone use it against us?"

"Everyone has enemies, Tyler, especially the rich and powerful."

Could Maddie be such an enemy? he wondered, half-shocked by the thought even as it made a terrible kind of sense. Because it wasn't a question his mother could possibly answer, he went back to his original point.

"Who, Mother? Who is my real father?"

"Your biological father," she corrected at once.

He sighed, but nodded. "Of course. Just tell me, please."

She seemed to be drawing on some inner courage before she spoke, but at last she said in a voice barely above a whisper, "Daniel. Your father is Daniel Corrigan."

Suddenly everything in his life clicked into place, as if a key piece of a jigsaw puzzle finally made all the rest fit. The bond between him and his boss—*his* father. The timing of Daniel's decision years ago to return to the rigs. His father's—Bryce's—resentment of Daniel and of Tyler's obvious affection for him.

"Does he know? Does Daniel know I'm his son?"

His mother nodded. "The moment I realized I was pregnant, I went to Daniel and told him. I also told him that, though I loved him dearly for what he had brought into my life when I desperately needed someone to pay attention to me, I wanted to stay married to Bryce if he would have me, that I needed to keep my family together."

"And he agreed?"

"He was furious at first, but he knew me well enough to know that I wouldn't change my mind. And he loved me enough not to fight me. Then I went to your father and told him. Confessing that I had betrayed him and that there was to be a child as a result was the most difficult thing I have ever had to do. Needless to say he was stunned, but being the kind of man he is, he accepted that some of the blame for what had happened belonged to him. And he loved me enough to forgive me, enough to accept you as his own. I'm not saying any of it was easy. It wasn't, and it didn't happen overnight, but the three of us sat down and worked it all out."

Tyler shot to his feet, thinking of them sitting around some stupid conference table, deciding his fate. "How terribly civilized of you, Mother. Did anybody stop to consider me in all of this?"

"You were the *only* person we considered. We did what we all thought was for the best. Your father and I took a long, hard look at our problems and our marriage and decided we wanted to be together, that our vows meant something, even though I had broken faith."

"And Daniel—did you consider his feelings at all? Did it matter that you were denying him his son?"

"He knew what we had was an illusion, a passionate interlude that never should have been, except that it gave you to us," she said, then added emphatically, "to *all* of us, Tyler. We've shared you through the years, albeit without you being aware of it. It's been a bitter pill for your father to swallow at times, seeing you go off to spend time with Daniel, but we agreed, just as Daniel agreed to keep his paternity a secret. He's an honorable man, too, Tyler, and for a time he brought me a joy that I thought had gone from my life."

Tyler struggled to accept the fact that his entire life had been built on a lie. People he had loved and trusted had lied to him about the most essential aspect of his life, his identity. An outsider had somehow picked up on it before he had.

He met his mother's gaze. "And Maddie knows all of this?"

"I think so—or at least some of it. She was asking about my marriage, if it had always been strong. She asked whether it could weather an affair."

Maddie had gone to his mother, not him. He wasn't sure whether to bless her for that or to strangle her. And why did any of this matter to her? Did she intend to use it in some way?

"Mother, she didn't threaten you, did she?"

"You mean blackmail?" his mother asked, seemingly shocked by the suggestion. "Good heavens, no. It was just that she was so close to hitting on the truth. I knew the secrecy had to end. That's what I found upsetting. I wasn't sure how you would take it."

Tyler wasn't sure, either. "It's a lot to absorb."

"Oh, darling, I know it is. But please don't hate me. Don't hate any of us. We did the best we could."

He walked to the door without responding. "Tyler, where are you going?"

"I honestly don't know," he said.

"Home?"

"I don't know where that is." Back to an apartment he had been sharing with a woman he clearly knew no better than he did his own family? Back to Baton Rouge and a job working for a man who just happened to be his biological father?

"Will you speak to your father before you go? Please," she said anxiously. "It will destroy him if he loses you. Never once, not in all these years, has he treated you any differently than he has Dylan, Michael or Jeb. You're as important to him as if you were his flesh and blood. Don't discount that."

Because even in his confusion he could see that Bryce Delacourt was as much a victim as he was, he nodded. "I'll talk to him," he promised.

He was about to open the door when he heard the catch in her throat and turned to see her holding back a sob. He had never been able to bear seeing her in pain. Even now he still couldn't. He walked back and pressed a kiss to her damp cheek.

"We'll work it out, Mother. It may take a little time, but we *will* work it out."

Then he hurried from the room and went looking for his father. He found Bryce Delacourt in his study, on the phone, making travel arrangements. Bryce barked something into the phone, then hung up the minute he saw Tyler. There was something that might have been a flicker of fear in his eyes.

"She told you, then?" Tyler nodded.

His father, always glib, seemed to be at a loss for words. "Thank you," Tyler said finally, not knowing what else to say.

His father stared at him in surprise. "For what?"

"For accepting me as your son." Even though he hated that the truth had been kept from him, Tyler knew that what his father had done had been the most unselfish and caring act a man could possibly do. He had given Tyler his name, his home and, most important of all, his unstinting love.

"You are my son," his father declared fiercely. "Never think that you're not." He sank back in his chair. "Though I suppose you'll want to go to Daniel and tell him that you know. I'll never get you back to the executive suite now that you know that you come by your love of the rigs naturally."

"That was a foregone conclusion, anyway," Tyler agreed with a half smile. "But I won't be rushing back to see Daniel, not until I've grappled with all of the implications."

"Damn that woman," his father said heatedly. "If she hadn't stirred all of this up..."

"Don't blame Maddie," he said. Her motives were something he needed to understand, something for which he might never forgive her, but the result of her actions had been that he'd learned a secret that never should have been kept from him for such a long time in the first place. "Whatever she said or did, it only brought out the truth. And the truth was long overdue."

"Perhaps so," his father said with a resigned sigh. "What will you do now?"

"I need to think. I need to see Maddie and understand her part in all of this."

"Will you be okay?" his father asked with obviously sincere concern.

Tyler nodded. "Of course, I'm a Delacourt," he said at once, then amended, "and a Corrigan. Can't get much more strong-willed than that."

His father gave a rueful chuckle. "No, I suppose not."

"Will you and Mother be okay?"

"We made our peace about this years ago, when I realized that my single-minded focus on work almost cost me her love. But to prove I haven't forgotten what's most important in my life, I just got off the phone with my secretary and with the travel agent. I'm taking your mother on a cruise. She's been clamoring to go around the world for years now."

If he'd announced a decision to forsake his worldly possessions and become a monk, Tyler couldn't have been any more shocked. "You're taking off on an around-the-world cruise? You do know how long they last, don't you? You can't have changed that much in the past half hour."

"Hardly," his father agreed with a rueful expression. "I figure two weeks in the Greek Isles will get our feet wet. Best to find out if either of us gets seasick before I plan anything longer." He regarded Tyler worriedly. "We could delay the trip if you'd like us to stay. I know you must have more questions that need answering."

"Whatever questions I have can wait. I think a cruise will be perfect for the two of you. I need time to myself, anyway."

"Will you tell your brothers and Trish? It's up to you. I can guarantee it won't change the way they feel about you. Through the years, seeing the bond among you proved to me that your mother, Daniel and I had made the right decision."

Tyler hadn't even thought of sharing the news, but of course he would have to eventually. Like his father, he didn't believe it would change his relationship with the others, but what if it did? Would he be able to bear it?

"I'll wait to tell them," he said finally. "Not for long, though. I promise."

"Your decision," his father said again. His expression turned sly. "Does the fact that you intend to hang around Houston for a bit mean I can leave you in charge of Delacourt Oil for the time being?"

Tyler laughed for the first time in what seemed like

an eternity. "Now I know we'll be all right. Nothing stops you from trying to get me behind a desk."

"Not while there's breath in my body," his father agreed.

"I'll try to keep things afloat," Tyler agreed. "Two weeks, though, not a day more."

"Agreed." His father's expression softened. "I love you, son."

Tyler blinked back tears. In all these years he had never had the slightest cause to doubt that. Even now, he didn't. "I love you, too, Dad."

He knew that as well as he knew anything. What he didn't know, anymore, was who the hell he was.

Thirteen

Maddie left Delacourt Oil and headed to the family's estate, determined to have it out with Bryce Delacourt before he left town.

"Please don't let Tyler be there," she repeated over and over as she drove.

But as she was parking her car along the edge of the curving driveway, she saw Tyler leave the house, shoulders hunched dejectedly, his expression bleak. His father, hers, the revenge she'd plotted for years, now all of it flew out of her head as she fought the need to go to him. She was forced to face the past versus the here-and-now.

She knew exactly what he must be feeling, because she had been there. Tyler, a man she cared for deeply, was hurting, and it was because she had deliberately stirred up a hornet's nest in his family. He had to be devastated by the discovery that his father had been having an affair. Once she linked that to the conspiracy to frame her father for embezzlement, his anguish would be even worse. She had set out to prove that his father had feet of clay and, in so doing, she had caused nothing but pain for an innocent man.

Just as Bryce Delacourt's insensitive actions had caused pain for her and her family, she reminded herself, but she couldn't take any comfort in that. Not any longer. The old adage about two wrongs never making a right had never seemed more true.

She stepped from her car, and the movement was enough to catch Tyler's attention. He stared at her as if he'd never seen her before or, worse, as if she didn't matter at all. That hard, flat look rocked her as nothing else could have. It was hard to believe that only a few days ago she had lain in his arms, and he had looked at her as if she were the most precious thing in his life.

"Tyler…"

He waved her off. "Not now, Maddie. I can't deal with you now."

"I need to explain."

He shook his head. "There is nothing you could say right now that I want to hear. *Nothing*."

He turned his back on her, climbed into his car, gunned the engine and sped down the driveway at a rate of speed that sent gravel spewing in every direction.

She leaned against her car and watched him go. "Dear God, what have I done?"

She glanced at the house and knew with sudden and absolute clarity that she couldn't go inside, couldn't even knock on the door and demand to see Bryce Delacourt, much less accuse him of destroying her father with his lies. She had spent years looking forward to this moment, and now that it was here, she found no satisfaction in it. In fact, she felt sick at heart.

"I'm sorry," she whispered, even though there was no one to hear, even though the man it was meant for was who-knew-where, suffering all alone.

She doubted that Tyler would ever want to see her again. As powerful as their passion was, she doubted it was strong enough to weather what he had to consider a betrayal. If he didn't know already that she was a reporter, it wouldn't be long before Dylan told him. It wouldn't matter to him that she had done what she had because of loyalty to her own father. All she could do for Tyler at this point was to leave him in peace.

Back at his apartment, she checked to make sure his car wasn't in his assigned parking space, then went upstairs. She hurriedly threw a few of her things into a suitcase. She planned to leave before he returned, knowing that her actions were cowardly but excusing them by telling herself that she was making things easier for Tyler.

In the living room she paused by the collection of framed snapshots and picked up one of all four of the Delacourt brothers wearing ragged jeans and faded T-shirts. Tyler had told her it had been taken after a tag football game on the beach. They were wet and breathless and covered in sand, but their laughter was contagious. Even now she smiled just looking at them.

Tyler's grin was widest of all as he triumphantly held a football aloft. "I'm sorry," she whispered once again as she gently placed the photo back in its place amongst so many happy Delacourt memories.

And then she left, wondering if she would ever see Tyler again.

Back in her car she reached for the key to start the engine, but her hand faltered. She suddenly realized she

had no idea where to go, no real destination, no one—
with the possible exception of Griffin Carpenter—who
cared where she was.

In the end it was the awareness that she owed Griffin an explanation that turned her toward Dallas. She
drove for hours, the image of Tyler, devastated and
angry, never far from mind.

Once she reached Dallas, she checked into a hotel
that she could afford on what truly were paltry savings. Her expense account days were over. She had no
appetite. She barely slept.

And for a solid week she did more soul-searching
than she'd ever done in her life. She didn't like the picture that emerged. Her determination to cling to the
past had come very close to costing her the one man
she thought might be able to make her truly happy. It
had stripped her of her journalistic ethics.

Whatever his father was, Tyler Delacourt was a
kind, decent man. She couldn't destroy one without
destroying the other. Praying that her father would understand her decision, she concluded that the price was
too high. Even if Tyler never spoke to her again, she
couldn't be responsible for putting his family's private secrets on the front page of Griffin Carpenter's
vicious tabloid.

Finally on Monday morning she picked up the phone
and called her boss.

"I need to see you."

"Where are you? What have you got for me?" he
asked at once. "I'm in Dallas. I'll be at your office in
twenty minutes."

"You ready to go to press?"

"We'll discuss it when I see you," she said, though

there was nothing to discuss. Her decision was made and it was final. If an exposé of the Delacourts was to be written, someone else would have to do it.

The moment she arrived at the *Hard Truths'* offices, she was ushered in to see Carpenter. He regarded her eagerly.

"Tell me everything."

She looked him straight in the eye and said, "There's nothing to tell."

He stared at her incredulously. "You must be kidding. You've been working this story for weeks. Are you telling me there is not one shred of dirt to be had on Bryce Delacourt?"

"None that I could find," she said evenly.

He slammed his fist on his desk so hard that a coffee cup bounced in its saucer. "Dammit, I don't believe it."

"I guess I'm just not as good a reporter as I wanted to believe," she said. "I'll save you the trouble of firing me, Griffin. I quit. Here's a check for my expenses so far."

She placed the check on his desk, then stood up and headed for the door. "Hold it right there, missy."

She paused, sucked in a deep breath, then turned to face him. "What?"

"I don't buy this, not for one single second. I know there has to be something. No one goes through life without making a few enemies, without cutting a few corners."

"I didn't find anything," she said again. "You can't print what isn't there."

"Oh, it's there. Maybe you just didn't have the stomach for finding it."

"Maybe not."

"Because of that man, am I right? He got to you. What did he do? Pay you off? Sleep with you?"

Ignoring the accusations with their ugly implications, she looked him straight in the eye. "Tell me something. Why do you hate Bryce Delacourt? Or is it even him? Do you simply hate anyone in the state who has wealth and power? That's what it looks like, you know. There's nothing honest or objective about this paper of yours. It's simply a tool for getting even."

"You were glad enough to use it when it suited your purposes," he accused.

"Yes," she said softly. "I suppose I was. But I learned something. Revenge isn't nearly as sweet as people say it is. You might want to remember that. Whatever satisfaction you take from your muckraking, it will never be enough to make up for whatever it was that happened in your past."

"You don't know what you're talking about."

"Yes," she said quietly. "I do. What was it, Griffin? What made you hate so many people you don't even know?"

"Oh, I know the bastards," he said heatedly. "I've made it my business to get to know all of them. I've made it my life's work to prove that they're no better than the rest of us mere mortals, despite what they'd have you think."

"Is that what happened? Did someone tell you once you weren't good enough?"

"They tried," he conceded grudgingly. "Told me I'd never be good enough for their daughter." A faraway expression crossed his face. "She was the best thing that ever happened to me, but all her folks could see was that I wasn't in their social class, that I was a little rough around the edges. It didn't matter that I would have given her the world or that she loved me. I just wasn't their kind. They sent her off to Europe, where she had my baby. When she came back, she was engaged to someone else, someone more suitable."

So that was it, she thought, the defining moment that had changed his life and made him go after not just those people, whoever they were, but all others like them. At heart, she and Griffin were all too much alike, but she wanted to believe she had changed...or at least that she could.

"They were snobs," she pointed out.

"They were ruthless, power-hungry fools," he retorted. "Which I was all too happy to point out in my first edition."

"And Bryce Delacourt was just one more target for you. You had nothing personal against him, did you?"

"No, but you did, and that suited me just fine."

"Has all this hate and anger, have all these exposés, given you what you need?"

"Of course," he said, but his expression seemed less certain than it had earlier.

"Do you have the woman you lost?"

"No."

"Or your child?"

"No," he said, his eyes filled with sorrow.

"Then it must be a hollow victory," she said. "I want more. I want to live well. I want to be happy. I want to put the past behind me, where it belongs. Maybe it's time for you to do that, too."

Of course, she thought as she left him, he wouldn't. Publishing *Hard Truths* defined him, gave him his own form of power, and he wouldn't sacrifice that easily.

If only she had understood all of this before she had turned Tyler's world upside down, she thought. But then she would never even have met him. She couldn't regret that.

Now she just had to find him and see if it was too late to make peace.

Tyler wasn't anywhere to be found, at least not in any of the places that Maddie tried. She staked out his apartment, sitting for endless hours in his living room, listening for the sound of his key in the door. She waited, ignoring Rodney's sympathetic looks and his insistence that Tyler hadn't been home for days. Finally she had to concede that the doorman hadn't just been putting her off.

She called the Delacourt house, the Delacourt Oil offices, then went to Baton Rouge. No one anywhere admitted to having seen him. She even tried the beach house, but it was deserted.

The possibility of Los Piños, where his sister and oldest brother lived, finally came to her. He had mentioned it often, talked about how content they were there. Perhaps he had taken refuge with one of them.

Rather than call and risk a rebuff, and because she had nothing else to claim her time, she drove across the state. She went to Dylan first.

"He's not here," he said tersely. "And even if he were, why should I tell you?"

"I know he must hate me," she began.

"You lied to him. You never told him you were a reporter. I know, because he was stunned when I told him. You deliberately set out to destroy our family and used him to do it. What else would you expect? That he'd forgive and forget?"

"I just want to explain, that's all. I have to. He might never want to see me again, but he needs to know I didn't do any of this to hurt him."

"So when's the story going to be in the paper, Maddie? Should we brace ourselves?"

"There won't be a story, at least not by me. I told Griffin I hadn't found anything, and then I quit."

"Well, bravo," he said sarcastically. "But it's too little too late. Leave Tyler alone. He doesn't need someone like you in his life."

Trish's response was much the same, though even less temperate. "Stay the hell away from my brother," she shouted, following Maddie onto the sidewalk in front of her bookstore, oblivious to the stares she was drawing on the otherwise quiet street. "How can you even bear to look at yourself in the mirror after what you've done to him?"

"I didn't do it to him," Maddie said, blinking back tears. "I know it must seem that way, but it was never about him."

"If you hurt one of us, you hurt all of us. Now Tyler has to figure out where he fits in our world."

Maddie stared at her in confusion. "What are you talking about? Have you all ostracized him or something because he brought me into the family?"

"It's not *us*. It's *him*. How do you think it feels to wake up one day and discover that you're not who you thought you were? Leave him the hell alone. If you don't, I won't be responsible for what I do."

Maddie had no idea at all what Trish was talking about. Why would Tyler be questioning who he was?

Finding him suddenly seemed more important than ever. She had to regroup, though. She'd searched every single place she could think of. Obviously his family had no intention of helping. And, truthfully, she could hardly blame them.

She walked into Dolan's, a drugstore next to Trish's bookstore. She sat at the counter and ordered a soft drink and a cheeseburger before she realized that everyone around her had fallen silent. Their gazes were avidly fixed on her. She winced as she realized they must have heard every word Trish had shouted. She was about to change her order to a takeout when an elderly man slid onto the stool beside her. He was a little frail, but his blue eyes snapped with intelligence and humor.

"Don't mind them," he said loudly. "They're just a bunch of old gossips, and nothing this lively has happened around here in ages." He gave a little nod of satisfaction when the conversations around them picked up again, then smiled sympathetically at Maddie. "I'm Harlan Adams. And you must be the notorious Maddie Kent."

She regarded him with shock. "How on earth did you know that?"

"In a town like this, word gets around. Trish and Dylan are like family to me. I've heard all about the nosy woman who stirred things up for their brother."

"I never meant to hurt him," she said for what seemed like the hundredth time. She didn't expect Harlan Adams to believe her, either, but he nodded.

"So what did you mean to do?"

Choking back a sob at the suggestion that he was

willing to listen impartially to what had happened, she shook her head. "There's no point in talking about it."

"There's always a point in getting to the truth," he said. "Tell me."

Suddenly she found herself spilling the whole ugly story, from what had happened years ago right on up to what had happened the previous week when she had quit her job with Griffin Carpenter.

"Sounds to me as if you were driven by loyalty to your father."

"Exactly," she said.

"Are you certain it wasn't misplaced?" he asked gently.

"Of course I am."

"You know for a fact that Bryce Delacourt framed him?"

She realized that she didn't, not with unassailable certainty. She had a theory and some evidence to support it, but not enough to print, not even enough to condemn the man in her own mind. She had seized on a few facts and twisted them to suit her. Even though she had balked at printing them, what did that say about her skill as a journalist?

"You can't be faulted for wanting to believe in your father," he said, clearly guessing that there were doubts she hadn't admitted aloud or even to herself until now. "But until you talk to Bryce Delacourt and know exactly what happened, you will never be able to put this to rest. It will eat at you."

"I've already decided not to do the story."

"Because your conscience kicked in, not because you believe Bryce Delacourt might be innocent, am I right?"

She finally nodded slowly.

"Then do what you have to do to get your answers, Maddie. Not for a story, but for yourself. Only when you have them will you be able to put this behind you and face this young man of yours."

"It's too late for Tyler and me. As for Bryce, he's out of the country."

"It's never too late for love, young lady, not while you can still draw breath. And if you want to talk to Bryce, I imagine I can wrangle a phone number from somebody. He could be in Timbuktu, but I imagine he's not out of contact with his office. Probably has a cell phone in his hip pocket."

She regarded him incredulously. "You would do that?"

"To help a friend, I would."

Maddie thought about it for no more than an instant. "Thank you, yes. I think I would very much like to talk to him and get to the bottom of this once and for all."

"Consider it done." He stood up, started around the counter, then beckoned for Maddie to follow.

"Sharon Lynn, we need to use the phone in the back room," he announced to the woman behind the counter, though he didn't wait for permission. He winked at Maddie. "Never could get used to cell phones myself, but who needs one when half the people in this town are related to me?" His gaze shifted to the woman. "Not a one of them will deny me a long-distance call or two, am I right, darlin' girl?"

"If I didn't offer it to you, you'd just take it, Grandpa," Sharon Lynn said, laughing. The look she cast at Maddie seemed a bit friendlier, too, as if her grandfather's acceptance of Maddie was good enough for her.

In the back room, in no time flat, Harlan Adams had Bryce Delacourt on the line. He was apparently on a cruise ship somewhere in the Mediterranean.

"Oh, stop bellyaching about the interruption," Harlan Adams said to him. "This is important and it won't take long. I've got someone here who needs to ask you something. And don't you dare hang up on her, either."

Though her palms were sweating and her stomach was churning, Maddie had to grin at his imperious tone. She took the phone he held out, swallowed hard, then said, "Hello, Mr. Delacourt. This is Maddie."

She heard a sharp gasp on the other end of the line. "Please don't hang up," she begged. "I promise you that I won't take more than a minute of your time."

"Why should I believe anything you have to say?"

"Because I have nothing left to lose. I just need the answer to one question from you and then I'll stay out of your life."

"And out of my son's?"

"If that's what he wants," she said, "and I imagine it is."

"Okay then, ask your question."

"Did you frame my father for embezzlement to protect Pamela Davis?"

"Embezzlement? Your father?" he asked blankly. "Who are you, anyway?"

"I'm Frank Kent's daughter," she responded.

"Dear God in heaven," he murmured. "That's what this is about? You came poking around in our lives because of Frank?"

"Just answer me. Did you frame him?"

"No," he said, his tone suddenly gentle. "I did not. I'm sorry, Maddie, but that's the truth. And when I get home I can show you every single piece of evidence to prove it, if that's what it will take.

"If only I'd known that's what you were after," he said with a sigh.

She heard the compassion in his voice and the absolute sincerity. He was telling the truth. She felt it in her gut. That didn't mean she didn't want to see it in black-and-white. "It's not that I don't believe you," she said finally. "But I would like to see whatever you have."

"Of course," he said at once. "Maddie, I truly am sorry. I liked your father. I tried more than once to get him to stop gambling. I did all I could to protect him. You know I didn't file charges. But I had no choice, I had to let him go. I couldn't keep him on if I couldn't trust him."

"Yes, I can see that," she said with quiet resignation, shaken by the fact that for all these years she had believed a lie, that rather than being a victim, her father had gambled away thousands of dollars, then stolen to cover the debt.

"I'll be in touch as soon as I get back. I wish you had just come to me in the first place."

"So do I," she murmured, then handed the phone to Harlan Adams and turned away, fighting tears. A moment later she felt his hand on her shoulder.

"Not the answer you were hoping for, I gather." She shook her head.

"It's never easy growing up and discovering that your parents have faults. It's even harder when they've died while you were at an impressionable age and there's an easy target to blame." He tucked a finger under her chin. "I never knew your father, Maddie, but I do know Bryce. He's an honorable man. A bit of a control freak when it comes to his kids, but as honest as the day is long."

"I think I knew that from the moment I met him," she said. "I just didn't want to believe it. It makes it so much worse. I did all this, hurt so many people for nothing."

"Then you'll make amends," he said confidently. "Starting with that young man of yours."

"I can't make amends if I can't find him."

"Mind if a nosy old man asks one more question?"

"Of course not."

"Do you love him?"

For all the good it did her, she thought disconsolately. "Yes," she said in a voice barely above a whisper.

Harlan Adams gave a little nod of satisfaction. "I didn't think my instincts had failed me. Now here's what you're going to do."

She stared at him incredulously. "You're going to help me? Won't Dylan and Trish be furious?"

He waved off the possibility. "They're used to me meddling and matchmaking. They'll get over it. You willing to listen to an old man?"

She thought of the stakes and nodded readily. "Absolutely."

"You get yourself back over to Houston. March yourself into Delacourt Oil and demand to see that young man of yours."

"He's there?" she asked, shocked.

"Well, of course, he is. Michael's on his honeymoon and his father's traipsing around the Greek Isles with his wife. Who do you think's running things? Don't you read the papers?"

"Apparently not the right ones," she said dryly.

"Well, you can bet that if Bryce and Michael are away, Tyler's running the ship. No matter what else has gone on, he wouldn't take off. The man's responsible. All of the Delacourts are."

"But I called there," she protested. "Talked to some secretary, I imagine."

"Yes."

"Who owes her paycheck to a Delacourt."

"I think I'm beginning to see what you mean. I guess I'd better get to Houston."

"Good girl," he said with an approving smile. "One last thing."

"What's that?"

"No matter what the outcome there, I want you to consider coming back here and working for the paper right here in town. It's not a big-city daily, but you won't be bored. And it seems to me we can always use someone with a conscience keeping an eye on things."

Maddie was flabbergasted by the suggestion, especially when she had all but admitted that she was a very flawed journalist. "Do you really mean that, even after everything I've told you?"

"It's because of what you've told me," he said. "Good luck, Maddie Kent. I hope to see you again soon."

"Thank you, Mr. Adams."

"Call me Grandpa Harlan. Practically everybody around here does."

Impulsively she pressed a kiss to his weathered cheek. "I'll be in touch, no matter what."

She spent the night in a motel on the outskirts of Los Piños, then drove back to Houston in the morning. It was late in the day by the time she marched past a startled security guard and an even more indignant secretary to throw open the door to Tyler's office. When she actually made it across the threshold, she suspected the two employees' hearts must not have been in the chase.

Tyler's head snapped up when she entered, and a frown settled on his face, but she noticed he waved off the guard and the secretary.

"Not going to throw me out?" she said lightly, trying not to show her relief.

"Not yet," he said quietly.

"Good, because I have a lot to say."

"Why should I listen to it? Why should any of it matter, when it's coming from a woman who has done nothing but lie to me from the day we met?"

"Because there was a time when I meant something to you," she suggested, praying it was true, praying that the feelings hadn't been one-sided.

"That time has come and gone."

She tried not to let the finality of his tone hurt, but it did. "Then how about because you still mean something to me?"

A flicker of emotion darkened his eyes, but then his expression hardened. "Heaven protect me from the sort of havoc you could wreak if you hated me."

"Will you listen?" she asked. "I mean really listen, not just sit there to pacify me?"

"Maddie, you're here. Talk. I'm not promising anything."

Unfortunately she couldn't think where to begin,

not with him looking at her as if she were lower than dirt, not with the shadows under his eyes a constant reminder of her betrayal. Overwhelmed by guilt, she lost her nerve. She closed her eyes and sighed, then stood.

"Never mind. I'm wasting my time and yours."

Her words hung in the air, along with the same thick tension that had been present since the moment she entered. She got as far as the door, had her hand on the knob, when he finally spoke.

"Don't go."

She turned at the command, drawn by the ragged sound of his voice. She saw the regret in his eyes that suggested he already wished he hadn't spoken.

"I can't do it, Tyler. I can't put my heart out there and let you trample on it."

"Then you are a coward," he said. "I thought so when you ran out without explaining anything, when you hid the fact that you were a reporter from me."

"There were reasons," she said defensively.

"Then tell me. I need to know, Maddie. I need to know where my judgment fouled up. I need to know why what we had was so unimportant that you could throw it away by trying to destroy my family."

Once again she sat down across from him, knowing that whatever she said might not be enough, knowing that this was her last chance to make things right.

And knowing that her heart would break if she couldn't.

Fourteen

From the moment she had set foot in his office, barreling past both a security guard and his secretary with a determined jut to her chin, Tyler had known he couldn't let Maddie walk out, not without answers. He didn't understand any of it, not his mother's revelations, nor Maddie's role in her deciding to make them. All he knew was that it was going to be a long struggle to make sense of it...and to forgive either of them.

Yet looking at the woman seated across from him, bright patches of color on her cheeks, turmoil in her eyes, he also knew that he wanted to find answers he could live with, answers that might justify his desperate yearning to have her back in his life.

"Tell me," he said again. "I need to know why you stirred everything up. What were you trying to do? Dylan said you work for Griffin Carpenter. I know what a snake he is. I also thought I knew the kind of woman you are. It doesn't make sense that you would work for him."

"I thought he was my only option," she said simply.

Her only option? What was that supposed to mean?

"Why? Dylan says you've worked for a number of papers, that all of your employers speak very highly of you. You left them. You were never fired. Why would you have to turn to a man like Carpenter for work?"

"Your brother is very thorough," she said wryly. "No wonder you turned to him, instead of asking me."

"I already knew you were lying to me," he said matter-of-factly. "I thought I had no choice."

"But you think I'll tell you the truth now?"

His gaze locked with hers. "I'm hoping you will. I need to know why my whole world is turned inside out."

She regarded him with a puzzled expression that didn't appear to be feigned. "Trish said the same thing. She said you didn't even know who you are anymore and that it's because of me. I don't understand."

"How can you not understand? You were about to print it all in Carpenter's rag, weren't you?"

"I considered writing what I thought was the truth about something that had happened a long time ago, but even before I learned that things weren't what they seemed to be, I changed my mind. I told Griffin I hadn't found anything worth printing."

"Why?"

"Because of you, because I couldn't bear to hurt the people you care about the way I was once hurt."

Now it was his turn to be confused. "Who hurt you?"

"I blamed your father, but it seems I was wrong. It was my own father who was responsible for everything that happened."

Completely at a loss, Tyler shook his head. "Maddie, maybe you'd better start at the beginning. None of this is making any sense."

"No, I suppose not," she said, then sighed. "Okay, from the beginning, and believe me, this is the short version. I told you that my father died when I was in my teens."

"Yes."

"He didn't just die. He committed suicide." Her gaze met his, then darted away. "I blamed your father."

Tyler was incredulous. "Why?"

"Because he had fired my father. My father was never the same after that. I suppose a doctor would say he became clinically depressed, but I only knew that day by day I was losing the father I had adored because of a ruthless man."

"My father?"

She nodded. "I came here to get even for that."

"Then you did set out to use me to get close to my father," he said flatly. Even understanding why she had done that didn't make him feel any better about it. Had there been one, single, honest moment between them? Was there anything about those weeks that he could believe, that he could trust?

Anything on which to build a future?

She twisted her hands in her lap, her expression filled with sorrow. "I hated what I was doing. The better I got to know you, the more difficult it became to go on deceiving you. I kept trying to keep some distance between us..." she said, leaving the rest unspoken.

Tyler filled in for her. "But I wouldn't let you."

"And I wanted that closeness," she insisted. "Not for the story, for me. No one had ever treated me the way you did, as if I really mattered."

"You did matter," he admitted reluctantly. He hadn't wanted her to, but she had. There was no point in denying it to her or himself.

"Not enough to keep my father alive," she said bleakly. "My mother, my brothers and I weren't enough reason for him to want to live. Can you imagine what that did to all of us?"

Tyler had told himself that he could never feel anything for Maddie again, but he did. He felt an unbearable sense of pity for that lost young girl whose father had chosen death, even when he had so much to live for.

"It must have hurt terribly," he said. "And it must have made you hate my father."

"I was devastated. And getting even with him, finding some way to bring him down, became the single most important goal in my life. That's what I came here to do, but I kept losing sight of my goal."

"Why?"

"Because I was falling in love with you," she admitted.

Tyler didn't want to believe her, because in some ways that would make what she had ultimately done even more difficult to bear. She had loved him, yet she had betrayed him in an unimaginable way. She had lied to him, not just once, but over and over. How could he ever trust a woman like that again?

"You came here digging for dirt," he summed up. "And you found it, not in my father's past, but in my mother's."

The disbelief that registered in her eyes appeared genuine. "Your mother? What does she have to do with it?"

"The affair," he said, hating the tawdry word. But

the truth was, he was alive because his mother had slept with another man.

"But it was your father..." she began slowly, then stared at him with dawning horror. "It wasn't, was it? He was never the one who cheated."

"No."

"Oh, my God, why didn't I see that?"

"Because you weren't looking for it, I imagine. Who would? I sure as hell didn't. My mother has made it her life's work to appear to be the devoted wife. And, as I understand it, ever since that one time, she has been exactly that. She and my father would probably have forgotten all about her lapse, if it weren't for one constant reminder."

"Reminder?"

"Me." Even as the word left his mouth, he saw her eyes widen in shock, much as his must have done as he'd listened to his mother destroy everything he'd believed to be true about his identity.

"You are not Bryce Delacourt's son?" Maddie asked incredulously.

He watched her closely and knew that not even this woman who had been deceiving him for weeks now could feign such a stunned reaction.

"You honestly didn't know, did you?"

"No."

"Then what the hell was this all about? Why were you questioning my mother, if you didn't know the truth, if you weren't planning to use this juicy Delacourt scandal to get your revenge?"

"I thought..." She waved off whatever she'd been about to say. "Never mind. Obviously I had it all wrong."

"Had what all wrong? Maddie, what did you think you knew? I think I have a right to know."

"I was convinced your father was having an affair with Pamela Davis in accounting, that he accused my father of embezzlement because he was covering for the woman who was really responsible."

Tyler had thought things couldn't get any more complicated, but *embezzlement?* Where had that come from?

"You're going to have to help me here. I'm lost again."

"While I was doing my research, I found a clipping in which my father was accused of embezzling money from Delacourt Oil. That was the reason your father fired him, not some simple accounting error, which is what I'd always believed. There was a woman in the accounting department, Pamela Davis, the only other person who would have had access to the missing funds. I asked some questions, then leaped to an apparently faulty conclusion that she and your father were involved. That's what I was trying to confirm when I had lunch with your mother. That's why I forced the issue with her, asked a lot of vague questions about betrayal and infidelity. I thought once I had all of the facts to humiliate your father, I could do what I'd come here to do and walk away. Because of my feelings for you, everything had gotten far too complicated."

"So even though you claim to have loved me, it wasn't enough to stop your vendetta?"

"Can't you see? I thought I owed it to my father. I know it was wrong and I'm sorry for the pain I caused you," she whispered. "This wasn't personal. If it had been, I could have used what you told me about Jen and your daughter. This wasn't about you. It was never about you."

"Well, pardon me if I think that discovering I've been living a lie my entire life is damned personal."

"I didn't know where this would lead, not when I started. Not even when I went to your mother. I just wanted your father to pay."

"Well, you certainly got what you wanted, didn't you? This will make tabloid fodder for weeks to come."

"No, it won't," she insisted. "I couldn't use anything I had…or thought I had. Even when I had enough information to cause your father and everyone in your family the kind of pain I felt years ago, I couldn't do it. I quit my job yesterday. And I paid back every penny Carpenter gave me. Now I really am looking for work again."

"Doing what? Destroying lives?" he asked heatedly.

"Never again," she whispered. "Not when I've seen what it can cost."

Tyler's gaze locked on hers. "Why the turnaround? I don't buy this sudden conversion to honest journalism."

"God help me," she whispered, "because I love you, because I didn't like the woman I had become, obsessed with the past and willing to hurt anyone because of it. I want to be the kind of woman you thought I was, the kind who deserves a life with a man like you."

Tyler wanted to protest that she didn't know the meaning of love, but she stepped close and touched a silencing finger to his lips. It was an innocent gesture, but it made him want things he'd sworn never to have again. It made him want her. It required every ounce of self-control he possessed to keep from reaching for her.

"I don't know if it will ever be possible for you to

forgive me, but I want you to remember one thing—in the end I couldn't go through with any of it, because I love you with all my heart. I knew it the day I saw you walking out of your parents' house looking as if your entire world had collapsed. You were all that mattered to me then."

"The damage has been done," Tyler said, his tone deliberately icy. "My life is a shambles. My parents are devastated. What does it matter that none of it will appear in a headline in Carpenter's rag?"

"I know, and I'm sorry. More sorry than you'll ever know." She looked him in the eye. "It probably doesn't seem that way now, but isn't it better that you know the truth? If only I had known the truth about my father years ago, none of this would have happened. Maybe, in the end, that was my father's worst betrayal."

Tyler couldn't deny that a part of him was glad to know about Daniel, even though he had yet to go and see him. It would take some time before he learned how to juggle his emotions when it came to these two very different fathers—the one who had given him life and the one who had raised him.

Maybe it was true what they said, that the truth would set him free—from Bryce Delacourt's control and from the demands he placed on himself to live up to his father's expectations. Right now, though, that seemed scant comfort.

"I wish I could let you off the hook that easily, Maddie, but I can't. There have been too many lies between us."

"Yes, I suppose there have been," she said, her expression sad, her eyes bright with unshed tears.

Shoulders squared proudly, she walked to the door

of his office, then turned back for one last look. "Good-bye, Tyler."

This time when she turned to go, he didn't try to stop her.

Maddie closed the door to Tyler's office, then leaned back against it and let the tears flow unchecked. She had never felt so alone in all her life, not even on the day she had buried her mother and stood beside that grave with absolutely no one to offer comfort.

There had been a hundred moments in Tyler's office when she had wanted to throw herself into his arms, when she had wanted to comfort him and beg for his forgiveness, but his rigid self-control had stopped her. Tyler might not hate her, but he definitely didn't want her in his life. That much had been clear.

"Are you all right?" his secretary asked, regarding Maddie sympathetically.

"No," she admitted candidly, then drew herself up. "But I will be." After all, survival instincts were second nature to her. Or were they?

She had survived her father's emotional abandonment and his suicide only by focusing on revenge. How would she cope with the loss of Tyler when there was no one to blame but herself?

She walked out of Delacourt Oil, then paused on the steaming pavement and looked up, trying to guess which was the office from which she had just come. In the towering skyscraper, there was no way to tell one window from another, but she wanted to believe—needed to believe—that Tyler was looking down, watching her walk away. That gave her the strength to keep her chin up and her step brisk.

The tactic was effective until she was all the way down the block and out of sight. Then her shoulders slumped and the tears stung her eyes again.

Just when she thought she couldn't bear it, her cell phone rang.

Surprised because very few people had the number, she fumbled in her purse and pulled it out.

"Hello."

"Maddie? Is that you?"

She recognized Harlan Adams's voice at once. "Grandpa Harlan," she whispered brokenly, trying the name out as he'd instructed, finding comfort in it in a way she hadn't imagined possible. Even if it was an illusion, she felt as if she had family, after all.

"You've seen him, then?" he said, his tone sympathetic.

"Do you have spies everywhere?"

"Just about, but it wasn't my sources who told me this. I could hear it in your voice. It didn't go well?"

"No," she said wearily. "It didn't go well. I've cost him too much."

"He'll come around, child. If the feelings were real, he will come around."

"Maybe they weren't real," she said, voicing her greatest fear.

"Then you'll have lost nothing and you'll move on," he said confidently. "So when can we expect you? Janet—that's my wife—is fixing up a room, even as we speak. And the editor of the paper is chomping at the bit to have you get started."

On the darkest day of her life, she finally had something that brought a smile to her lips. "Awfully sure of yourself, aren't you?"

"If you don't have faith in yourself, who will? Now get yourself behind the wheel and point that car of yours in this direction."

"I don't know," she began, wondering if she shouldn't stay right here.

Maybe force Tyler to deal with her in due time.

"If you're worrying that Tyler won't know where to find you, I think you can count on his brother and sister to see that he knows."

"They won't welcome me," she said.

"They're good people. They will eventually. You have any place you'd rather be?"

"Alaska has crossed my mind, but it's too darned cold."

"Then stop arguing with an old man and come on. If you don't like it over here, you can move on, but for now think of it as a safe haven while you get your bearings."

A safe haven? Maddie certainly needed one. She had to face the decisions she'd made. There were the mistakes, too. So many of them.

She thought of Bryce Delacourt's promise to show her the evidence of her father's embezzlement, then dismissed it as a poor reason to stay in Houston. If the papers existed, she could see them anytime. Now they would be only an excuse to linger as she waited to see if Tyler would ever change his mind about her.

"I'll be there tomorrow," she promised Harlan Adams.

"You won't regret it," he said. "This is a good place to live and an even better place to heal."

Maddie hoped so, because healing was what she desperately needed.

Fifteen

Tyler's parents had been back from their trip for two weeks, looking rested, tanned and more devoted than ever. He knew he could no longer postpone going back to Baton Rouge, not just to work, but to see Daniel.

As he had when Jen had died, he longed for the hard, physical labor that would tax his energy and keep his thoughts at bay. He was less anxious to see the man who was his biological father. There were too many conflicting emotions.

He was stunned, therefore, when his father called him into his office and asked bluntly, "When are you going back? It's about time, don't you think? You can't put it off forever."

"I never thought I'd hear you encourage me to go back to working on the rigs."

"It would suit me just fine if you never set foot on another one," his father said. "It's… Daniel you have to deal with."

"Frankly, I never thought I'd hear you say that, either."

His father sighed. "I never thought I'd have a need

to, but the truth is what it is. There's no ignoring it and no turning back. To be perfectly honest, it's a relief having everything out in the open. I've spent the past twenty-some years waiting for the secret to slip out, resenting every minute you and Daniel spent together. I think I finally realize that there's room in your heart for both of us. I just hope you realize that, too. It doesn't have to be a contest, Tyler, even though for years I tried to make it one. I hope you'll forgive me for that."

Tyler heard the regret in his father's voice, and he trusted that as he'd trusted very little in recent days. "There's nothing to forgive. No man could have a better father than you've been to me."

"Or a better mother," his father said pointedly. "You haven't seen her since we've been back. It's tearing her heart out."

"I don't know what to say to her."

"How about telling her that you love her no matter what?" Bryce suggested mildly. "That would go a long way to easing the tension she's under. The rest can be worked out with time."

Tyler nodded. "I can do that."

"Soon?"

"Today, if it'll get you off my back."

His father grinned. "It will, for the time being, anyway." His expression sobered. "What about Maddie?"

"I don't want to talk about Maddie."

"You have to. I've done little else the past few days myself. Think about that little girl who lost her father. How can you blame her for wanting to lash out? You're a grown man, and *you* want to strike out against your mother and Daniel."

"I don't," he denied, then sighed. "Yes, I suppose I do. But I would never set out to destroy them."

"Because, despite everything, you knew you always had their love and mine. Maddie lost everything. And her target was me. You just got caught in the cross fire."

"She *used* me." He still couldn't get over how deeply that hurt him.

"But she also backed away from using what she had on me because of her feelings for you."

"The way I hear, what she had wasn't exactly on the money."

"Perhaps not, but Griffin Carpenter's not above using half-truths if they suit him. And Maddie didn't know what she had was only a part of the story. She wanted to believe the best about her father. Then, when she was confronted with what he'd done, she fought like crazy to prove it had been a mistake."

"I can't forgive her, Dad."

"Well, that's up to you, of course, but in case you change your mind, you might want to know she's living in Los Piños now."

Tyler regarded his father in stunned disbelief. "How the hell did that happen?"

"Harlan Adams took her under his wing, the way I hear it. He heard your sister giving her a tongue-lashing on your behalf and went to bat for her. Not with Trish, of course. Nobody would want to tangle with your sister when her protective instincts are aroused, but Harlan spent a little time with Maddie, found her a job on the paper over there and took her into his home till she gets back on her feet. Trish is still spitting mad about it, but she concedes that Maddie's already doing a good job for the paper. She can't find a single fault with her reporting, much as she'd like to for your sake."

"I can't believe it," Tyler said. For some reason he'd just assumed Maddie had stayed in Houston. Maybe he'd wanted to believe that she would be nearby whenever he was ready to go looking for her. Obviously, she had taken him at his word, that he wanted nothing more to do with her. Her leaving bothered him more than he cared to admit.

Why? he asked himself. Was it because it was proof that she thought she could make a life for herself without him? Was it because she might meet someone over there in that blasted town where his sister and his brother had both met their soul mates? Harlan Adams was a notorious meddler. If he'd taken a shine to Maddie, it wouldn't be long before he tried to find someone for her to marry, Tyler thought, feeling thoroughly disgruntled by the prospect.

First things first, though. He had to see Daniel. "Okay, you win," he told his father. "I'm taking off."

"For?"

"The house to see Mother, then out to the rig to see Daniel."

"And Maddie? I saw the way the color drained out of your face when you heard she was in Los Piños. You afraid of what Dylan and Trish might do, or are you worried about Harlan and his matchmaking?"

"I wish to hell I knew," he said honestly.

A half hour later he was sitting across from his mother getting a similar lecture about not letting Maddie slip through his fingers.

"What is it with you and Dad?" he demanded.

"Shouldn't you hate her for busting in here and stirring things up?"

"She was just protecting her own, or thought she was. It seems to me that a woman like that would make some man a good wife. She'd be someone he could count on, someone who'd be in his corner no matter what."

Tyler shook his head. The whole world was going loony on him. He leaned down and gave his mother a kiss and a warning.

"Stay out of my love life."

"From where I sit, you don't have one," she said tartly. She grabbed his hand when he would have walked away. "Tell Daniel…" Her voice trailed off and she sighed.

"Tell Daniel what?"

"What I would have told him if I'd seen him—that I'll always be grateful to him."

"For?"

"Why, you, of course," she said with a tender smile.

Tyler found Daniel in his office, his expression grim as he grappled with a list of figures that apparently weren't doing his bidding. "Blasted numbers," he grumbled when he saw Tyler. "Don't know how I ever let your father talk me into running this operation."

Tyler met his gaze, then said quietly, "I think I know how."

Daniel's expression faltered. "What is it you think you know?"

"The truth."

"Is that so? How did you come upon this truth you think you know?"

"It's too complicated to explain, so let's just leave it

that I know you're an honorable man and you agreed to come back here rather than stay in Houston and stake a claim on your son."

The color washed out of Daniel's face. "Stop talking crazy, boy."

"I know everything," Tyler said. "Mother told me."

Of all the shocking statements Tyler had made since entering Daniel's office that was the one that seemed to shake him the most.

"But why?" he asked, regarding Tyler with total disbelief. "We'd made a promise, all of us."

"She was afraid it was going to come out in a tabloid. She wanted me to know first."

"And your father agreed to that? Over the years he's warned me on a regular basis that we had an agreement. As if I could have forgotten," he said with a shake of his head. "What changed his mind?"

"Mother didn't give him a choice."

He chuckled at that. "Helen always did have a stubborn streak. She and I locked horns on more than one occasion while we were…" His voice faltered.

"Lovers," Tyler said. "It's okay, Daniel. I'm old enough to know that's how I came to be. She said to tell you she's grateful for that, by the way."

"No more than I am," he said. "You've made me proud, Tyler. Even though I wasn't the one who raised you, and have no right to take the credit, I can't help feeling proud of the man you've become. You're strong and decent and honorable."

"A part of the credit for that does go to you," Tyler insisted. "Don't you know what an influence you've been on my life? Don't you know how much I've relied on you, even without knowing that you were my father? Look at Jen. You were the only one I trusted with that."

"It broke my heart when she and my granddaughter died," Daniel said. "It broke my heart even more to see you grieving so." He studied him intently, then said with his usual lack of subtlety, "I thought maybe that young woman who was here a few weeks ago might be changing that."

Tyler groaned. "Not you, too."

"What?"

"I'm not discussing Maddie with you. I've already had an earful from Mother and Dad."

Daniel chuckled. "Then I'm sure that was more than enough." He regarded Tyler with a hopeful expression. "You coming back to work?"

Tyler almost said yes, seizing on the suggestion as a way to put off what he knew he had to do where Maddie was concerned. "No," he said reluctantly. "Not just yet. There's one more person I have to see."

He just wished to hell he knew what he was going to say when he saw her.

Maddie was slowly but surely falling in love with Los Piños and the people in it. Harlan Adams and his wife were at the top of the list. They had made her feel a part of their extended family from the moment she had stepped across the threshold.

Her job was…well, it was safe, after the walk she had almost taken on the journalistic wild side. She was getting back to basics, covering everything from weddings to cattle rustling and being meticulously accurate about all of it.

She was also willing to admit that she was content

living in Los Piños partly because there were Delacourts living here, and she knew that, sooner or later,
Tyler would come to visit. Maybe she would eventually
catch a glimpse of him, though not if Trish or Dylan
had their way.

Dylan usually muttered a greeting when their paths
crossed, but Trish scowled and turned away. They were
still treating her as if she were a carrier of the bubonic
plague or worse, but she could understand how they
felt. She had hurt their baby brother and their parents.
Their attitude was simply the price she had to pay for
the damage she'd caused to their family.

Whatever happened with Tyler or the rest of the
Delacourts, she was determined to make the most of
the opportunity she'd been given to start over. She
wanted to prove that she could be a different kind of
journalist, one who stuck to the facts and—even more
importantly—one with heart.

Harlan Adams certainly seemed to think she had it
in her. He continued to amaze her. She'd interviewed
him on his ninetieth birthday, sprinkling bits of his
wisdom on life and love and family through the article. The story had been picked up around the state. She
couldn't help wondering if Tyler had seen it and, if so,
what he'd thought, especially about Harlan's declaration that love should never be squandered but rather
seized and savored, no matter how difficult the path
sometimes seemed.

"Did you send a copy to your young man?" he'd
asked, once he read it.

"Of course not."

"Then maybe I will. There's a message in here, if
only he's bright enough to find it."

"Don't you have enough people falling in with your plans without going after Tyler?" Maddie asked.

"You changed your mind about wanting him?"

"No, but—"

"No buts about it," Harlan said emphatically. "Sometimes people need a little nudge." He folded up the clipping and stuck it in an envelope. He started to hand it to Janet, then snatched it back. "Never mind. I think I'll put it in the mail myself."

His wife regarded him indignantly. "Harlan Adams, are you suggesting I can't be trusted with a piece of mail?"

"Now usually the answer to that would be an unequivocal no, but sometimes you tend to take the short-sighted view when it comes to my matchmaking." He patted his pocket. "I think I'll play it safe."

Janet looked at Maddie and rolled her eyes. "The man's had a few little successes with getting his grandbabies married and settled down. His ego's out of control. Lord help the great-grandchildren."

Maddie met his gaze. "Would it matter if I asked you not to send that clipping?"

"No," he said flatly. "And it has nothing to do with my ego. I just know a thing or two about love."

Maddie resigned herself to the inevitable. "I'm out of here."

Harlan regarded her with alarm. "What do you mean by that? You're not leaving just because I won't back down, are you?"

She laughed at his stunned reaction. "No, actually, I'm just going to cover a town council meeting, but I'll have to remember that threat for another time."

He scowled at her. "You go, missy, but you'll thank me in the long run."

The town council meeting was uneventful, but on the walk back to her office Maddie saw a man step out of the shadows. She knew at once who it was, because the jolt of her pulse had less to do with fear than anticipation. He had come, and it hadn't taken a letter from Harlan Adams to get him here. She considered that promising.

"Tyler," she said, hoping her voice sounded far calmer than she felt.

"Can we talk?"

"Of course."

"Where?"

"I was on my way to the newspaper office. There won't be anyone else around at this time of night."

"Fine."

She led the way down the block, then used her key to enter the darkened office. All the while, her pulse was scrambling, her thoughts racing.

"Coffee?" she asked, more for something to do than out of politeness.

"If it's no trouble."

She filled the coffeemaker, then turned it on. After that she was at a loss. Her gaze kept straying to the man perched on a corner of her desk. She couldn't seem to get enough of just staring at him. He looked tired and maybe a little thinner than he'd been the last time she'd seen him.

When she finally poured their coffee and sat down opposite him, he slid a thick envelope across the desk toward her.

"What's that?"

"It's from my father. He said you'd understand."

It was the file he'd promised her, the one she'd concluded she didn't need to see. Maybe someday she could look at it with objectivity and try once more to understand why her father had done what he'd done, but not now. She tucked it into the back of a drawer.

Tyler seemed surprised by her action. "You're not going to look at it?"

"I know what's in it. The evidence of my father's embezzlement, the proof of his gambling debts."

"I'm sorry," Tyler said. "That must be very painful."

"The pain is going away. I just have to keep reminding myself that what happened was in the past." Because she wanted to concentrate on the present, she asked him, "Are you back at work on the rig?"

"Not yet. I've taken some time to do some thinking."

"About who you are?"

"That, and about what I really want."

"Have you reached any conclusions?"

"Just one."

She studied his face, searching for a clue, but his expression was blank. "Which is?"

"You're too important to me for me to walk away without giving us a second chance."

Maddie almost sagged with relief, even though he hadn't sounded especially overjoyed about his decision. A chance was all she wanted, all she needed. For the first time in weeks she began to have hope.

"I've spent weeks trying to see all of this from your perspective," Tyler said. "I think I understand your motives, but the rest of it, the way you used me, I'm not sure I'll ever be able to get past that."

"I know," she said, because it was true and nothing excused it. She'd been wrestling with that herself.

He regarded her evenly. "To be honest, I was hoping that when I saw you again that would be the end of it, that it would be over, that I wouldn't feel a thing. That's why I came here."

Her heart began to thud dully. "And?"

"It's not over, dammit. I look at you and I want you." He sounded angry and confused, not at all like a man in love.

"Wanting's not enough."

He rubbed a hand across his face. "I know. That's the trouble. There's so much more. I go to sleep and there you are in my dreams. I think about those weeks we were together and I remember all the good times. Even though they were based on a pack of lies, I can't forget about them. We had something, Maddie. I lost Jen and my daughter. They're dead. I can never get them back. But you're here and very much alive. No one knows better than I do how precious and fragile love is. How can I turn my back on it without a fight?"

Maddie heard the doubts in his voice, even as he claimed to want what she wanted, a future for the two of them. "So, what are you saying, Tyler? I've told you that I love you. I've said I'm sorry. I'm not going to spend the rest of my life apologizing. Either we pick up and go on or we forget about it."

"Can you do that? Can you forget?"

"No," she said softly. "I'll never forget you. No matter what happens you'll be the man I loved with all my heart, enough to give up everything I thought mattered in my life."

She forced herself to meet his gaze. "Do you want to know what I learned from you? I learned that family is what really matters. I thought that was a lesson I already knew. I thought it was why getting even was so important to me, but then I realized that family hadn't mattered at all to my father. If he had cared about us, he wouldn't have left us. He would have worked harder to make the most of the chance your father gave him by not pressing charges. It also made me realize that I need to find my brothers, mend some fences if that's possible."

Tears welled up as she said it, tears for the weak man she had adored, for the strong man across from her she might well be losing. Suddenly she felt Tyler's hand close over hers.

"Don't," he said softly. "It's going to be all right, Maddie. Somehow we're going to make it right."

She lifted her gaze to his. Hope blossomed in her heart. "We are?"

"I'm not saying it's going to be easy. I'm still trying to figure out exactly who I am, how I fit in."

"You're a Delacourt," she said. She was able to say it emphatically because it no longer mattered to her, but it very much mattered to him.

"So my parents keep telling me," he said wryly. "And I guess I've got the Delacourt stubbornness, even if I only learned it by example. That's what makes me believe we can make it." He grinned. "Love and determination, Maddie—we've both got more than our share."

"We do, don't we?" she said, matching his grin, feeling her heart lighten.

"Shall we put them to the ultimate test? Just plunge in with no safety net? Will you marry me? You can't very well nurse a grudge against the Delacourts if you're one of us."

"I stopped nursing a grudge against the Delacourts

months ago—when I fell in love with one of them," she admitted.

She lifted his hand and brushed a kiss across the scarred, familiar knuckles, felt the heat stir inside her. It was time, she thought, time to put the past solidly where it belonged, in the past, and take the first step into the future. This must be what it felt like to Tyler working on the rig, putting his life on the line—risky and exhilarating.

"What kind of wedding do you think we can have if your sister's not speaking to me and your mother blames me for all of this?" she asked by way of a response.

"If you're saying yes, they'll be there," he said, a smile tugging at the corners of his mouth as he grasped what she was really saying. "Mother's actually relieved that the secret is out in the open, and Trish will come just to keep an eye on you."

"Maybe we could elope," she suggested half-seriously.

"Not a chance. They might forgive you for a lot of things, but not for depriving them of a wedding."

"And you? Can you forgive me for a lot of things?"

"I think if you were to kiss me, it might be a good start," he teased, his gaze locked with hers.

"If that's all it takes, then we're definitely on our way," she said, moving into his arms.

It wouldn't be this easy, of course. Maddie knew that. But he was willing to put his faith in the two of them, on the line. He was ready to make a commitment to her, despite everything.

And because of that she would spend the rest of her life proving to him that his faith hadn't been misplaced.

Epilogue

The baby squalled all the way through the baptism in the small, crowded church in Los Piños. Tyler glanced over at Maddie, saw the embarrassed blush in her cheeks and winked. Their son already had a mind of his own, and having water sprinkled on his forehead did not, evidently, have his approval.

"I baptize thee, Daniel Bryce Delacourt, in the name of the Father, the Son and the Holy Ghost," the minister said, ignoring the baby's bad temper to bless him, anyway.

Tyler had a feeling that with his heritage, baby Daniel was going to need all the heavenly intervention he could get. His biological grandfather and namesake and his Delacourt grandfather—also his namesake— were already engaged in a tug-of-war over who got to hold him the most. Maddie managed to keep both of them pacified, but she had laid down the law when the gifts started arriving at their new home in Los Piños.

"I will not have a nursery that looks like a branch of FAO Schwarz," she told Tyler emphatically.

"Hey, I'm not the one doing the shopping on the

Internet. Speak to Dad and Daniel. While you're at it, you might want to speak to Grandpa Harlan, too. He's the one who had the swing set installed in the back-yard while we were still at the hospital."

Maddie had only laughed. "I've already learned that Harlan Adams does what he wants around here. It would be a waste of breath to try to stop him."

"Then you can't very well deny Daniel and my fa-ther the same right. We'll have a rebellion. They'll re-tire and settle in Los Piños right next door, and we'll never have any peace."

The comment had been made only partially in jest. Neither of the men were happy about his decision to leave Delacourt Oil and go to work for Jordan Adams's oil company.

"You're doing it to spite me," his father had declared.

"You're doing it to keep peace between your father and me," Daniel had said. "Don't you think we can manage to be civilized, especially now that the truth is out? Whether you work for him in the office or me on the rig, it's your call."

"I'm doing it because Maddie is happy in Los Piños and I want to keep her that way," he'd retorted to both of them.

It was evident that neither of them had believed him, but it was the truth. If Maddie had wanted to live on an island with absolutely no natural resources that could be mined or drilled for, he would have found a way to accommodate her, especially after she had told him they were expecting their first baby. It was just a side benefit that Los Piños happened to have the headquar-ters of a reputable oil company.

He gazed down at his son and felt his heart begin to

expand in his chest. The boy was a miracle, no doubt about it. Even if his full-volume cries were disrupting the solemn ceremony. Because of him, Maddie had even reached out to her brothers, tracking them down with Dylan's help to invite them to today's family celebration. They had declined due to their own family obligations, but their promise to come for a visit had satisfied her for now.

Tyler knew if they didn't back up their words with action, Maddie was more than capable of going after them, now that she'd made up her mind to get them back in her life. She'd been pleased to discover that both had let go of past ill-advised behavior and settled down with wives and children of their own.

When the service ended, Maddie reached for Daniel. "I'll take him. I need to feed him."

She slipped out the door, while the rest of the family was busy slapping Tyler on the back.

"Hey, where'd my grandson go?" Bryce demanded.

"Maddie's gone home to feed him," Tyler said. "You'll see him when we get to the house."

"Here, you can hold your other grandson," Dylan said, slipping his eight-month-old boy into Bryce's arms.

"What about me?" Trish's daughter demanded, looking up at her grandfather and pouting.

"I guess we're just going to have to move here," Helen Delacourt said. "That's the only way we'll get to spend enough time with the new generation of Delacourts. Even Michael and Jeb's children love it over here and come to stay every chance they get."

"No need," Harlan Adams said slyly. "I'll look after 'em."

"Over my dead body," Bryce retorted. "You've got your own family, old man. This crowd belongs to me."

Tyler left them squabbling and went in search of Maddie and baby Daniel. When he walked through the front door of the house they'd built, a feeling of absolute contentment stole over him at the quiet serenity. In a few minutes, when the others arrived, chaos would erupt, but for now this was his world, his and Maddie's.

From the moment he'd uttered his proposal, he'd felt the rightness of his decision, but never more so than when he stood in the doorway of the nursery and saw her with his son.

She seemed to feel his gaze and glanced up, a smile on her lips. "Is everyone here?"

"Not yet. I snuck out of the church while they were trying to mark their turf."

"All of them?"

"Mainly Dad and Grandpa Harlan. It's killing my father that so many of us have defected into Harlan's world. Mother's making noises about moving over here."

"That would be wonderful," Maddie said.

"Would it? You wouldn't mind having Dad underfoot?"

"Of course not. I love your parents."

He never ceased to marvel at the fact that she really did. As if she read his mind, she chided, "Tyler, I've put the past behind me. Thankfully, so have your parents. Can you say the same?"

He sighed. "When I look at you and little Daniel, I have everything I need. The past doesn't matter, only the present and the future."

She reached for his hand. "Ditto."

The front door banged open and three masculine voices called out in unison. Tyler recognized his father and Daniel and Grandpa Harlan, all of them sounding impatient. He grinned at Maddie. "His royal subjects await. Is he ready?"

"He is," she said at once, laughing. "Are you?"

"If you're coming, I'm ready for anything."

With Daniel snuggled firmly against Tyler's chest, he and Maddie walked hand in hand to the top of the stairs. Before they could start down, he pulled her to a stop, leaned down and kissed her.

"I love you, Maddie Delacourt."

"Maddie Kent," she corrected automatically.

"Are you sure it was professional reasons that kept you from taking my name?" he teased.

"You'll just have to trust me on that."

Tyler stared into her eyes, saw the indisputable love shining there. "I do," he said. And he knew with every fiber of his being that by some miracle, he did. He thought of Jen and Rachel and of what Mrs. Andrews had said to him when he and Maddie had visited, that they had died for a reason, because God had another plan for him. Maddie and his son were in his life because of that loss. They would never replace Jen and his little girl in his heart, but one thing the past months had taught him: When it came to love, there was more than enough room for everyone. And that was a lesson he and Maddie would certainly pass on to the next generation of Delacourts.

* * * * *

THE PATERNITY TEST

Prologue

Next Saturday's baby shower would be the fifth Jane Dawson had been invited to in the past three months. Every time she turned around, it seemed, another friend or another co-worker was having a baby. She was being overwhelmed by the sight of rounded tummies, radiant faces and silver rattles.

She'd become such a regular at Annie's Baby Boutique that Annie routinely called when something special came in. They'd become fast friends, and the boutique had become Jane's favorite after-school haunt for a cup of tea and some girl-talk.

As a result, Jane's biological clock was ticking so loudly, she was sure it could be heard throughout her hometown. She would be thirty in July, not so old for having babies these days, but definitely getting up there, especially with no prospective father in sight.

Once again back at Annie's, this time specifically to buy a present for Daisy Markham's shower on Saturday, Jane rubbed her fingers over the cheerful yellow gingham liner in an antique carved oak crib that was Annie's latest treasure and sighed heavily. She'd been sighing a lot lately. Wishing, too, and dreaming.

It was getting more and more difficult to hide her envy, as well. *Oohing* and *ahhing* over one more hand-knitted pair of booties, one more tiny outfit, might send her over the edge. Today, she thought looking at the crib, could very well be the day.

"What do you think?" Annie asked, glowing with pride over the refinished piece. She still had streaks of wood stain and polish on her hands. Her no-nonsense short hair was mussed and she hadn't gotten around to so much as a dusting of powder across her face, much less any lipstick.

"Is that not the most beautiful crib you've ever seen?" she demanded.

Jane tried to hide her own yearning to possess that crib—to have a reason to possess that crib—and nodded. "It's lovely."

"Can you imagine?" Annie asked indignantly, buffing the already gleaming surface. "I found it stuck way back in a dim corner of an antique place out on Route 3. You should have seen it. It had been painted half a dozen times at least. Stripping it, I went through layers of white, blue, pink and several more of white paint. It was caked on so thick, it wasn't until I got almost down to the wood that I saw the carving."

The shop's owner rubbed her fingers lovingly over the intricate design. "A little angel. Have you ever seen anything so precious?"

"Never," Jane said, her yearning to claim it deepening.

Annie grinned. "Well, I know it's too extravagant for a shower present, but I just knew of everyone who comes in here, you'd appreciate it the most. I had to call the minute I put it in the store. Sometimes the urge to share my finds overwhelms me. I hope you don't mind that I left a message at the school. It's not like I'm trying to make a sale. I know perfectly well you don't need a crib."

Something inside Jane snapped at Annie's offhand remark. "I'll take it," she said as if to prove her wrong. "Just the way it is with the yellow gingham liner and all. Put it on my account and send me the bill."

Almost immediately she regretted the impulsive words as Annie gaped. "But—"

Jane cut off the shocked protest. "You can have it delivered to my place, right? John will bring it by Saturday morning, won't he?" she said, referring to Annie's husband, who frequently helped out with deliveries on weekends.

"Of course, but—"

"Thanks," she said, cutting off her friend's questions, logical questions for which she obviously had no rational answers. "I've got to run. I have a PTA meeting tonight. All the teachers have to be there early to greet the parents. We're trying to butter them up so they'll help us raise the money to upgrade the cafeteria. Don't forget to wrap up that little pink sweater and bonnet for Daisy's shower. It's Saturday afternoon. You can send the package along with the crib."

"Of course."

Jane felt Annie's puzzled, worried gaze follow her as she left the store and walked up the hill toward the old brick school.

Not until much later, after the PTA meeting, after she was back home and sipping a cup of tea, did she concede that Annie might have cause to wonder what an unmarried, uninvolved woman was going to do with a baby crib. Hopefully she could come up with a plausible explanation before everyone in town concluded that she'd turned into an eccentric old spinster whose hormones required serious adjustment.

Annie's devoted husband, still handsome and fit at fifty, delivered the crib at 9:00 a.m. on Saturday. He set it up in Jane's spare bedroom and never once asked why in the world she'd bought it. Jane swore her undying gratitude to the man for that.

After he was gone, she made herself a cup of raspberry tea and sat down in the tiny bedroom to admire the crib. She dreamed of the day when she'd have a baby of her own sleeping on the pretty yellow sheets, when she could decorate the walls of the room with bright paper and a border of ducks and rabbits and put a rocker in the corner. The image was so clear, she felt an incredible pang of longing to make it real.

"But it's not real," she told herself sternly, forcing herself to leave the room and close the door firmly behind her. The purchase of that crib suddenly seemed foolish. She was months, if not years, ahead of herself.

This time it was her friend Daisy who was having the baby, her third. She already had two boys and had discovered that this one would be a girl. She and her husband were over the moon about it, even though the boys were teenagers already and this baby had been a huge surprise.

Jane told herself that the sharp stab of envy she felt was normal, the alarm going off on her biological clock, so to speak. Buying a crib, however, was a bit of an overreaction. Maybe she should call Annie, admit she'd made a ridiculous mistake and have John pick up the crib and take it back to the store. She even reached for the phone, but she couldn't seem to make herself dial.

If only…

She brought herself up short. There was no sense looking back. Mike Marshall, the love of her life, was in her past. They had made a rational, mature decision together to end the relationship nearly a year ago when he'd been offered an incredible job in San Francisco. A clean break, they had decided. No looking back.

Mike had always dreamed of the kind of opportunities this new company would give him. He'd craved the recognition it could bring him as an engineer, the financial stability of the salary a big firm could offer.

Jane's dreams were different, simpler—a home, a family, roots in a community where neighbors knew each other and cared about each other. It was almost the way she'd grown up, the way she wanted her own children to be raised, quietly and with a greater sense of stability in their lives than she had had with a father who'd always been running off.

Since Mike had gone, she'd told herself a thousand times that they'd made the right decision, the sensible decision. Love sometimes meant letting go. If they'd been meant to be together, they would have walked down the aisle years sooner, but Mike had always held back, needing the proof that he could support a family in a style his own background had never provided.

But Jane still cried herself to sleep thinking about him. Being sensible, she'd concluded, sucked.

Since he'd gone, she'd hidden her favorite snapshot of him deep in the bottom of her drawer, but every now and then she stumbled across it and each and every time it brought tears to her eyes. The sale of his old house, right next door, had made his move final and the permanency of it had left her shaken for months. Lately she'd told herself she was over him, that she *had* to be over him. But she wasn't, not by a long shot.

Once they had talked about a future, about having babies and growing old together, but that golden opportunity in California had been too powerful for Mike to resist. She wouldn't have let him turn it down, even if he'd wanted to.

And she hadn't been ready or willing to leave the town and the job that suited her so perfectly. Both of them had dug in their heels, unable to see any way to compromise. And so a relationship that had once meant the world to both of them had ended.

By now he'd probably found someone new, someone more suited to a big-city lifestyle, someone whose social life revolved around more than baby showers and picnics and an occasional movie. She hoped he had. She didn't want him to be as lonely and miserable as she was.

What if he was, though? What if he missed her as desperately as she missed him? If that were the case, though, wouldn't he have called?

No, of course not, she told herself, not if he took their agreement as seriously as she did. Not if that famous Irish pride of his had kicked in as viciously as hers had. When it came to pure stubbornness, they were a perfect match.

She opened the door to the spare room and stared at the crib again, imagining her baby there, hers and Mike's. A chubby, strong little boy with round cheeks and thick black hair just like Mike's. Or maybe a rosy-cheeked little girl with glints of red in her hair just like Jane's.

Had she closed the door on that dream too soon? Had she accepted Mike's departure too readily, conceding defeat when she should have been fighting tooth and nail to find a way to make it work?

Finding that crib at Annie's had forced her to face emotions she had convinced herself were dead and buried. If she still loved Mike as deeply as ever, didn't she owe it to both of them to see him again, to see if there was anything left now that he'd had a chance to test his wings in the kind of job and city he'd always dreamed of?

Spring break was just around the corner. So was Mike's birthday, though she'd always been more sentimental about such occasions than he had been. After she paid for the crib, her savings account was going to be low, but there was enough left for a trip to San Francisco without dipping into the rainy day money her mother's small insurance policy had left her. Could there be a better investment of her savings? She couldn't think of one.

Maybe they would fall in love all over again. Or maybe they would sleep together one last time for old times' sake.

Maybe by some glorious fluke they would make a baby, she thought wistfully. Okay, it was highly unlikely, but what a joyous blessing it would be! Whether their relationship resumed or faltered, she would treasure a child of theirs, raise it on her own, if need be.

The decision to go to San Francisco was made as impulsively as the purchase of that crib. It took an hour on the phone with the travel agent to nail down all the arrangements. By the time she was finished she was late for Daisy's shower.

The party was in full swing when she arrived, the laughter and teasing audible from outside. When she walked in, the group fell silent and stared.

"Where on earth have you been?" Daisy demanded, hefting her bulky figure from a chair and rushing over to hug Jane. "You're never late."

"We tried calling the house a half-dozen times but the line was busy," Ginger added. "Donna was about ready to drive over there."

"So? What happened?" Daisy prodded. "Don't tell me Mike showed up on your doorstep after all these months."

"Nothing like that," Jane said. "I just lost track of the time."

"You never lose track of the time," Daisy protested.

"Well, this time I did," she said, a defensive note in her voice that clearly startled them.

Donna, who'd known her since first grade, studied her intently. "Okay, maybe he didn't show up, but it has something to do with Mike, doesn't it? Did he call?"

"No, he didn't call."

"But it does have something to do with him?" Donna persisted with the unerring accuracy of such a long-time friend.

Jane wasn't ready to discuss her plans with anyone, not even her closest friends. She forced a brilliant smile. "Hey, forget about me, okay? I'm here now and I want to see the presents." She handed her own to Daisy to add to the pile beside her. "Get busy. You look as if that baby could pop out any second now. I want you to finish opening all these before it does."

With some reluctance, everyone finally turned their attention back to the gifts. Jane *oohed* and *ahhed* with the rest of them, but her mind was already somewhere else, in a city she'd never seen, with a man who was part of her soul.

One

Engineer Mike Marshall had had more adventures than most men twice his age. Most of the riskiest had come in the past twelve months, since his move to San Francisco. Until today—his thirty-second birthday—it hadn't occurred to him to wonder why he was suddenly so willing to put his life on the line.

The truth was, he'd always been eager to take risks. As a kid, he took every dare ever offered. Now, though, he didn't even wait for the dare. If an overseas assignment for his company didn't satisfy his hunger for adventure, then he scheduled a trek up Mount Everest or a rafting trip on the Snake River. It had been months since he'd had a spare minute, much less a moment's boredom.

And yet, something was missing. He knew it, just the way he knew when a design for a bridge or a dam wasn't quite right. He stared out his office window at the Golden Gate Bridge emerging from a thick fog and tried to put a name to what was missing from his life.

Not excitement, that was for sure. Every day was packed with it.

Not companionship. He'd met a dozen women, beautiful, successful women, who shared his passion for adventure.

Not money. His salary was more than adequate for his needs, more than he'd ever dreamed of making back in Virginia. For the first time in his life, he felt financially secure, able to support a wife and family if the right woman ever came along.

Not challenges. The partners in his engineering firm only took on the most challenging jobs.

What, then? What was the elusive something that made him feel as if the rest hardly mattered? What was behind this vague sense of dissatisfaction?

It irked him that he couldn't pin it down.

To his relief, the buzzing of his intercom interrupted the rare and troubling introspection.

"Yes, Kim. What is it?"

"You have a visitor, sir. She doesn't have an appointment," she added with a little huff of disapproval.

Mike grinned. Kim Jensen was a retired army drill sergeant with closecropped gray hair and the protective instincts of a pit bull. She maintained his schedule with the precision of a space shuttle flight plan. Flexibility was not part of her nature.

"Does this visitor have a name?" he asked.

"Jane Dawson, sir."

The clipped announcement rattled him as nothing else could have. His heart slammed to a stop, then took off as if he'd just been advised that it was his turn to bungee-jump from the penthouse floor of a Union Square office building. The reaction startled him almost as badly as the mere thought of Jane in San Francisco. Jane, who'd never flown in her life, had come clear across the country, out of the blue, with no warning? He had to see it with his own eyes.

"Send her in, by all means."

"Are you sure, sir? You have an appointment at fourteen hundred hours. Sorry, sir. I mean in ten minutes."

"Send her in," he repeated and stood up, wondering at the astonishing sense of anticipation that was zipping through him.

"Just plain Jane," as she'd been known a dozen years ago, was in San Francisco? The woman who'd vowed never to leave their small Virginia hometown had braved her first flight on a whim, just to say happy birthday, perhaps? The concept was so out of character he found it almost as impossible to grapple with as the design for a sturdy, yet inexpensive bridge in some third world country.

But unless he'd imagined Kim's announcement, Jane was here, on his turf, and his heart was beating as rapidly as it had the day he'd stolen his very first kiss from her. At the same time a long-missed sense of calm settled over him.

The door to his office opened, Kim stepped aside and Jane walked past her. His mouth dropped open. He'd known her his whole life and he almost didn't recognize her. Her old high school nickname was hardly appropriate anymore. There was nothing plain about the woman before him. She was wearing a lime green suit that flattered her coloring and slinky heels that flattered her long legs. Her hair was shorter, with a sassy, trendy cut that feathered against her cheeks, then skimmed to her shoulders in layers. The red highlights glinted brighter than ever. She looked more sophisticated than he remembered. Sexier, too. Then her familiar sweet, shy smile came and went and his heart flipped over, just as it always had.

"Hello, Mike. Happy birthday."

His own grin broadened. "I can't believe it. Come here, you."

He opened his arms and, after an instant's hesitation, Jane stepped into the embrace. When she was settled against his chest, her head tucked under his chin, the oddest sensation crept over him. It was as if he knew, at long last, what had been missing.

But, of course, that couldn't be. He'd put Jane Dawson firmly in his past when he'd made the move to San Francisco. He'd given her his word that the break would be clean and he'd kept it. With his parents dead, his brothers and sisters scattered and the family home sold, there'd been no reason to go home again. He hadn't looked back, not once. Well, hardly more than once.

He stepped back eventually and looked her over. "You look fabulous. Sit down. Tell me what you're doing in San Francisco. Is it a teachers' convention of some kind? Why didn't you let me know you were coming? How long are you staying?"

She laughed at the barrage of questions, the sound as clear and melodic as a bell. "Last question first. I'm here for a week. I didn't let you know because I didn't know myself until the last minute. Spring break crept up on me and I decided not to spend it cleaning the house the way I have every other year since I started teaching. This is pure vacation."

She regarded him uncertainly. "I hope you're not about to take off on an assignment or something. Will you have time to have dinner at least? We haven't missed celebrating your birthday together since we were kids."

"Dinner will be a start," he agreed, thinking of all he could show her in a week, imagining her excited reaction. That was the thing he had loved about Jane. She brought such enthusiasm to every discovery, whether it was finding an arrowhead in the clay banks of the Potomac River or seeing the first crocus pop up in the spring. It was the quality that made her such an excellent teacher. She was able to communicate that enthusiasm to her students.

She'd always been able to communicate it to him, as well. Maybe that was why they'd been so good together, even though her pursuits were far more sedate than those he might have chosen for himself. Once they'd toured Stratford Hall, Robert E. Lee's birthplace, together. When she'd suggested it, Mike had shuddered at the prospect. He'd been barely into his teens and a whole lot more interested in playing ball than touring a musty old plantation.

Afterward, to his amazement, he'd felt as if he'd been caught up in the middle of an incredible family drama that had eventually played itself out on a Civil War battlefield. There was no denying that Jane had a gift for teaching, a gift for firing the imagination.

At the moment, with her looking the way she did, his imagination was taking off in a much more provocative direction, remembering the feel of her in his arms, the burning of her lips on his.

His intercom buzzed way before he was ready for the interruption.

"Sir, your appointment's here," Kim announced with a touch of triumph and the obvious expectation that he would promptly shoo his unscheduled visitor out of his office.

"Get him a cup of coffee or something and tell him I'll be right with him," Mike told her. He turned back to find Jane staring out the window, her eyes wide and shining with excitement.

"It's something, isn't it?" he asked, moving up behind her to gaze at the Golden Gate.

"Better than the pictures," she agreed. She turned. "I can see why you were drawn here. The Golden Gate always did inspire you. Even when we were kids, that was your favorite picture in the encyclopedia. You must have sketched it a million times. Now it's right outside your window."

For a few weeks that had awed him, too. Then he'd begun to take it for granted, just as he once had the love of the woman standing here with him now. The sound of his buzzer reminded him that he had a prospective client waiting and an impatient secretary who wasn't likely to let him forget it.

He touched Jane's cheek with regret. "I do have to take this meeting. Where are you staying?" he asked. "I'll have Kim clear my schedule this week. I'll be by at six to pick you up."

"Are you sure? I don't expect you to drop everything for me."

"I'm sure," he said with no hesitation at all.

In fact, he hadn't been more sure of anything in a very long time.

Jane still couldn't believe it. Her first flight had been a real nail-biter even before the first pocket of turbulence, but it was nothing compared to walking into Mike's office, staring down that snippy, protective secretary of his, then actually seeing him again. She'd been stunned by the surge of old feelings, startled by an unfamiliar rush of uncertainty until she had seen the warm welcome in his eyes.

Now, a few hours later, she realized that their very first date hadn't shaken her nearly as badly as dressing for this one nearly sixteen years later. Of course, she'd never before prayed so intently for a date to wind up in bed. For once in her life, she wanted to make something happen, to risk everything to make her dream come true. She'd been obsessing on having his baby ever since the possibility had first crossed her mind. She wanted desperately for it to happen, wanted him to want her as he once had. But as badly as she wanted his baby, she wanted him more.

Her hands shook as she fumbled with the clasp on the gold locket. Would he remember? Mike had given her the locket on her sixteenth birthday. His picture was still inside. Glancing in the mirror as the locket settled between her breasts, she wondered if it was the wrong touch. Was she counting too much on sentiment and old yearnings, instead of the here and now? If so, her presents were all wrong, too, chosen to remind Mike of all he'd left behind.

If only she could be cold and calculating, intent only on getting pregnant by a man who had once been her best friend, as well as her lover. But five minutes alone with Mike in his office had told her that, for better or worse, she was still in love with him. It remained to be seen how he felt about her or whether they would be any better at compromise now than they had been a year ago.

Her fingers faltered when she heard the impatient knock on her door. She almost dropped the tiny, very expensive bottle of French perfume she'd indulged in. She managed one last dab of the scent between her breasts, then went to the door.

Mike never failed to startle her when he was all dressed up in a suit and tie. Used to seeing him in jeans and T-shirts for so many years or even in a dress shirt with the sleeves rolled up and his tie askew as he had been in his office earlier, she wasn't prepared for the full impact of a light gray suit, white shirt and teal-and-gray silk tie with Mike's dark hair and perpetually tanned skin. When she wasn't looking, the boy next door had turned into a sophisticated man. Odd how she'd never noticed that before he'd left, even though he'd been thirty-one by then.

His approving gaze swept over her, heating her flesh. An impudent grin spread across his face and the boy next door was back. "Did you buy an entire new wardrobe for this trip?" he asked.

"Of course not," she lied, unwilling to let him see just how much she'd invested in this supposedly impromptu visit. She wondered if he'd guessed that her new haircut and the glistening highlights were courtesy of a San Francisco stylist to the tune of over two hundred dollars. She'd turned pale when she'd seen the bill, but one glance in the mirror told her it had been money well spent.

"I've never seen that dress before," he insisted. "I definitely would have remembered."

"You've been gone a year. Naturally I've bought a few new things in all that time."

His gaze narrowed perceptibly. "Was the dress for a special occasion?"

Jane couldn't prevent the laughter that bubbled up. "Mike Marshall, you're jealous."

He looked appalled by the suggestion. "Don't be ridiculous."

"You are. You have never made such a fuss about my clothes before."

"Because you were always in sedate little outfits suitable for teaching fifth-graders," he muttered. He gestured toward the dipping neckline and clinging silk. "This is something else."

"Want me to change?" she asked.

"Oh, no. You can wear that dress for me anytime."

"Just not for anyone else."

"I didn't say that."

She grinned. "You didn't have to." She linked her arm through his. "Come on. Let's get out of here before you start getting ideas."

"Honey, if you don't want me getting ideas, you'd better pull a sweatshirt on over that dress."

Jane shook her head, deciding she liked this newly discovered power she had to turn him on. "Not a chance. I'm all dressed up with a handsome man at my side. I want to go out on the town. I'm not wasting a single minute of this trip. I want to see and do everything."

"Then we'd better get started. This isn't our hometown, where we could cover everything in a weekend. San Francisco will take a little more time to explore."

They started with dinner across the bay in Sausalito, followed by a stroll along Fisherman's Wharf and an Irish coffee on the waterfront. Jane fell in love with the twinkling lights, the riot of sights and sounds and smells. Questions tumbled out so quickly that Mike had a hard time keeping up with the answers.

It was almost two in the morning by the time they made their way, exhausted, back to her hotel. He paused at the door to her room.

"I should say good-night here," he said, his knuckles resting against her cheek as he toyed with a strand of her hair.

Familiar, never-forgotten sparks shot through her at his touch. "You should," she agreed, then stood on tiptoe to brush a kiss across his lips. "But I hope you won't."

"Jane—"

"Don't argue. Besides, I haven't given you your birthday presents yet."

It was exactly the right incentive. Despite his claims of indifference, Mike had never been able to resist a present. When they'd first met as kids, he'd been uncomfortable with the way her mom went all out on special occasions, especially birthdays. His own family barely acknowledged birthdays, maybe because there were so many of them and so little money for extras.

Jane had always treated Mike's birthday as if it were a national holiday. She'd baked a cake, found half a dozen small, special treats and wrapped them as if they were solid gold trinkets. She'd done the same this year. She'd even arranged for the hotel to deliver a birthday cake to her room while they were out. A bottle of champagne was on ice beside it. Mike stared at it as if she'd ordered a feast.

"How did you manage this?"

She grinned. "It is San Francisco, after all. Anything's possible. Isn't that what you told me when you were trying to convince me to move here with you?"

"I'll bet the cake's not my favorite," he said, already poking a knife speculatively through the thick coating of whipped cream frosting.

"Oh, but it is. Chocolate with raspberry filling," Jane confirmed.

He turned and smiled at her. "You're amazing."

"So you've always told me. I suppose I'll always have to go to extraordinary lengths to live up to my reputation." She opened a drawer and extracted three small, brightly wrapped packages. "These first, then cake."

As he always had, he opened the smallest one first. It was a gold key ring with a bright beach design enameled on it and Virginia written in bold red letters.

"Afraid I was going to forget home?" he asked, laughing.

She gazed at him, then said quietly, "I was afraid you already had."

His laughter died and his gaze locked with hers. "Never."

Jane swallowed hard, then looked away. She couldn't read too much into that, she didn't dare. "Open the biggest one next," she insisted.

"But I always save that for last."

"Not this year."

"Okay, okay," he said, picking up the flat, ten-by-twelve-inch package. As if to taunt her, he took his own sweet time with the ribbon and paper. When he finally had it open, she saw the heat rise in his cheeks as memories tumbled back. He glanced at her, his astonishment plain.

"It can't be."

"Oh, but it is," she assured him. "It's a picture of your car, that old blue convertible you loved so much." She paused, then added softly, "The one we made love in the first time."

"Where on earth...? I thought for sure this was on the junk heap long ago."

"Nope. I was walking through town one day and heard the sound of that engine—"

"Who could ever mistake that?" he asked, chuckling. "It sounded like a lawn mower on speed. The word clunker was coined for that engine."

"Maybe so, but that clunker still runs, and a teenager, one of Velma Scott's boys, has it now. He thinks he's the hottest kid in town."

"Just the way I did."

"You were the hottest boy in town," Jane said softly. "Anyway, I asked him if he'd take me over by the river and let me take a picture for you."

"I hope you didn't tell him why," Mike said.

She chuckled. "Didn't have to. He figured that part out all on his own. He said he remembered watching the two of us in that car when he was just a kid."

"Hopefully not while we were parked by the river."

Jane laughed at his horrified expression. "It was ten years ago when you sold it. He was maybe eight at the time. I doubt he was allowed out at midnight."

"Thank God for that." He ran his fingers over the glass as lovingly as he once had touched the finish on that beloved car. He met her gaze. "Thank you."

"You're welcome."

"Can I ask you something?"

"Sure."

"Why the trip down memory lane?"

She shrugged, trying to feign indifference. "I don't know. I suppose I was feeling nostalgic when I realized it was your birthday and it would be the first one in years we hadn't shared."

"Have you missed me, Jane? Is that it?"

She forced herself not to look away, not to skirt the truth. If ever an occasion called for honesty, this was it. "I missed you, yes. More than I'd imagined possible."

"Oh, baby," he whispered, gathering her close. "I've missed you, too."

He tilted her face up, then slowly—inevitably— lowered his mouth to hers. And with the touch of their lips, passion raged and a lifetime of memories came flooding back.

Two

No one back in Virginia would have called Jane plain if they could have seen her tonight, Mike thought as his touch brought color to her cheeks and a flare of heat to her eyes. He'd always thought she was pretty, but tonight he was certain he'd never seen any woman more beautiful.

Cupping her face in his hands and gazing directly into her eyes, he asked, "Are you sure? We promised we wouldn't do this again. You said—we agreed—it would only drag things out, complicate them."

"I haven't had a decent complication in my life in a long time now. I'll take my chances," she said, her gaze steady. "Please, Mike, I want you to make love to me again. I've missed being in your arms. I've missed the way I feel when you touch me."

"Like this?" he asked, caressing her. "And this?" His hand slid lower, caught the hem of her skirt and lifted it as he stroked the inside of her thigh above the sexy black hose she wore.

Her familiar whimper of pleasure was his answer. Teasing and taunting, he came closer and closer to the hot, moist place between her thighs, never touching it, until she was arching against his hand, demanding more. In bed, her natural shyness had always vanished. She let him know what she needed, provoked him into giving it to her, then shared every bit of her pleasure with him. She was doing the same thing now.

His own pulse was racing, his body hard, but still he concentrated on Jane. He took her to the edge, then retreated, until she was gasping and pleading with him to come inside her.

He wanted to. Oh, how he wanted to, but he hadn't come prepared. Making love had been the last thing he'd imagined them doing tonight, because they'd both so vehemently declared the relationship over. He'd figured he'd be lucky if she allowed him to steal the kiss he'd been wanting since she'd waltzed into his office earlier.

"Mike, please," she whispered against his ear. She reached between them, sought his erection and almost jolted him off the bed with her cleverly wicked touches.

"We can't. I don't have anything with me," he said, sorrier than he could say.

"It's okay," she insisted, arching against him.

He regarded her doubtfully. They'd never taken chances before. "You're sure?"

She shoved his clothes aside and feathered kisses across his belly, then lower. "I'm sure," she insisted, then touched her tongue to the tip of his arousal. "I'm sure."

Mike never questioned her sincerity after that. This was the first woman he'd ever loved, the woman whose body and responses were as familiar to him as his own. Urgency wiped out all rational thought as he stripped away his clothes and then the last scraps of hers. Her skin was hot and damp when he finally poised above her. Slowly, savoring every sweet sensation, he sank into her, sheathing himself in slick velvet heat.

For a moment that was enough, just being inside her again, just feeling the stirring of his body, the pounding of his heart. Then he wanted more, so much more. Jane's cries echoed in his head as each thrust went deeper and deeper, joining them in a frenzy that went beyond lust.

It had never been like this before. They'd never made love with such uninhibited abandon, as if each sensation were wild and reckless and new. No dare he'd taken since leaving her had been this exciting, this thrilling. Maybe he'd always held back something, knowing that one day the right job would come along and he would leave. Maybe she'd always held back, knowing she would stand aside and watch him go.

Now, though, it was as if they had reached that hurdle and pushed past it. Whatever happened to them, the chemistry between them would triumph. This was the proof of that. The past, the future, neither mattered. It was now, this moment they were living in.

Thinking of it, Mike smiled. Jane caught him. Entwined in his arms, their bodies slick with sweat, she tilted her head and assessed him curiously.

"Something about this amuses you?"

"It's you," he said at once. "You amuse and delight and thrill me."

"Prove it," she dared, wriggling her hips provocatively.

"You just wait," he taunted, rolling until he was on

his back and she was astride him. "I'm going to let you have your way with me."

He linked his hands behind his head and leaned back against a pile of pillows. "I'm all yours, Janie."

Her eyes widened. "But—"

"Just use your imagination. Anything goes."

A grin spread slowly across her face. "Big mistake, Mike. I have a very inventive imagination and months alone to let it run wild."

To his astonishment and delight, she pretty much exhausted him proving it.

When they'd finally collapsed and were nestled in each other's arms again, Mike listened to the soft sound of her even breathing, then sighed. "Oh, Janie," he murmured. "How am I ever going to let you go a second time?"

He would have to, too. There wasn't a doubt in his mind about that. He loved San Francisco and his job, the life he'd built for himself, the sense of security that had been such a long time coming. And as much as he wanted to, he couldn't deny that Jane belonged in the town where they'd grown up. Her roots ran deep, her feelings for the place and her friends ran even deeper. In a few short days she would go back and he'd be left to make do with these new memories and a cold, lonely bed.

Waking up to find Mike still beside her, his breath on her shoulder warm, his arm across her middle heavy, Jane smiled contentedly. It wasn't over between them, not with such powerful chemistry exploding at the slightest touch. They had six more days to figure out a solution that would keep them together. She felt more hopeful than she had since the night he'd told her he was leaving.

"You look awfully smug," Mike murmured, his voice gravelly with sleep.

"Do I? Maybe that's because I actually managed to distract you not only from opening your third present last night, but from your birthday cake and champagne."

"And you consider that a coup?"

"I consider it a miracle."

"Where is that present?"

She shrugged. "On the floor somewhere, I suppose."

"I hope to heaven it wasn't breakable."

She grinned as she thought of what the box contained—glow in the dark condoms. They'd been meant as a joke...and as a last resort if the picture of his old car hadn't gotten him into bed. Mike was a healthy, virile male, unlikely to resist such a blatant message. And, as he'd said the night before, they'd never taken chances. She hadn't deliberately set out to take one last night. The condoms, she reassured herself, were proof of that.

Even so, she couldn't help whispering a little prayer that she had gotten pregnant. Not to trap him, never that, but to give herself the child she wanted so desperately. Mike's baby.

"Jane?"

"Hmm?"

"The present. It's not breakable, is it?"

"That's definitely something you don't need to worry about," she assured him. "These are guaranteed not to break."

"These?"

She scrambled off the bed and found the box, then tossed it to him. He shook it, obviously intrigued by the light weight. When he ripped off the paper and saw what was inside, he chuckled.

"Insurance?"

"There are twelve of them. As I recall, there was a time you would have considered that a dare."

He winked at her. "Still do. Order up a huge breakfast so I'll have the strength for it and we'll try to make a dent in the supply."

They saw very little of San Francisco that day or the next, but Jane couldn't have been happier. She had come to see Mike, not the city. This was the honeymoon they'd never had, the one she'd been envisioning since she first knew what the word meant. It didn't seem to matter that the wedding she'd also envisioned had never happened. If anything, their appetites for each other were more insatiable than ever. They talked, made love, ate, made love, slept and made love again. It couldn't have been more perfect.

On her fourth day in San Francisco, she awoke to hear Mike in the shower, humming an off-key rendition of an old Johnny Cash song. The sound was so familiar, had once been so much a part of her daily life that she had to remind herself sharply that it might be only temporary. Sooner or later they were going to have to talk about something besides what to order from room service and which color of condom to try next. She picked up the box and shook it. There were none left. That pretty much eliminated one of their favorite topics.

She slipped out of bed and crept into the bathroom.

When she opened the shower curtain, Mike grinned at her.

"Lonely?"

She nodded. When he beckoned, she stepped under the shower. Mike's hands, slick with soap, began to explore. It took only a heartbeat for both of them to become as steamed up as the room and thoroughly aroused. Her body was sensitive to the slightest brush of his fingers. In the blink of an eye he was lifting her, guiding her until he was deep inside and her legs were wrapped around his waist, her back pressed against the cool tile.

"Oh, yes," she murmured, as the hot spiraling need slashed through her yet again.

Mike's head was thrown back, his muscles tensed as yet another climax tore through them both.

When the aftershocks were over, he released her slowly. Her body slid along his until her feet touched the tile floor. Jane was shaken by how quickly he was able to shatter her, how attuned her body was to his. She had always enjoyed sex with Mike, thrilled to his touch, but in the past few days, they had moved to some new level of neediness. She couldn't believe what he was able to do to her with little more than a slow, seductive look.

"I can't believe what you do to me," Mike said, echoing her thoughts, looking at her with amazement once they were back in the bedroom dressing. "We were always good together, but this…"

"I know. It's astonishing."

"Scary, too," he said.

Jane stilled, gazing at his reflection in the mirror in front of her. "Scary? Why?"

"What will happen when you go home again in a few days? This intensity isn't something you can just walk away from and forget." He studied her intently. "Or is it?"

So, she thought, they were going to have this conversation now. She'd hoped to put it off a little longer, hoped to have time to put her own feelings into perspective.

"What are you asking me?"

"I suppose I'm asking what happens next. Do you just go back home and pretend that this was just a romantic interlude, a spring break to remember, something you can tuck away in a mental scrapbook? Or does it mean something to you?"

Hands and knees trembling, Jane sank down on the edge of the bed. "Do you want it to mean something, Mike?"

He came and sat beside her and took her icy hand in his. "Yes, I want it to mean something," he said fervently. "I want it to mean that this time we'll figure out a way to make things work. I want our love to last this time. I want it to mean that you'll stay here and marry me."

Jane swallowed hard. It was what she wanted, what she'd prayed for…almost. "Here," she repeated, unable to hide the note of defeat that crept into her voice.

"Yes, here," he said, the old familiar defensiveness promptly coloring his words. "Why not here? It's a beautiful city. It's exciting. There are thousands of people who would give anything to be able to live here, especially in the style I can afford." He frowned. "But you're not one of them, are you? You won't even give it a chance."

"That's not true. I came here, didn't I? It's not entirely my fault that we've barely left the hotel."

Mike sighed. "You have a point, which is why I'm already dressed, instead of taking you back to bed again. I want you to see the city, see my place. I want you to meet my friends. I want to take you sight-seeing and shopping until you fall in love with it all the way I have."

Jane's spirits sagged. Couldn't he see that she was in love with him? Wasn't that enough? Why did San Francisco have to be part of the bargain?

"Please," he said softly, as if he'd read her mind. "Just give it a chance, keep an open mind. That's all I'm asking."

It was only fair, she supposed. She reached up and touched his cheek. "I'll give it a chance," she promised, then turned away before he could see the tears gathering in her eyes as she saw part of her dream already slipping away.

Three

Jane dedicated herself to getting to know San Francisco, to giving it a fair chance. Mike could see the grim determination in her eyes when she sat down with a guidebook over lunch on Fisherman's Wharf and chose the spots she wanted to visit. She mapped out a rigorous, dutiful schedule his secretary would have admired.

Once they'd started, though, her attitude began to change. As he'd anticipated, she was entranced with everything, almost despite herself. The transition over the next couple of days was slow, but unmistakable. She peppered him with more questions than he could answer, delighted in the strange and exotic food, the sight-seeing ride on a boat on San Francisco Bay, the opening day ball game he'd committed to attending with clients he couldn't offend. Jane charmed them and cheered as if she'd been a loyal Giants fan her whole life.

But there was no mistaking the sense that she was on vacation, enjoying an interlude, rather than settling into a new routine. Maybe that was his fault. Maybe he shouldn't have taken the time off. If he'd left her to her own devices, maybe she would have begun to adapt as if she lived there, instead of taking it all in as a tourist.

As it was, there was a sinking sensation in the pit of Mike's stomach as Sunday rolled in. He sensed that she would leave and nothing at all would have been resolved by this visit. He was at a loss over what else he could possibly do to win her over.

There was no question in his mind that their love was as strong as ever, even after a year's separation. The sex was extraordinary. Their thoughts meshed on so many topics, disagreements were rare. It was just that the one subject about which they disagreed was a doozy, the kind that could make or break their future.

They awoke at dawn on Sunday, this time in his bedroom, rather than her hotel. When he pulled her into his arms, when he made love to her, he couldn't hide the fierce desperation in his heart. It was in his every frantic, possessive touch, in every kiss.

And in hers.

When it was over and he held her, he felt the dampness of her tears falling on his chest and knew that he had lost the battle once more.

"You're going to leave, aren't you?"

"Of course," she said briskly, then added with a catch in her voice, "school starts again tomorrow. You knew that."

"It'll be out in June," he said, struggling to keep his tone even. "Will you be back then? Can't you at least give it a three-month trial run? You could move in here with me, really get to know the city. We could spend weekends exploring all of California. Don't we deserve that much?"

She looked at him briefly, then her gaze skittered away. "Maybe. I don't know, Mike. What would be the point? Your life is here. Mine's there. Teaching matters to me. My friends matter. And we can't do this to each other over and over again. It's not like this is around the corner from home. We can't exactly commute."

"There are teaching jobs here. You liked my friends. They adored you. Okay, maybe there's not the long history you share with Donna, Ginger, Daisy and the others, but these are good people, too. You loved the museums, the restaurants. I don't get it. What's the problem?"

Tears clung to her lashes. "It's not home," she said.

For her it was as simple—and as complex—as that. Anger ripped through him. Unreasonable fury stripped away any pretense of calm. He stood up and began to pace. It was happening all over again. She was throwing away what they had as if it had no importance whatsoever. He tried telling himself that she was throwing it away, not him, but it felt the same.

"You could come back," she suggested tentatively. "Obviously your company respects your work. Maybe you could make some sort of an arrangement with them. It would mean traveling, but you do that now, right? You're not even in San Francisco most of the time."

"That's not the point. This is where the headquarters are, where clients meet with us. If I'm not underfoot, I won't be the one they think of when a big job comes in. I'll get the leftovers. Then one day they'll wake up and discover they don't need me anymore at all." He'd been through enough firings and downsizings with his father to know what emotional devastation that wreaked on everyone around. He would wind up resenting Jane for having put him in that position.

He and Jane had been over the same ground a hundred times before he'd left for San Francisco the first time. Nothing had changed...in her position or his. And it broke his heart.

If only this visit had gone badly, if only the feelings had died. Instead they were stronger than ever. He loved Jane. He wanted her as his wife. He wanted their children. He just couldn't see any way to make it work, not when she was so totally unyielding, not when he couldn't see any way to bend.

"We'd better be getting to the airport," he said finally. "You wouldn't want to miss your flight."

He refused to acknowledge the hurt in her eyes. It didn't make sense that they both had to be in this much pain. There had to be an alternative, one they hadn't thought of, but damned if he could see it.

They rode to the airport in silence. Inside the terminal, as she prepared to go to the gate, he pulled her into his arms and kissed her with a hunger that left them both shaking.

"I love you," he said fiercely, as if she needed the reminder.

"I love you," she whispered. "Will you call?"

He hesitated. "I don't know. I don't know if I can go through this again, if you should go through it again. We're just making each other miserable."

A tremulous smile quivered on her lips. "Only when we say goodbye. The rest is magic."

"But we seem doomed to keep saying goodbye," he told her with regret. "Maybe this should be the last time."

Tears spilled down her cheeks. "Or maybe we just need to learn to believe in the magic," she whispered, and then she was gone.

Maybe she was right, he thought as he watched her go. Maybe the magic would come through for them yet, but he was far too practical a man to count on it.

When the phone rang at ten o'clock on Sunday evening after she'd gotten home, Jane's heart began to race. It was Mike. It had to be. No matter what he'd said about making this latest goodbye the last, he hadn't meant it. He couldn't have. Her hand shook as she reached for the receiver.

"You're back," Donna said, sounding relieved. "How was your spring break? Was it wonderful? Are you going to tell me now where you went?"

"Not tonight," Jane said, trying to hide her disappointment at the sound of her best friend's voice. "I'm beat. It's been a long day."

"Are you okay? You sound funny."

"I'm fine, just a little tired."

"Then we'll go out after school tomorrow. Dinner's on me. Darryl's coaching Little League tomorrow night and I can't wait to hear all about this mysterious adventure of yours."

When Jane was about to beg off, Donna said, "No excuses. If you say no, I'll know something's wrong."

"Okay, fine. Dinner will be great." All she had to do was get through it without bursting into tears.

The next day after the last of the kids had cleared out and Jane had done every last bit of paperwork she could find to delay the inevitable, she looked up and spotted Donna in the doorway to her classroom.

"The kids have only been back one day. You can't possibly have any more papers to grade," she told Jane.

"No, I suppose not," Jane said with regret, glancing around just to be sure.

"Then let's get out of here. It's a beautiful day, or haven't you noticed?"

"I noticed." The damp morning fog had drifted away by noon, leaving behind a sky so blue it made her eyes ache looking at it. It reminded her of the days she'd spent in San Francisco.

"Where do you want to eat?" Donna asked.

"Doesn't matter. You pick."

"Emilio's, then. I'm in the mood for Italian with lots of cheese and garlic."

"And cholesterol," Jane teased.

"I lived on little more than trail mix for an entire week," Donna countered. "Darryl takes his camping seriously. I deserve real food."

Jane thought of all the excellent meals she'd eaten on her own vacation, every ethnic variety imaginable, each one more delectable than the one before. "Well, not me. I should be dieting for the next month."

Donna grinned. "Then you went someplace with terrific restaurants. Now we're getting somewhere."

Whey they arrived at Emilio's, Donna led the way into the restaurant and picked a table in the corner. "More privacy back here, so you can tell me all the details."

Emilio brought them both huge glasses of iced tea, took their orders, then vanished into the kitchen to shout orders at the chef, who also happened to be his wife.

"One of these days she's going to chase after him

with a butcher knife," Donna observed, just as the deb-
onair Italian came scooting back into the front.

"Maybe she just did," Jane said, chuckling at his
chagrined expression as he retreated to his post at the
door.

Her gaze was still on poor Emilio, when Donna
asked casually, "How's Mike?"

Jane's head jerked around. "Mike? What made you
bring him up?"

"That's where you went, isn't it? To see Mike in
San Francisco?"

"Where would you get a crazy idea like that?"

"Oh, give it up, Janie. You've got that wounded look
in your eyes again, just the way you did when you two
split up last year. I take it it didn't go well."

"You're wrong."

"Wrong about where you spent spring break or
wrong about how it went?"

Jane sighed. "Can't I have any secrets?"

"Not from me," Donna said easily. "I've been your
friend for too many years now. Now, spill it. I want to
hear everything. Is Mike spectacularly successful?"

"So it seems," Jane said with a trace of bitterness.

Donna stared. "Hey, what's that all about?"

"I'm sorry. I'm pleased for him, really I am. It's
just that it would be so much easier if he hated it, if he
wanted to come home again, but he doesn't. The job
is a dream come true. He loves everything about San
Francisco."

"And you don't, I suppose."

"It's a wonderful city. I had a terrific time," she
claimed, but even she could hear that her tone was flat.

"But?"

"This is home."

"Jane, aren't you being the teensiest bit stubborn?"

"Ornery as a mule, to hear Mike tell it," she admitted.

"Well, maybe you should give a little."

"And do what? Go out there, marry Mike, then discover that I'm so homesick I can't stand it?"

"Were you homesick this week?" Donna asked.

"Of course not, but it was just a week." She smiled. "And Mike did keep me very busy." There was enough innuendo in her voice that no one could have mistaken her meaning, especially not someone as attuned to her as Donna.

"And you still walked away," Donna said with a shake of her head. She regarded Jane with a genuinely puzzled expression. "Are you crazy or what?"

The pressure of the week in San Francisco, the still-unresolved conflict with the man she loved and now Donna's unsympathetic reaction were all too much. Jane snapped.

"How can you even ask me that?" she demanded angrily. "You of all people know what it was like in my family. My dad had the world's worst case of wanderlust. He took off whenever the mood struck him. When he was here, he felt trapped and we all paid for it with his foul moods. When he was gone, it was no better, because then my mom was miserable. I won't set myself or Mike up for the same kind of anguish."

"Fine. I see where you're coming from, but have you ever explained all of that to Mike? Maybe he's never made the connection."

"How could he not have made it? He lived next door. He saw it."

"He was a kid," Donna argued. "Do you have any idea how oblivious kids can be? You should. You're a teacher. Besides, unless I miss my guess, you were as tight-lipped then as you are now. You probably never let him know what was going on." Her gaze was penetrating. "Did you?"

Jane sighed. "Probably not. I would have felt as if I were betraying my dad if I'd talked about it. In those days, I only wanted to please him so he'd stay."

"Then tell Mike how you felt, why you're afraid going to San Francisco could turn out the same way. He deserves to know what's going on in your head. All of it. Right now he probably just thinks that he's not important enough for you to take a risk that seems perfectly reasonable to him. He's offered you marriage, right?"

Jane nodded.

"And you turned him down?"

"Yes."

"Again."

"Yes."

"Can't you see what that must do to his ego?"

"Yes, but—"

"But what?" Donna countered impatiently. "No excuses, Janie. You have to tell him everything or else close the door on the best thing that ever happened to you. In the end how happy will you be here if the man you love isn't in your life?"

"I thought you weren't all that crazy about Mike," she said, confused by her friend's sudden defense of him, this unexpected push into his arms.

"I wasn't, not when I thought he was the one totally at fault, but I'm seeing another side to this now. Tell him, Janie."

"There still won't be a way to compromise."

"Maybe there shouldn't be a compromise," Donna suggested carefully. "Maybe just this once you should give in and follow your heart. I know how much a home means to you, but that house of yours isn't a home, not unless you manage to fill it with love. Last time I checked the love you want is several thousand miles away."

"Why do I have to be the one to put everything on the line?" she asked plaintively. "Why is it my sacrifice to make?"

"It's not a contest," Donna countered. "If you look at it that way, you're both bound to lose. In this case, you're the one with the options. He has a job there that he can't equal back here, at least for now. You could teach there, as well as here. Mike's ready to make a home for you there. Isn't that really what you've always wanted—a house, kids, a man who really loves you?"

The idea was tempting. It always had been. "He said the same thing," she admitted.

"Then maybe it's time you listened to him." Donna regarded her intently. "Or is the real truth that he just doesn't matter enough?"

"How can you say that?"

"Because, sweetie, actions speak louder than words, and you're still here."

Four

Mike wasn't going to call Jane. He made a solemn vow to himself about that. She was the one who'd walked away…again. The door to their future had slammed closed when she'd gotten on that plane.

It was amazing, though, how the color had gone out of his life when she left. San Francisco had had its own unique charm before she'd come. Now, having seen it all over again through her eyes, he should have been doubly enchanted by all it offered. Instead it felt empty and lonely and bland.

The excitement had gone out of his work, too. His boss had offered him a plum assignment just that morning and all he'd been able to do was nod and take notes on the details. The job meant spending two months in Canada planning a new bridge project. He should have been elated. Instead he saw it only as a way to escape the bittersweet memories San Francisco now held for him. Even at that, he debated turning it down. He'd promised his boss an answer before the day ended.

It was hard to believe that just over a week ago he'd been wondering what was missing in his life. Now he knew and he couldn't think of a single way to change things and get what he wanted, what he needed.

No, that wasn't entirely true. He could quit his job and go back to Virginia. Jane would marry him then, but he would wind up restless and bitter, just the way her old man had been.

Oh, he'd seen what a hell Johnny Dawson had put his family through, though Jane had done everything in her power to hide the dissension from him. For a long time he'd ached for the little girl whose life had been turned upside down every few months. He'd done as well as any kid could to offer the stability she didn't have at home. That's when the bond between them had been forged. He'd been so sure it would last a lifetime.

He'd seen the look in her eyes when he'd told her about San Francisco, the hurt and betrayal. At that moment, she had lumped him in with her father and that had been that. She couldn't see how different it would be for the two of them. He would have to travel, yes, but he would always come home. He would never leave her in any doubt about that, not the way her father had.

He wondered if it would do any good at all to tell her that, then concluded that it wouldn't. If she couldn't see it, then all the words in the world wouldn't convince her. And she wouldn't take the risk necessary for him to convince her with actions.

Which meant there were no answers, not now, anyway. He walked down the hall and told his boss he'd take the Canada assignment. He was on a plane the next day, grateful to be running from the memories that now haunted him everywhere he turned.

* * *

Jane hadn't needed the home pregnancy test or the visit to her doctor to confirm that she was pregnant. She had known it for weeks. Her body was as reliable as a clock. When she missed her period, there wasn't a doubt in her mind about the reason. Joy flooded through her, though, when the doctor actually said the words.

"You're going to have a baby," Dr. Laura Caine said. "Right after the first of the year."

Tears slid down Jane's cheeks. "You're sure? There's no mistake?" She didn't think she could bear it if she got her hopes up, only to discover there'd been an error in the lab.

"No mistake," Dr. Caine assured her. "I take it, despite the tears, that you're happy about this."

"Oh, yes," Jane breathed, cradling her stomach. "Oh, yes."

"There will be complications."

Jane's heart slammed against her ribs. "Complications? What sort of complications?"

"With the school. Parents might object to having an unmarried woman teaching when she's carrying a child."

"I don't care," Jane said, chin tilted defiantly. "I'll take a leave of absence, if I have to. I want this baby, Doctor."

"Can you manage a leave of absence financially?"

"If I have to," she said, thinking of the money her mother had left her. If ever there was a rainy day need for it, this was it. "You'll get paid. Don't worry about that."

"For heaven's sakes, Jane, I'm not concerned about

your bill," the doctor said, clearly insulted. "I'm worried about the stress you'll be putting on yourself and the baby."

"Oh." She flushed. "I'm sorry."

"Don't worry about it. Look, if there's anything I can do to make it easier for you, if you need a letter for the school, whatever, let me know."

"Thank you."

"What about the father?"

"What about him?"

"Will you tell him? He could help out if you're out of work."

"No," Jane said quietly. "I won't be asking him for help."

That night, though, as she sat in the room she already thought of as a nursery and contemplated her wonderful news, an image of Mike kept intruding. He would be happy about this. She knew he would. And he had a right to know. Common decency told her that. It didn't have to mean marriage or child support or any of those things. He just had a right to know he was going to be a father.

It took her a week to work up the courage to call. When she'd left three unanswered messages at his apartment, she guessed that he was off on an assignment. She finally took a deep breath and forced herself to call his office, bracing herself for an inquisition from that ogre who answered his phones and guarded his door.

"Mr. Marshall is out of town," Kim told her, giving away nothing about his whereabouts.

"Can he be reached?"

"In an emergency."

"This qualifies as an emergency," Jane insisted. "Ask him to please call Jane Dawson as soon as possible. He has the number."

"I'll give him your message when I hear from him."

Jane lost patience. "Is that how you handle an emergency? You just sit around and wait for him to check in?"

"Those were his instructions."

Suddenly Jane was a twelve-year-old girl again. She'd fallen from a tree and broken her arm. She remembered desperately wanting her daddy, needing him, crying for him, only to be told by her mother that they had no way at all to reach him. It wasn't going to be that way for her child. She would see to that.

"Never mind," she said dully. "Don't bother telling Mr. Marshall I called."

That night, for the first time since she was twelve, she cried herself to sleep over a man who was too far away to care.

The Canadian project took forever, far longer than anyone had anticipated. Mike could have left someone else in charge once the work was underway, but his boss agreed with him that the client deserved Mike's personal attention. And Mike had no reason to go back to a lonely apartment in a city that had lost its luster. It was early December before he finally returned to San Francisco.

Spring, summer and fall had passed in a blur. Not a moment had gone by, though, that he hadn't thought about Jane. He'd missed her, longed for her and cursed himself for the weakness.

Obviously, though, she hadn't been thinking about

him. If she'd called, Kim would have given him that message.

On his first night home, he knew he would be too restless to sleep. He drove straight from the airport to the office and found himself faced with a mountain of files and old message slips. He was about to toss the messages, when Jane's name popped out at him. He glanced at the date: *May 27.* Cold fury ripped through him. Why the hell hadn't he gotten the message way back then? Why had it been left on his desk all these months?

He noted that Kim had first written "emergency" in the message space, then crossed it out and written, "never mind."

Dear God in heaven, what sort of emergency had there been? Why hadn't Jane been given his Canadian number at once? Oblivious to the hour, he called his secretary at home, waking her from a sound sleep.

"Kim, I'm at the office. There's a message here from last May from Jane Dawson. Why wasn't I told about this? She said it was an emergency. What kind of emergency?"

"Wait, let me think," she said, instantly alert. "It was right after you left. Oh, yes, I recall. When I told her you'd left instructions that messages were to wait until you called in, she told me to forget it. I should have just thrown the message slip away, sir. I'm sorry."

"No, what you should have done was give me the damned message," he shouted. "Never mind," he said, slamming the phone down, then dialing Jane's number. His heart pounded, thinking of her needing him and then being brushed off.

It had to be nearly dawn in Virginia, but Jane's

phone rang and rang. Not even her answering machine picked up. At least the number hadn't been disconnected, he told himself, but that was small consolation.

He had a bad feeling about this, a very bad feeling. He called the airlines, then left the office. At home he heard three more messages from Jane, probably left months ago, as well. More panicked than ever, he threw some clean clothes into a suitcase and headed straight for the airport. He would be on the first flight out in the morning.

On the long drive from the airport to the riverfront town about eighty miles away, he told himself over and over that there was no reason to worry. Her answering machine was probably just broken. She'd probably just left the house earlier than usual that morning. He would find her at home when he arrived.

As he drove into town, he tried to see it through her eyes, tried to imagine it as a safe haven. True, the streets were clean and lined with large homes with gracious front porches. The old oaks were bare now, but in spring and summer their shade would provide welcome relief from the penetrating glare of the sun. Instead of being gray and choppy as it was now, the river would be a glistening blue.

The downtown section was barely more than a half dozen blocks of tidy storefronts and blinking neon signs. In summertime, the sidewalks were bustling with locals and tourists, but at this time of year, with the wind bitingly cold off the river, they were practically empty. One shopper, head lowered against the wind, rushed toward the blinking lights of the small gift shop, intent on Christmas shopping, no doubt.

Why didn't all of this beckon to him, as it did to

Jane? It wasn't that he hated it or held bitter memories. Simply put, it had never been enough. It had lacked the opportunities he'd craved.

A few minutes later he was sitting in front of Jane's house, staring at the drawn blinds and remembering the first time he'd seen the little girl who lived there. She'd been his shadow from that first meeting.

He never even glanced next door at the house that had been his home for most of his life. He was too stunned by the bleak darkness of her house. There were no signs of life at all, no indication of Christmas preparations inside. Jane had always decorated and baked with a fervor for the holidays. That sick feeling in the pit of his stomach intensified.

What if something had happened to her? What if she'd been ill and needed him? A thousand *what ifs* ran through his head, each one worse than the one before.

The school, he thought finally. There would be answers at the school. He drove the few blocks without even noticing what he passed. He was tearing up the walk, when he ran smack into Donna Iverson exiting the building. He'd known her almost as long as he'd known Jane, but she'd never much liked him. Now she stared at him incredulously.

"Mike?"

He grabbed her shoulders. "Where is she?" he demanded, not even trying to hide his worry. "Where's Jane?"

He saw the caution spread across her face. "Dammit, Donna, tell me. Has something happened to her?"

"It's taken you long enough to get around to asking that question," she said heatedly. "It's been months since she called you."

"I just got her message last night. I've been in Canada for months. You have to believe me—if I'd known she was looking for me, I'd have gotten back to her." He ran his fingers through his hair as he thought of how Jane must have felt when he didn't return her calls. Compassion threaded through his voice as he imagined her pain. "She must have felt so abandoned when I didn't call."

"She did," Donna agreed, regarding him evenly, clearly not intending to give an inch.

He felt the need to defend himself to her. "But I didn't know she needed me. I swear I didn't. I would have called—hell, I would have been here—if I'd had any idea she needed me."

Something softened in her expression then. "You love her, don't you? You really love her?"

"Always have."

Donna nodded, clearly accepting it as the truth. "I thought so. I told her there had to be some sort of mix-up, some reason you hadn't called. I begged her to keep trying, but she refused."

"Then tell me where she is. Let me try to straighten this out."

"Come on over to my house," she said. "We need to have a talk."

He wanted answers here and now, but he could tell he didn't have a choice. Donna intended to do this her own way. He followed her to a small brick house with black shutters, went inside and accepted the cup of coffee she offered him. "You are going to tell me where she is, right?"

"After we talk. I want to be absolutely sure I'm doing the right thing."

Mike grinned despite himself. "I always knew I was going to have to ask permission to marry her. I never figured you were going to be the one I'd have to ask."

"Oh, there's a whole slew of us around here who care about Jane. You're just lucky I'm the first one you ran across. Darryl wants to cut your heart out."

She said it with such cold-blooded sincerity, he shuddered. "Then I'll be sure to steer clear of Darryl."

"Maybe not. I married him six months ago. He'll be home any minute now."

Mike had an image of Darryl Smoot left from high school. The boy had been as big as a house and mean to boot, at least on a football field. Off the field, he'd cultivated the same image, but the rumor had been that it had all been for show. Mike prayed that the rumors were true.

He and Donna were still skirting the subject of Jane's whereabouts when Darryl came through the door. He was still huge, but he was all muscle now and the scowl that spread across his face when he recognized Mike was intimidating enough to give Mike a few bad seconds. Then Darryl turned his back on him as if he didn't exist and gave his wife a resounding kiss.

"What's the story, sugar? When did he turn up?" He gestured in Mike's direction.

"He's looking for Jane."

Darryl turned a fierce look on him. "Maybe Jane doesn't want to be found, same way you didn't when she called looking for you."

"That was all a big mistake," Mike explained again.

"So you say."

"It's the truth, dammit. Just tell me where she is. Is she okay? What the hell is going on?"

Donna snagged her husband's arm, then shot a look at Mike. "Excuse us a minute, please."

He heard their whispered exchange outside the kitchen door, but he couldn't make out a single word. He guessed they were debating how much to tell him. If the circumstances had been different, he'd have told them what they could do with their games, but they were his best hope for getting at the truth in a hurry. If anyone knew Jane's secrets, it would be Donna. And like it or not, he'd rather tangle with her and Darryl than try to get information out of the principal of Jane's school.

Finally, when he was about to lose it, the kitchen door swung open and Darryl came back alone. He held out a piece of paper.

"Here's her address." He positioned himself so he was in Mike's face, literally and figuratively. "You do anything to hurt her again and you'll deal with me. Is that understood?"

"Understood," Mike agreed, then moved around the man. When he was at the door, he glanced back. "I'm glad she's had you in her corner all this time," he said with absolute sincerity.

"Should have been you."

Mike sighed heavily. He could see Darryl's point. "Yes," he agreed without reservation, without even knowing what it was Jane had been left to face alone. "It should have been me."

Five

Jane had baked ten dozen batches of Christmas cookies since dawn. She'd only burned the first three dozen,
trying to get the timing down in the ancient oven in the
tiny furnished apartment she'd rented until the baby
was born. The apartment itself wasn't bad, with its
huge windows overlooking the river and its bright cur-
tains and overstuffed furniture. The appliances, however, were a very different story. The stove was turning
her holiday baking into an adventure.

She'd taken a leave of absence for an entire school
year, rather than battle the board of education over her
suitability to teach. She had enough money left from
her mother's insurance policy to cover her expenses,
including this apartment in a town just far enough from
home to protect her reputation. Maybe it was a foolish, old-fashioned ruse, but she had to try to give her
child a start that didn't include speculation about his
or her paternity.

She had debated just staying in her own house and
weathering the gossip, but in the end she'd concluded
she and the baby would both be better off if they just

turned up again in the spring. Maybe she was only postponing the inevitable questions, but she'd felt she would be better able to cope with them after she'd gotten through the pregnancy and had a healthy baby.

There was an ironic twist to her decision, of course. In the end, she'd done exactly what she'd refused to do for Mike. She had left the hometown she loved.

But it wasn't as if it was going to be forever, as it would have been if she'd married Mike. And she was still close enough to have lunch every couple of weeks with her friends. They met at a restaurant midway between the two towns, caught her up on all the news and brought her anything she needed from her house. They were scheduled to get together again on Saturday and she intended to have her usual packages of Christmas cookies ready for them since it was likely to be the last time she saw them before the holiday.

The apartment smelled of cinnamon and sugar and ginger and echoed with the sound of Christmas carols being played at full volume. In fact, the CD player was so loud, she barely heard the knock at the door. She turned the sound down, then listened just to be sure.

"Who on earth…?" she murmured, wiping her hands on a paper towel and grabbing the last batch of cookies from the oven before going to the door. It was probably a neighbor complaining about the volume of the music or her landlord coming to beg a couple of cookies. The man had an insatiable appetite for sweets and a constantly—and futilely—dieting wife who refused to bake them for him.

With her cheeks flushed from the heat of the oven and probably streaked with flour, Jane suspected she was quite a sight. Judging from the impatient pounding on the door, though, she didn't dare pause to make any improvements in her appearance.

"Okay, okay," she muttered under her breath, throwing open the door.

Her mouth gaped. "Mike? How on earth did you find me?"

He shook his head, still staring. "Doesn't matter."

No, she supposed it didn't. The point was, he was here. She wasn't sure which of them was the most stunned. His gaze went from her face to her unmistakably huge belly in the blink of an eye, then remained there as all the color drained out of his face.

"You…you're…"

"I'm going to have a baby," she said, supplying the words that eluded him. She regarded him intently. For a rugged man, he looked awfully shaken. "You aren't going to faint, are you?"

"Of course not," he said at once. "But—"

"I think you'd better come in and sit down," she said, though that was the last thing she wanted. For months she'd dreamed of finding Mike on her doorstep, but the dream had eventually died. Now her own reaction was nothing like what she'd anticipated. She felt nothing, or so she swore to herself. She was just surprised, that explained the sudden racing of her pulse, the lurch of her heart.

To give herself a little time to gather her composure, she left Mike in the living room and went into the kitchen to pour him a cup of coffee and herself a glass of milk. She added a handful of cookies to the tray and carried it back into the living room. Mike still looked dazed.

"What? When?" he asked, apparently incapable of forming a coherent sentence.

If she'd imagined him sweeping her up and dancing around at the sight of her body swollen with his child, this stunned reaction would have been a serious letdown, but she'd stopped counting on anything from Mike Marshall. Still, she had no intention of lying to him.

"The baby's due in three weeks, right after New Year's. I got pregnant in April."

"April," he repeated, then his gaze shot to hers. "You mean?"

She tried not to be hurt that he hadn't guessed it at once. "Yes, the baby's yours, Mike."

The confirmation snapped him out of his daze. "Why the hell didn't you tell me?" he demanded angrily.

So much for the joy she'd hoped for. Jane stared him down, then said quietly, "I tried."

"Well, you didn't try hard enough."

"I left messages at your apartment," she said pointedly. "I called your office, only to be told you were away and weren't to be bothered. What more would you have had me do?"

"Write me a letter, keep calling." He ran a hand through his hair in a familiar gesture of frustration. "Dammit, Janie, you should have found a way."

"Did it ever once occur to you to call me?" she retorted. "You knew we'd taken chances. Maybe you should have been responsible enough to check to see if there were any consequences."

"So now it's my fault for not checking with you?

Don't you dare try to pull that, Janie. You know perfectly well you told me there was no risk."

She flushed at that. "That's not exactly what I said," she argued, but without much spirit.

"It's sure as hell what you implied."

She couldn't deny that was exactly the impression she'd meant to give him. "Mike, it doesn't matter, not now. I'm having the baby in a few weeks. I don't expect anything from you. Not a thing. You're off the hook. You can hop the next flight to San Francisco and forget all about this."

He stared at her as if she'd lost her mind. "And what if I don't want to be off the hook? What if I want to be a father to this baby?"

She fought the little frisson of hope stirred by his words. He was just feeling territorial.

"Then we'll work something out," she said evenly. "I would never try to keep you from your child. That's why I called you in the first place."

"But you still won't marry me?"

"Now? Under these circumstances?" she asked incredulously. "No, of course not. A baby doesn't solve the problems we were having. It's just an added complication."

"That's how you view our child, as a complication?"

"No, never," she said fiercely. "That wasn't what I meant at all."

"What, then?"

"Just that it was difficult enough figuring out what to do when it was just the two of us involved."

"A baby should simplify it. We should both be thinking about what's best for our child."

"But we obviously don't agree on what that would be. We never have."

"How the hell do you know that? I only found out about this baby a few minutes ago. I don't even know what I think." He stared at her in frustration. "Jane Dawson, you are the most pigheaded woman I have ever known in my life."

"That kind of attitude will certainly win me over," she said dryly.

"I'm not trying to win you over. Obviously I've lost that battle. But I'll tell you one thing and make no mistake about it," he said, his voice climbing, "I am going to be a father to this baby and you can damned well get used to the idea."

"Well, that's just fine," she shouted back.

In the silence that followed, another CD slid into place on the player and the pure, clear notes of "Joy to the World" filled the air. Jane couldn't help it...she began to chuckle. When she glanced at Mike, she saw the fierce expression on his face begin to give way to a smile.

He sighed, then said softly, "Merry Christmas, Janie."

"Merry Christmas, Mike."

"Think we can discuss this rationally?" he asked.

"Maybe in the spirit of the season, we can try," she conceded, then gave a little gasp as the baby walloped her with a ferocious kick.

"What is it?" Mike demanded at once. "Are you okay?"

"It's nothing, just a little reminder that your kid's getting restless. The baby gets a little rambunctious around this time of day, probably because it's time to eat. A couple of cookies aren't going to do the trick."

"We'll go out," Mike said at once.

"I can fix something here."

"Do you have to argue about everything?"

She grinned. "Pretty much."

"Well, just this once give in gracefully, okay?"

His gaze settled on her stomach and a look of such yearning came over his face, that Janie felt something inside her shift. She had always imagined Mike looking at her with exactly that expression of awe when she was carrying his child. She had always imagined them sharing the wonder of it. Impulsively she moved across the room and stood in front of him.

"Give me your hand."

He stared at her. "Why?"

"Do *you* have to argue about everything?" she teased, echoing his accusation against her.

He held out his hand and she placed it against her stomach. The baby didn't disappoint her. The kick was another solid wallop. Mike's eyes widened and he stared at her incredulously.

"Oh, my God, that was him, her, whatever?"

Jane nodded.

"Do you know which it is?"

She shook her head. "I didn't want to know." The truth was it would have hurt too much to know if it was going to be the little boy she'd dreamed of giving Mike. She hadn't wanted to deal with that until she had to.

"It's a boy," Mike said with utter confidence. "If it's not, we're never going to have to worry about anybody messing with our daughter. She'll blow 'em away." His gaze on her softened. "You're okay? No problems with the pregnancy?"

"I'm healthy as a horse," she assured him.

"I want to know every detail," he said fiercely. "And

I want to go to your next doctor's appointment with you."

Jane stared at him in shock. "You'll be here that long?"

"Honey, you couldn't get me out of town now if you wanted to. I'm here for the duration."

When she opened her mouth to argue, he cut her off. "Get used to it, Jane. I'm here to stay."

"But your job…"

"I've worked nonstop ever since you left San Francisco. I'm due for some time off. I'll call tomorrow and make the arrangements."

The thought of Mike being around for the birth of their child left her feeling shaken. If he stayed that long, if he took care of her as he obviously intended, if he reminded her of how deeply she loved him, how would she ever manage to say goodbye again?

Mike didn't sleep a wink that night. Only a part of his restlessness could be blamed on the too-short, lumpy sofa in Jane's living room. There hadn't been any question of him sharing her bed. When they'd gotten back from dinner, she'd walked into the bedroom and shut the door. A moment later she'd emerged and tossed some sheets and a pillow in the direction of the sofa. He'd gotten the message. What he hadn't gotten was a moment's sleep.

He was still wrestling with the idea that he was going to be a father. He and Janie were going to have a baby. The thought boggled his mind. Over dinner he had pumped her for every single detail of her pregnancy, trying to hide his resentment over having already missed so much of this miraculous process.

To think that she could have had this child and he

might never have learned of it. The very idea of that made him so furious he wanted to break things. When he got past wanting to throttle her for not seeing to it he was informed, he thanked God over and over that she had decided to go through with the pregnancy. His next hurdle was to convince her to marry him so their child would bear his name.

He could hardly wait to hear the explosion likely to greet that plan. He'd spent the whole night trying to come up with the right words to convince her. In the end he'd concluded he would just drag her off to a church and let a minister persuade her that her child deserved to be born within the sanctity of marriage. He liked that. It was exactly the right button to push.

However well she might seem to be coping, it was obvious to him that she'd left her home because she didn't want the stigma for herself or her baby of being an unwed mom. That stigma wasn't likely to go away just because everyone back home missed the actual pregnancy. The only way to make things right for all of them was to get married. He just had to get the timing perfect.

Jane was a morning person. She always had been. He figured she'd be up with the birds, which meant he had to get busy. He dug around in the kitchen cupboards and came up with the best china the place had to offer. He found a couple of candles tucked in a drawer and put them in the middle of the table in the apartment's tiny dining alcove. Then he went to work in the kitchen.

He made biscuits and an omelet and squeezed fresh juice from the oranges he found in the refrigerator. He had coffee perking and a glass of milk poured by the time he heard the first stirrings in her room.

A few minutes later, she wandered into the dining area, barely covering a yawn. She stared at the fancy table and the huge breakfast, then sank into a chair.

"You've been busy," she said, regarding him warily.

"You told me to make myself at home. Do you want jam for your biscuits?"

"Yes, please." She toyed with the food on her plate. "Mike?"

"Yes."

"You can't keep doing this."

"Why not?"

"I'll be big as a barn."

"Maybe a bungalow," he said, grinning. "Never a barn. It won't matter anyway. I'll still think you're beautiful."

"That's only because you haven't seen my swollen ankles," she said, holding out her feet. She was wearing fluffy blue slippers. "Look. And this is at the beginning of the day. They'll only get worse."

"That's because you've been on your feet too much. That's going to stop, now that I'm here. You can keep them propped up."

"And do what?"

"Watch TV, read a book, crochet little booties."

"I don't think so."

"Jane, I intend to pamper you." He glanced at her plate. "Finish your omelet. The baby needs protein."

"How do you know?"

"I read that book you left by the sofa. Milk and protein for the baby's bones, plus plenty of fruits and vegetables."

She regarded him with amusement. "Mike, I'm eight and a half months pregnant. I know what to eat. I know how to take care of myself. If you're going to hover, you can leave now."

"I'm going to hover," he said, then added with a touch of defiance, "And I'm not going to leave. Get used to it."

Six

Mike was very big on routine. He always had been. Growing up in his household of rambunctious brothers and sisters, order and routine had been in short supply. He had always craved it. Jane suspected that was one of the reasons he'd been drawn to the calm and serenity in her house. Now he'd taken that need for order to new heights.

By the third day of his visit, Jane was fairly sure he'd missed his true calling…drill sergeant. When he wasn't stuffing her with food, promptly at seven a.m., noon and six with a couple of snacks thrown in at precisely two-thirty p.m. and eight, he was pushing the latest child care books on her to read. Judging from the stack he'd accumulated, she doubted there was a single title on parenting or prenatal care left in the local library.

And then there were the walks. Not the sort of strolls she'd grown accustomed to taking every afternoon, no. These were more like forced marches. By the time Saturday rolled around, she could hardly wait to get out from under his watchful gaze for a few hours while she met her friends for lunch.

When she appeared in the living room wearing her favorite maternity dress, the only outfit that didn't make her look like a blimp, he popped up out of his chair.

"Where are you going?"

"I'm meeting Donna and some others for lunch."

"Where?"

"At a little restaurant and craft shop in Lottsburg. I doubt you've ever been there."

He looked horrified. "But I know where Lottsburg is. It's on a back road in the middle of nowhere. You can't drive over there by yourself. I'll take you."

"Mike!"

"Stop arguing. I drive or you stay here."

"Dammit, Mike, I am not helpless."

"No, but the baby's due any second. What if you go into labor while you're on that country road all alone? Or what if there's an accident? The steering wheel could hurt the baby." He shuddered visibly. "No, I'm going and that's that."

"Mike, if you'd been this bossy when we were together, I'd have thrown you out on your ear."

"You weren't having a baby then," he said, as if that were explanation enough for his overprotectiveness.

Jane sighed and followed him to the car. "You'll sit at a separate table," she informed him as they drove.

"Whatever."

"In fact, you could wait in the car."

He grinned at her. "Don't push your luck, angel."

"Okay, a separate table will do."

Naturally, though, it didn't work out that way. All of the women she knew were well acquainted with Mike. They had all pretty much guessed that he was the fa-

ther of her expected baby, even if they hadn't said as
much to her face. The minute she and Mike walked in
the door together, the others crowded around, assum-
ing that his presence meant a wedding was just around
the corner. Jane guessed from Donna's satisfied expression that she was the one who'd steered Mike to
Jane's apartment.

"Feeling smug?" Jane inquired, choosing a seat by
her friend.

"Hopeful," Donna replied. "He's still around. That's
a good sign, isn't it?"

"Depends on your point of view," Jane grumbled.
"He's fussing over me as if I were the first woman on
earth to have a baby."

"And your complaint about that is?"

Jane sighed. "It's not going to last. Sooner or later,
he will go back to San Francisco."

"You don't know that. He looks content enough to
me. This could be just what he needs to decide he wants
to stay in Virginia."

"He spends an hour or more on the phone to his office every day when he thinks I'm taking a nap. Doesn't
that tell you something?"

"It tells me there are twenty-three hours he's devot-
ing to you. Be grateful. Most husbands don't give their
wives that much attention, ever."

"You don't understand," Jane said. "I can't let it
matter. I just can't."

"You still love him, don't you?"

"Yes, but…"

"Then use this time with him to come up with a
workable arrangement." She regarded Jane slyly.
"Maybe you should think about the fact that you've

been living away from home and away from teaching for months now and it hasn't been as awful as you feared it would be."

"Because I still talk to all of you and see you. And at first I was so exhausted, I slept all the time. I wasn't awake long enough to miss teaching."

"Honey, that's why they invented long-distance phone lines and airplanes. As for the exhaustion, wait till you have a toddler around the house." She patted Jane's hand. "Think about it, okay? Promise me."

Jane nodded. "I promise."

Donna grinned. "Good. Now, then, let's get this party underway."

"Party?"

"Annie?" Donna called. "Are you hiding back there?"

"I'm here," Annie called back and wheeled in a cart laden with packages as all the others shouted, "Surprise!"

"A baby shower. I can't believe it," Jane whispered, tears in her eyes. Mike made his way to her and put a hand on her shoulder and squeezed. She looked up at him and caught the way he was eyeing all the presents. She was probably going to have to fight him for the right to open them.

"After all the baby showers you've attended for the rest of us, it was the least we could do," Daisy said.

Jane thought back to Daisy's shower the previous March. That was the event that had triggered all of this. That was when she'd realized just how desperately she wanted a baby of her own. That was when she'd bought that wonderful antique crib from Annie.

It was also when she'd begun thinking of Mike again, wishing that they were together just like this.

Well, almost like this. She'd hoped for a more traditional arrangement, but she was having his baby and he was here at her side. That counted for a lot.

As she opened the presents, *oohing* and *ahhing* this time over her own gifts, a feeling of absolute contentment stole over her. She wouldn't have done a thing differently, she realized now. Whatever difficulties lay ahead, she wanted this baby—Mike's baby—with all her heart. If she couldn't have Mike with her for the rest of her life, at least she would have a permanent reminder of the love they'd once shared.

When the last present had been opened, and the last crumb of cake had been devoured, she made a decision. She turned to Mike. "I want to go home," she whispered.

"Okay. I'll get all of this stuff in the car and then we'll go back to the apartment."

She shook her head. "No, I mean I want to go home, to my own house. I want to put these things in the nursery. I want to stay there. I want to spend Christmas in my own place, to be there when I go into labor."

He studied her worriedly. "Are you sure? You've gone to this much trouble to hide your pregnancy. Do you really want to go back now?"

"I'm sure. I don't want to hide out anymore. Will you come with me?"

"You know I will." He knelt down and brushed a strand of hair back from her cheek. "In fact, if you want we can stop at St. Mary's on the way and see about getting married."

"Married?" she said as if she'd never heard the word before, never heard him propose the same thing a dozen different times. Sneaking it in again now, when she was so clearly vulnerable, was a low-down, dirty trick. She wavered.

"If you won't do it for yourself or for me," he added, "let's do it for the baby."

She wanted to. Oh, how she wanted to, but a marriage that from the very start wasn't meant to last? Wouldn't that be worse than no marriage at all?

"Think about the baby," Mike persisted, when she remained silent, repeating a now-familiar refrain. "The baby deserves to have the father's name, my name. We've loved each other our whole lives. Surely we can do this one thing together for the baby we've created."

It was the right thing to do for the baby. Jane could see that. But was it right for the two of them? How much heartache could they bear? The time would come when Mike would leave. It was inevitable.

"Darling, stop thinking so hard. Stop trying to gaze into a crystal ball and figure out what will happen tomorrow or a month from now. Right now all that matters is the baby and what's best for his or her future."

He made his case passionately and persuasively. If he couldn't say the exact words Jane wanted to hear, if he couldn't promise to stay in Virginia, well, that wasn't the only thing that mattered under the circumstances.

"We can talk to the minister," she said at last and wondered if she'd just made the best decision of her life…or the worst.

It took some doing, but when Mike wanted to make something happen, he pulled out all the stops. By nightfall, they had moved Jane's belongings back into her own home, met with the minister and arranged for a quiet, private ceremony to take place two days before Christmas. Donna and Darryl had agreed to stand up for them.

On the morning of the wedding, they found the church already decorated for Christmas with huge baskets of poinsettias. The candles were lit, giving off a soft glow around the altar. Jane had bought a new, cream-colored silk maternity dress and shoes to match. Mike was wearing a black suit with a crisp white shirt and black tie.

Even though the marriage would be only temporary, little more than make-believe, Jane couldn't help trembling as she looked around at the beautiful old church. It was just as she'd always imagined her wedding would be, except in most of those daydreams she hadn't been almost nine months pregnant.

Just before the ceremony was to begin, Mike gave her a bouquet of a single white poinsettia surrounded by white roses and tied with white satin ribbons. He tilted her chin up and gazed into her eyes.

"Everything okay?"

Jane managed a wobbly smile. "Everything's fine," she assured him, thinking to herself if only…

If only it were for real, if only it were forever.

When the minister read the vows, she repeated them in a voice that trembled, while Mike's rang out clear and sure. It almost sounded as if he meant every word, but she knew better. This was for the baby, nothing more. Pride should have kept her from saying yes, but for once pride had mattered less than doing what was best for her child. And she would have a few days or weeks with Mike that she could cherish forever.

In a few weeks it would all be over, the baby would

be here and Mike would leave. Her life would go on. Tears tracked down her cheeks as the minister pronounced them man and wife. Other brides had surely cried, she thought, but none from the sort of heartache she was feeling.

When Mike bent and kissed her and tasted the salty dampness on her lips, he regarded her with surprise. Instantly concerned, he whispered, "Oh, baby, it's going to be all right. I promise."

Jane wanted to believe him. He'd always made good on his promises.

This one, though, seemed to be beyond his capabilities.

Donna and Darryl gave them a moment alone, then swept in and announced they'd arranged for a wedding lunch.

"That wasn't necessary," Jane said, touched by their attempt to make this occasion seem real and special, even though both of them knew the circumstances were anything but normal.

"Of course it was," Donna insisted. "Come on. We even have a limo waiting and sparkling grape juice in the back so we can toast the newlyweds on our way to the restaurant."

They were halfway to Fredericksburg when Jane's back began to ache. They were almost on the doorstep of the restaurant when the first contraction hit. She doubled over and clasped Mike's hand.

"Dear heaven, what is it?" Mike said, the color draining out of his face. "Janie, talk to me. What's wrong?"

When the hard grip of the contraction loosened, Jane managed a smile. "I'm not sure, but I'd say we got married in the nick of time. Unless I miss my guess, this baby's coming now."

"Now?" Three voices echoed with shock.

"Oh, yeah," Jane said as she was seized by another contraction.

Donna patted her hand as Mike guided her back into the limo. "Don't you worry about a thing," she told Jane. "The hospital's practically right around the corner and years from now you can tell your kid that he made the trip in a limo instead of an ambulance."

"As long as he's not delivered in the back seat of a limo," Jane said. She glanced at Mike. "How are you holding up?"

He swallowed hard. "To tell you the truth I'm feeling just the slightest bit superfluous. You're the one who's got to get the job done."

"Oh, no, you don't," Jane muttered. "You're not running off with Darryl to buy cigars or something. You're going to be in that delivery room with me."

"But I trained as your coach," Donna protested. "Are you sure you want to change at the last second like this? Does Mike even know how to do the breathing exercises?"

"Don't go getting territorial on me," Jane said. "You can coach. Mike can hover. It's something he does very well."

Darryl grinned. "I guess that leaves me to pace and buy the cigars."

The limo screeched to a halt at the emergency room entrance and Mike and Donna butted heads trying to be the first one out. Darryl took off out the other side. It was several seconds before anyone noticed that Jane was still inside.

"Hey, guys," she called out plaintively. "You can't do this without me."

Mike scooped her up and carried her inside. An orderly swooped down on them and took them straight up to labor and delivery, where less than two hours later black-haired, blue-eyed, David Michael Marshall entered the world screaming his head off to protest the indignity of it all.

By nightfall Donna and Darryl were gone and Jane and Mike were alone with their son. They regarded the six-pound-three-ounce baby with awe.

"How did we ever create anything so beautiful?" Mike wondered.

"He started out with a pretty decent gene pool on his daddy's side," Jane said pointedly.

"Better on his mother's."

"Do you want to hold him?"

There was no hesitation at all. Mike reached for him eagerly and settled into the rocker beside the bed. As Jane drifted off, the last thing she heard was Mike explaining to his son that he would always, always be there to protect him.

"You can count on it, son." He glanced at Jane. "So can you." But she had already fallen asleep.

Seven

Mike couldn't seem to take his eyes off of his son. From the moment he'd held the baby in his arms at the hospital, he'd felt an incredible mix of love and pride and joy. Nothing had prepared him for the overwhelming sense of protectiveness that had washed through him.

David was so tiny, so astonishingly fragile, yet the boy could bellow loud enough to be heard from the hospital nursery all the way to Jane's room. He was clearly going to be a kid who would make his displeasure known.

Staring down into that tiny face, Mike wondered if his father had felt the same way after the birth of each of his kids. It made him think about the way his father had struggled over the years trying to support his family, trying to protect them, always falling just a little short. He'd seen how defeated his father had looked every time he failed to be promoted, every time another job ended.

Mike had watched, felt his father's pain and vowed never to let that happen, to always go the extra mile for his employers, to be so good at what he did that he'd be indispensible. He knew that was what was driving him now, that it was behind his refusal to give up the opportunity he'd been given in San Francisco. That job enabled him to give Jane and his son anything they wanted or needed. How could he walk away from it?

And yet that job was the very thing that seemed destined to keep them apart.

He sighed, glanced over at Jane and smiled. She was finally asleep. She had shown amazing strength and bravery in the delivery room. He'd been in awe of her. She deserved to sleep for a month and he intended to see to it that she got all the rest she needed for as long as he could. He just wasn't sure how long that would be.

He'd told his bosses he'd be back in San Francisco after the baby's birth. He'd assumed that would be sometime in late January. Since the baby was a few weeks early, they would expect him sooner, probably right after the first of the year.

He couldn't help wondering what Jane's reaction was going to be when he said he had to go. He wanted desperately for her to come with him, but nothing in the past couple of weeks had indicated she'd softened her stance against leaving her home. And he knew that jobs as satisfying and challenging as the one he had in San Francisco were too few and far between to walk away from.

Was he being selfish to want to hold onto that kind of career satisfaction and financial security for his family? Or was it Jane who was at fault? One thing was for certain: Neither of them seemed willing to break the stalemate. Love, which supposedly conquered everything, couldn't seem to make a dent in this.

The door to Jane's hospital room opened and a nurse stepped in just as the baby began to whimper in his arms again.

"Just in the nick of time, I see," the woman said, reaching for the baby. "I'll take him for his bottle and put him down in the nursery so you and your wife can get some rest."

Mike relinquished his son with reluctance.

The nurse grinned. "Don't worry. I'll bring him back first thing in the morning. I promise. Believe me, you'll be glad you've had a full night's sleep tonight, once you get him home. This may be the last you have for some time to come."

Mike sighed when they'd gone. She had no way of knowing that his sleepless nights would be over in a couple of weeks at most. Then Jane would be left with the full burden of two a.m. feedings and pacing the floor with a cranky baby.

How could he let that happen? How could he possibly leave the two of them behind and go back to San Francisco? What kind of pleasure and satisfaction could he take from a job that had cost him his brand-new family? What good was financial security if it cost him the very family he was trying to protect?

He was still struggling with that when he realized Jane was awake, watching him. His mouth curved.

"Hey, you, why aren't you sleeping?"

"Where's the baby?" she asked.

"Back in the nursery, so you can sleep. The nurse suggests we both take advantage of the peace and quiet while we can."

"He's okay, though?" she asked, gazing worriedly toward the door.

"He's perfect."

"You're sure?"

"Janie, you saw him. He couldn't be healthier or more beautiful."

She struggled up. "I want to see him."

He recognized the stubborn jut to her chin and gave up the fight. "Let me get you a robe. Donna ran out and brought one back from the mall. She said you'd want to wander out of here in the middle of the night and you couldn't do it with your backside showing through that indecent hospital gown."

"I knew there was a reason she was my best friend."

Mike wrapped the robe around her, then tucked his arm around her waist. "Ready? Do you want me to get a wheelchair?"

As he'd anticipated, she frowned at the idea.

"I can walk," she insisted, setting out a little stiffly.

Outside the nursery window, she scanned the bassinets until her gaze fell on their son. "There he is, Mike. Look, he's blowing little bubbles in his sleep."

"Just like you," he teased.

She regarded him with indignation. "I do not."

"Sure, you do. I was just sitting there watching you. You're both adorable when you sleep."

"Mike Marshall, you are a bald-faced liar."

He chuckled. "Okay, maybe I was wrong about the bubbles, but you do snore."

She swatted him. "You're just saying that so you won't feel so bad about the fact that I haven't let you in my bedroom."

"I was in your bedroom not five minutes ago," he reminded her. "That's how I know for a fact that you snore."

"If you want me to believe that, you'll have to tape-record it."

"Then you'll have to let me move into your room with you. It could take several nights to get convincing documentation."

"Oh, no, you don't. If you can't get it in one night, right here in the hospital, then it doesn't happen."

"Come on back to bed. I'll get one of the nurses to come in and witness it firsthand. Will you believe an impartial observer?"

"Not likely," she said, after taking one last look at the baby. "You can charm those women into saying anything you want them to. I saw you wheedle a dinner tray out of one of them."

"That was for you," he protested, walking her slowly down the hall. "I knew you had to be starved."

"The point is you were able to get your way, even though it was way past dinnertime."

"If I'm so good, how come I can't talk you into coming back to San Francisco with me?"

For just an instant, he thought he saw pure longing in her eyes, but then it was gone. She crawled gingerly back into the bed without answering.

"Jane?"

"I can't," she whispered. "I want to, but I can't."

"Couldn't you just give it a try?" he pleaded. "Maybe for a few months? They're not expecting you back at school this year anyway, right? Come home with me and see how it goes. Let me give you the perfect life we always imagined we'd have."

A tear spilled over and washed down her cheek. Mike relented. "Never mind. It's not the time to talk about it."

"I'm sorry."

"Don't be," he said, trying not to blame her for feelings that were so entrenched they might never get past them. He tucked the covers back around her, then brushed a kiss across her forehead. "Get some sleep."

Her eyes drifted closed, then struggled back open. "Mike—"

"Hush. It's okay."

"No, you don't understand. I just wanted to say thank you."

"For what?"

"For being here. For my baby."

"Our baby," he said fiercely. "He's our baby, Janie." But she was already asleep.

The baby's homecoming was as triumphant as if he'd been royalty. It might not have been marked by media attention, but all of Jane's friends were there when Mike drove up.

Inside, Jane found the house decorated for the holidays and the nursery filled with all the supplies the baby could possibly need. Everything was perfect, or would have been if she hadn't had this sick feeling that it was all about to end. She forced a smile when Donna came over with outstretched arms.

"Let me hold my godson," she said.

"Don't go getting any ideas," Darryl warned, coming up behind her. "We've agreed to wait another year."

"I know. That's why I need to hold this one as much as Jane will let me," Donna said.

Mike joined them. "Hand him over," he said. "You'll get your turn when I'm gone."

Jane felt the salty sting of tears at the reminder that

this whole homecoming was bittersweet. It marked a new beginning for her and the baby, but the clock was already ticking toward the end of her brief marriage to Mike. No doubt he'd want to set a divorce in motion before he left. What was the point of staying married when there was going to be an entire continent between them? The baby carried his father's name and that was what this whole sham of a marriage had been about in the first place.

Suddenly she couldn't bear it another minute. She ran from the room. As she let the kitchen door slam behind her, she was dimly aware of Mike's muttered curse, then pounding footsteps chasing after her.

"Jane!"

He caught her heaving shoulders and turned her around. "Oh, baby, don't cry. Dammit, I keep getting it all wrong."

She looked up and caught the tormented expression on his face. "It's not you. It's us. One minute I can almost believe that all of this is real, that we really are a family, just the way I always dreamed we would be. The next I realize it's make-believe."

"It's not make-believe," he said. "It doesn't have to be. I love you, Janie. And you love me. I know you do."

"Yes," she agreed, her voice ragged. "But that doesn't change anything. You're going to leave. You have to do it. I understand that."

He stared deep into her eyes. "Do you? Do you really understand it?"

She nodded. "Yes, but I hate it, Mike. I really hate it."

He gathered her close. "I know, baby. I know. It's just like it was when your dad used to go away, isn't it?"

Startled, she met his gaze. "You know that?"

"Well, of course. Remember, I was the one you used to run to every time he'd go. Not that you ever talked about it, but I could see the hurt in your eyes, the fear that he wouldn't come back. I hated him for doing that to you." He sighed. "And now I'm doing the same damned thing. Telling you I love you one minute, then saying goodbye and walking out the door."

He tucked a finger under her chin and tilted her face up. "There's one difference, though."

"What's that?"

"You can count on me coming back."

Hope stirred inside her. "You'll be back?"

"Whenever I can. Our boy is not going to grow up wondering if his father cares about him. It may not be a perfect arrangement, but I promise you we'll make it work."

Something died inside Jane as she realized what he meant, that the separation would go on forever. "I guess we'll be no different from a million other divorced couples," she said bitterly. "Shipping our child back and forth on a plane."

He stared at her. "Who said anything about a divorce?"

"You did."

"No, what I said was we would make this arrangement work."

She stared at him, appalled by the suggestion. "You expect me to just hang around here, waiting for the moments you can spare us? I don't think so, Mike Marshall. I do not intend to live my life in the same sort of emotional limbo that my mother did. Go or stay, it's your choice. But let me be very clear about one thing, if you go, it will be the end for the two of us. I'll file for divorce the day you get on the plane."

She whirled around and went back inside, making very sure that she was always in the middle of a throng of friends, so Mike couldn't challenge her about her threat. She knew that a confrontation was inevitable. She couldn't ask her friends to hang around all night to prevent it, but for once she felt she was in charge of her own destiny.

If Mike chose to go—and she told herself she was prepared for that possibility—then he was the loser. There would never be anyone who could love him as she did, never be anyone to compare with his firstborn son. Her life was here, and so was his, if only he could recognize it in time.

Eight

Christmas came and went, then New Year's. On the second day of January, Jane was sitting in the nursery rocking the baby, when she caught a glimpse of Mike in the doorway. She could tell from his expression that the time had come and he was going to say goodbye. Tears flooded her eyes and streamed down her cheeks. He saw them and was by her side in an instant.

"Janie, don't cry." He pulled out a handkerchief and dabbed at the dampness on her cheeks.

She shrugged off his touch. "It's okay. Just roller-coaster hormones."

"Is that all?" he asked, watching her worriedly.

She forced a smile. "Of course." She met his gaze evenly. "What about you? You seem upset."

"We can talk about it later." His gaze settled on his son. "How's my boy doing?"

"Your boy has a full tummy and is sound asleep," she said. "I should put him in his crib, but I love sitting here holding him in my arms and rocking him. I still can't quite believe he's real."

A ghost of a smile passed over Mike's face. "Yeah, I know what you mean."

"Want to trade places?"

"Sure."

He said it so eagerly that she laughed. "Here, then. I'll go do the latest mountain of laundry. I never imagined that a guy this little could generate so many dirty clothes."

Mike traded places with her, settling Davey against his chest and humming to him. She would have given anything for a picture of the two of them, but her camera was out of film. They'd gone through three rolls in the past week and she'd neglected to pick up more. She'd have to remind Mike to get some when he picked up the prints later.

Unless he was going to leave before that. That was what he'd been about to tell her. She was sure of it. She wouldn't cry when he said the words. She wouldn't. Why make it harder than it had to be? They'd both known this day was coming.

But knowing it intellectually and facing it were two very different things. She listened in dread for the sound of his footsteps coming from the nursery. When he finally walked into the kitchen a half hour later, she was dry-eyed.

"We need to talk," he said, gesturing toward a chair. When she was seated, he asked, "Want some tea?"

Jane shook her head. Her stomach had knotted the moment she saw him.

Tea wouldn't help. Nothing would.

Mike sat down opposite her and drew in a deep breath. "I'm leaving tomorrow."

Even though she'd anticipated the words, shock rippled through her. "I see."

"But I have a request before I go."

She regarded him warily. "What kind of a request?"

"A few days back you threatened to file for divorce the minute I left. I'd like you to wait."

"Why, Mike? Why wait?"

"Because I don't think we should throw our marriage away like this."

"We're not throwing it away," she said angrily. "It never had a chance."

"And whose fault is that?" he demanded, then closed his eyes, visibly struggling for calm. "I'm sorry. I know it's not your fault or mine. This goes deeper than pure stubbornness. I know that, too. We both have reasons for feeling the way we do."

"Reasons that won't change over time," she said. "We were apart for a whole year and nothing changed."

"Because neither of us made the effort."

"What's different about now? What kind of effort are we supposed to make?" she lashed out. To her shock, she thought she saw tears in his eyes.

"Please, Janie, don't write us off yet," he pleaded. "There has to be some way to make it work. I have to leave here believing that."

"I wish I could say I agreed with you, but I don't. Some impasses just can't be broken. Why prolong this?"

"Because we made vows," he said fiercely. "Despite the circumstances, those vows meant something to me. If they meant anything at all to you, then you have to give us more time." He gazed at her intently. "Did they? Did they mean anything at all to you?"

"You know they did," she said in a whisper. "They meant everything." He stood up and gathered her into his arms. "Then you have to wait. Don't file those papers, Janie. Please."

Engulfed by the pure masculine scent of him, surrounded by his heat and his strength, she couldn't have refused him anything at all.

"I'll wait," she said at last. "For whatever good it will do, I'll wait."

If there was any shred of hope at all for the three of them to be together always, she would cling to it.

In the middle of March, Jane had a call from the principal of her school. The teacher who'd taken over her classes was ill. The principal wanted to know if there was any chance that Jane could come back to finish out the school year.

"Of course," she said eagerly. Staying home was driving her batty. Davey didn't need her attention every second. And if she was going to be a single working mom, the sooner she set the pattern for it, the better. "When do you need me?"

"Monday will be fine."

"Thank you. I'll be looking forward to it," Jane said. Only after she'd hung up did she realize that in accepting the job, she was conceding that she would never leave home to join Mike.

Donna stopped by later that afternoon. "I hear you're coming back to work on Monday."

"The grapevine in that school always was remarkable."

"What's Mike going to say about it?"

"Mike doesn't have anything to do with it. He's in California. I'm here. I always intended to go back to work. This is just a little sooner than I planned."

"But you still haven't filed for divorce and neither has he. Shouldn't you talk this over?"

"No. It's only a matter of time. We talk almost every day but nothing's really changed. He keeps holding me to the promise I made before he left, that I wouldn't file for a divorce until we agreed that there was no chance we could make it work."

"Is he coming back any time soon?"

"He hasn't mentioned it and I haven't asked."

"Do you miss him?"

Jane sighed. "My heart breaks every time I hear his voice. I want him here with me more than anything in the world. And I know it's crazy, but I think Davey misses him, too. He's been fussier since Mike left, as if he knows he's lost someone important."

Donna regarded her sympathetically. "I hate this. I really do. You two belong together."

"I always thought so," Jane agreed. "But maybe Fate had something else in mind."

Jane went back to work the following Monday and quickly settled back into a routine that had once been as familiar to her as breathing. Because it was such a small school, she already knew many of the kids in her class. The substitute teacher's gradebook and detailed progress reports on each student filled in what she didn't know.

By the end of the first week, she felt as if she'd put her life in order and resigned herself to the idea that Mike would never be a part of it. She even dropped by Annie's Baby Boutique after school on Friday just as she had before she'd gotten pregnant with Davey. Now, though, she could shop to her heart's content for her own child.

At home, the minute she stepped inside, she sensed

that something was different even before she spotted the pile of suitcases in the hallway. Her heart slammed against her chest, then began an unsteady rhythm.

"Mike?" She hurried down the hall toward the nursery, knowing instinctively that was where he would be. "Mike?"

He was in the rocker with the baby in his arms. The sight of the two of them made her breath catch in her throat.

He glanced up. "Hey, pipe down, will you? I've just gotten him settled down."

"And what have you done with the baby-sitter?"

"Sent her home. The kid and I don't need any help."

She grinned at him. "Is that so? Did she, by any chance, feed and change him before she left?"

"Of course."

"No wonder you're so confident, then." He did look confident, too. He also stared at her as if he couldn't wait to devour her. She felt the heat of that look all the way across the room.

Finally she dared to ask, "How long will you be here?"

His gaze locked with hers. "For good."

This time she was pretty sure she stopped breathing altogether. "For good?" she repeated in a shaky voice. "Why? How?"

"Later," he said. "Right now, how about getting over here and giving your husband a proper welcome-home kiss?"

Dazed, Jane crossed the room and bent down to brush a quick kiss across his brow.

He scowled at her. "You call that a proper kiss?"

She grinned. "That's exactly what I call it—very, very proper."

"Then I guess what I'm after is something else entirely." He reached up and curved his hand around her neck and drew her back down. When their lips were barely a hairbreadth apart, he paused. "I love you, Janie."

And then he kissed her and there was nothing the least bit proper about it. In fact, the kiss devoured, sending heat and need flooding through her. When he finally released her, she frowned at him.

"You'd better have meant it," she said.

"Meant what?"

"You'd better be staying for good, because I'd have to slug you if you were kidding around."

"No kidding," he vowed. "In fact, I think I'll just put Davey here in his crib so I can take his mommy to her bed and prove just exactly how serious I am."

The minute he had their son settled in for his nap, he turned and the fire in his eyes set off butterflies in Jane's stomach. When he swept her into his arms and headed across the hall to her room, she pushed aside every last reservation she had and let the sensation of being in his arms overwhelm her.

Explanations, everything could wait until later, she thought as she gave herself up to the tender glide of his hand over her flesh. His caresses, the heavenly feel of his mouth on her breasts, the wicked demand of his fingers probing her moist, secret places, all of it carried her off to a place where everything was perfect and love was eternal.

Slick fire raged between them as their bodies joined. Each thrust lifted her higher until she was crying out for release, crying out for Mike, then shuddering as he took her over the top and beyond.

Tears streamed down her cheeks when it was over, tears of joy, but Mike stared at her with concern.

"Janie, what is it? Did I hurt you?"

He started to move away, but she held him tightly. "No, please. It's just that we've never made love like this before. It's never felt like this."

"Like what?"

"Like the start of forever." She searched his face. "That is what it meant, isn't it?"

He brushed the damp tendrils of hair back from her cheeks. "Yes, that's what it meant."

She sighed then and fell asleep. For the first time in months, she slept peacefully.

Mike stared down at the woman in his arms and wondered how he could ever have convinced himself to leave her. This was where he belonged. It had taken some ingenuity on his part and a whole lot of understanding and cooperation on the part of his bosses, but he'd finally found a way to get back to her.

Jane sighed contentedly and opened her eyes. She reached for his face and touched her fingers to his cheek, then smiled.

"You are here. This is real."

"It's real."

"You aren't going back to San Francisco?"

"I'll have to go occasionally, but this will be home."

"You didn't quit your job?"

"I threatened to." He described the scene in which he'd told his bosses that he was going to have to make the most difficult—most impossible choice of his life.

"Then I offered them an alternative. I suggested we open an East Coast office. We're getting more and more business on this coast anyway. It made perfect sense."

A smile of pure joy spread across her face as she grasped the implications. "And it made perfect sense to put you in charge of it," she guessed.

"That's pretty much it. The office will be in northern Virginia, but the commute's workable. Once in a while I may have to stay over up there if a meeting's going to run very late, but they'll be paying me enough that we could even get a small apartment if we wanted to." He grinned at her. "Our own private little love nest."

"Now that's an interesting spin to put on a place you'll need because you're tied up in business meetings," she teased.

"I figure that's only one use we can put it to. Once we have a bunch of kids underfoot, we're going to need a little privacy every once in a while. We can go to the Kennedy Center, have a late-night supper, then spend all night making love and come back to our kids like a couple of rejuvenated newlyweds. What do you think?"

She knelt on the bed beside him and peppered his face with kisses. "I think that you are the most inventive, smartest man on the face of the earth. You've done the impossible."

He traced a line from the pulse at her throat down between her breasts and on beyond. "Just wait till you see what I can do with the possible," he said.

The first sparkle he'd seen in ages lit her eyes. "Dare you to show me," she said at once.

So he did.

* * * * *

Keep reading for a special sneak peek at
Seaview Inn, *from #1* New York Times *bestselling author Sherryl Woods. Coming in June 2024!*

One

Hannah Matthews prided herself on being sensible and responsible. A single mom and a public relations executive handling several very demanding but fascinating clients, she was the person to turn to in any crisis. She claimed there wasn't a superstitious bone in her body, but she was beginning to wonder if there wasn't something to the old adage that things happened in threes, especially bad things. She was also losing her faith that God never gave a person more than they could handle, because she was definitely on overload.

Not quite three months past her final chemo treatment for breast cancer and less than a month after her mother's death from the very same disease, here she was back in a town she hadn't been able to flee fast enough, standing in front of the bed-and-breakfast that had once been her much-despised home. Worse, she was facing the arduous prospect of trying to convince her stubborn eighty-five-year-old grandmother that it was time to move into an assisted-living community and sell Seaview Inn. Life couldn't get much more stressful than this, or if it could, she didn't want to find out how.

"Hannah, why are you just standing out there day-dreaming?" her grandmother demanded from behind the inn's screen door, her tone every bit as querulous and demanding as Hannah remembered from her last visit home. "As hot as it is, leaving this front door wide open is a waste of air-conditioning. And why weren't you here this morning? You *told* me you'd be here this morning. I've been sitting on the porch watching for you most of the day. The heat finally drove me inside."

Hannah bit back a sigh and grabbed the handle of her suitcase to pull it along behind her. "My flight was delayed, Gran. Remember, I called you from the airport in New York to let you know?"

Her grandmother's faded hazel eyes filled with confusion, yet another recent change from her once astute demeanor. "You did? Are you sure?"

"I'm sure, Gran, but it doesn't matter now. I'm here."

"And about time, too," her grandmother added with a little *humph.*

Hannah placed an arm around her grandmother's frail shoulders and gave her a peck on the cheek. "You look good, Gran. Are you feeling okay?"

Truthfully, her grandmother looked as if a strong wind would blow her away. She'd lost weight she could ill afford to lose. Her face, filled with eighty-five years of lines and wrinkles, was sallow. Losing her only child, Hannah's mother, had taken a lot out of her. Her friends in town had called Hannah to let her know that Jenny had rarely left the house since the funeral. She'd been skipping the meetings of her quilting circle and, more telling, Sunday services at church. They were worried about her. "She's just going to fade away, die of a broken heart all alone, if you ask me," Rachel Morrison had said when she'd called.

Hannah hadn't missed the critical note in Rachel's voice, the unmistakable hint that Hannah had been irresponsible to run off right after her mother's burial and leave her grandmother to cope with her grief and Seaview Inn all on her own.

Though her family knew what she was struggling with, Hannah had been unwilling to share her own cancer crisis with any of these well-meaning neighbors. She'd been unable to defend her actions in any way that might have satisfied them. How could she possibly tell them that seeing her mom's quick decline and painful death while in the middle of her own treatment had left her terrified? She hadn't been able to get away from Seaview and the memories of her mother's final days fast enough. She believed that a positive attitude was an essential ingredient for surviving cancer, but it was almost impossible to maintain that attitude in the face of her mother's death from a recurrence that had come less than two years after she'd first been diagnosed.

So, instead of explaining, Hannah had succumbed to guilt and dutifully taken the remaining two weeks of leave she'd accumulated during years of ignoring vacation time and socking away sick days to come here. That two weeks was all that was left after the time taken for her mastectomy and then the chemo, which had knocked her for a loop despite her stubborn determination to pretend she was just fine. Her boss had grudgingly agreed to let her off, but he'd made it plain he wasn't one bit happy about the timing.

In less than twenty-four hours, she'd flown back to Florida, rented a car, driven for an hour, and then taken a ferry out to Seaview Key, a tiny island community of less than a thousand full-time residents just off Florida's west coast. Once there, she'd had to deal with traffic jams caused by winter tourists. All of which, given her current frame of mind, was trying, to say the least.

Worse, she had exactly fourteen days to convince her grandmother to sell the inn—which was also the family's longtime home—and move into a retirement community where she'd be well cared for. Since Grandma Jenny's parents had opened Seaview Inn when the island had been little more than a fishing village reached by boat, Hannah had a hunch her work was cut out for her. Her grandmother sometimes exhibited a tenacious streak of sentimentality that overrode common sense.

"I know it's only four o'clock, but we'll eat supper now," Grandma Jenny declared. "I missed lunch and I'm hungry. You can unpack your things later." She glanced at the suitcase Hannah had left at the bottom of the staircase that led up to the family's private quarters on the left and to the sprawling wing of guest rooms on the right. "Didn't bring much, did you? You having the rest of your things sent?"

Hannah stared at her blankly. "Why would I do that?"

"Because you're moving home, of course." Jenny's tone was matter-of-fact. "I've told everyone in town who's been asking that we'd have the inn up and running again in another week or two, a month at the outside. While your mother was sick, we let a few things slide, but with the two of us working that should give us enough time to get things shipshape, don't you think so? There's still a couple of good months of the winter season left, and we'll draw some folks from the mainland in April and May. Of course, a lot of our regulars had to make other arrangements, but they'll be back with us next year, I'm sure."

There were so many things wrong with her grandmother's assumptions, Hannah couldn't decide where to start. It didn't matter, anyway, because Grandma Jenny hadn't waited for a reply. She was already heading toward the kitchen at a clip that belied the reported evidence of her declining health. In fact, Hannah very much suspected that Grandma Jenny would outlive her and do it with gusto.

All during their early supper of broiled snapper and fresh tomatoes and strawberries from the local farmer's market, Grandma Jenny continued to bombard Hannah with her plans for reopening Seaview Inn as quickly as possible. She was as alert and strong-willed as ever.

"You can put that PR experience of yours to good use," she told Hannah. "Get some ads running up north. A lot of our regulars in Ohio and Michigan who come later in the season need to know our doors are open again. Maybe you can even do something on the Internet. I hear that's the best place to advertise these days. Or we can send postcards. I have the addresses for most of the customers who've stayed here in the past few years. Had 'em back to the beginning, but I figure those people are mostly dead and gone. What do you think?"

Hannah put down her fork and tried to find the right words to tell her grandmother that instead of spending time and money on advertising, they needed to be thinking about finding a good real estate agent. Then it occurred to her that a little renovating would give the place the kind of curb appeal needed to result in a quicker sale. Maybe she didn't have to discuss selling it just yet. She could wage that battle another day, when she wasn't quite so exhausted.

"I'll think about it," she said at last. "First thing tomorrow, you and I can take a look and see what needs to be done, okay?"

"Why wait?" Gran said, bouncing up, her eyes sparkling with enthusiasm. "Daylight might be scarce at the end of January, but we've got an hour or so till the sun goes down. We can check out the exterior first. I've been thinking a new coat of paint should be the first order of business, something bright and cheerful, maybe a nice turquoise with white trim."

Hannah winced, envisioning a garish result that would rob the inn of whatever tiny scrap of class it had.

"Well, come on," her grandmother called back. "Daylight's wasting."

With a sigh, Hannah followed her outside.

Over the years, the inn had grown from the original sprawling, two-story beach house that had been built in the thirties as a private home. Because of its size and her great-grandparents' enthusiasm for meeting people, they'd opened their spare rooms to paying guests. That first experimental season had been so successful, they'd officially named it Seaview Inn and expanded over the next few years, adding one section in the early forties, another in the fifties, operating much like the bed-and-breakfasts that had come along later.

Unfortunately, there hadn't been much attention to architectural detail in the additions. Wings jutted out haphazardly, one on each side, angled so that the guest rooms on the right and the big formal dining room on the left, with its soaring windows and hodgepodge collection of antique tables and chairs, and the second-floor family quarters all had a view of the beach across the road. To Hannah's disapproving eye, it looked like a cross between a halfway decent home and a seedy motel.

It would take more than a coat of paint, no matter the color, to fix it.

Her favorite part was the porch, which stretched across the front of the original house with a row of white rockers and a collection of antique wicker chairs with fading flowered cushions. In past years there had been hanging baskets of flowers, but this year neither her mother nor grandmother had had the time or energy to spare on such things.

As a child, Hannah had had tea parties with all her dolls on the porch. Sometimes her mom and her grandmother had joined her. Those afternoons had been the best. Later, as a teenager, the porch had been a place for sharing dreams and plans with her friends over sodas and snacks. Eventually her first kiss had been in the shadows on the porch.

Now, bathed in the light of a spectacular sunset, the inn didn't look as bad as it had at first glance. She could almost see its idiosyncratic charm and understand why her grandmother wanted to keep it open and in the family. The problem was that Grandma Jenny couldn't possibly do it alone and there was no one in the family to help her. Hannah didn't want to leave New York, especially with her team of physicians there, to say nothing of the demanding career she loved. Her twenty-year-old daughter, Kelsey, would probably wind up staying in California once she completed her studies at Stanford. Why keep the inn now, only to sell it to strangers in a few years, anyway? Her grandmother deserved to enjoy whatever years were left to her, not to spend them working her fingers to the bone waiting on strangers.

Hannah turned and caught her grandmother eyeing her speculatively.

"It's a good time of day, isn't it?" Grandma Jenny said quietly, her expression nostalgic. "Your grandfather and I spent many an evening out here watching the sunset with music drifting out the downstairs windows. And before that, my parents would spend their evenings doing the same thing. We didn't sit inside and stare at a TV screen the way folks do today. We talked, getting to know the people who stayed here. We enjoyed the beauty God gave us in this place." Her gaze met Hannah's. "You loved it, too, once. Do you remember that? There were nights we could hardly drag you home from the beach." Suddenly Hannah remembered being maybe five or six and working all day on a sand castle, then being called inside. The next morning she'd rushed across the road to see her handiwork, only to discover that the tide had washed it away overnight.

It had been her first hard lesson in the fact that some things simply didn't last, no matter how well built and solid they seemed. Sometimes it was the foundation that mattered, not the structure, and sand had a way of shifting underfoot, much as her own parents' marriage had crumbled a few years later.

As the years had passed and she'd developed more insights, there'd been little question in her mind that after the divorce her mother had felt trapped here by circumstances. What else could she do with a daughter not yet in her teens and no work experience beyond the family inn? "I remember," she said at last, but it was said in a faintly bitter tone that drew a sharp glance from her grandmother.

"There *were* good times, Hannah, whether you choose to remember them that way or not."

"I wonder if Mom felt that way after Dad left. Wasn't there a time in her life when she dreamed of going away and doing something else? He got to run away from her and from all of his responsibilities, but she was stuck."

"What are you suggesting?" her grandmother asked indignantly. "That I kept her here when she wanted to go? Nothing could be further from the truth. She loved it here. She knew it was the best place to raise a child, surrounded by family and friends."

"Dad obviously didn't love it," Hannah said.

"Oh, Hannah, that's not so. Surely by now you've learned that relationships are complicated. Your parents were happy for a time, and then they weren't. It had nothing to do with Seaview Key or the inn."

Hannah didn't waste her breath trying to argue. How

could she? She'd been so young, just on the verge of adolescence. It was entirely possible that she'd been totally oblivious to whatever rifts there had been in her parents' marriage. She relented now just to keep peace. "I suppose."

Her grandmother's shoulders seemed to sag. "I need to sit down," she said flatly, clutching the railing tightly as she climbed the steps to the porch. She sank into her favorite rocker as the sun slowly slid into the waters of the Gulf of Mexico, leaving the sky painted with streaks of orange and gold.

"Gran, are you okay?"

"Just a little tired. You go on in, if you want. Get yourself settled. I'll just sit here for a while and enjoy the evening. Leave the dishes. I'll do them when I come inside. Won't take any time at all."

"But we haven't even started the list of renovations you want to do," Hannah protested, feeling vaguely guilty for dampening her grandmother's high spirits.

"You said it yourself. Tomorrow's soon enough."

Oddly reluctant to go inside and leave her grandmother alone, Hannah stood in the doorway for a few minutes.

As twilight fell and a breeze stirred, the streetlight on the corner came on, illuminating the porch and yard. That was when Hannah noticed the tears glistening on her grandmother's cheeks.

"Mom, what on earth are you doing in Florida?" Kelsey demanded when she called Hannah's cell phone later that night and woke Hannah out of a sound sleep. "I called your office earlier and your secretary told me you'd taken time off again to go to Seaview. I've been trying to call all day, but you must have had your phone turned off. When you didn't return my calls, I got worried. Is Grandma Jenny okay?"

Hannah sat on the side of the bed, almost regretting that she'd remembered to turn the phone back on before going to sleep. There had been five increasingly impatient messages from her boss and three from Kelsey. For once, she'd ignored them all, grateful that it was too late to call the office and deciding she really didn't want to discuss this situation with Kelsey just yet. Now she had no choice.

"You mean besides her delusion that I'm going to give up my career and move back here to run the inn?" she replied.

"Oh, boy," Kelsey muttered. "Is she serious?"

"She spent an hour at dinner talking about how we need to spruce this place up and get it open again in two weeks," Hannah said. "I'd say she's serious."

"But you're not going to do it, are you? You hate Seaview Key and the inn."

"Of course I'm not going to do it," Hannah said emphatically, then sighed. "Actually, I was thinking it might be a good idea to do a few renovations."

"But why, if she's not going to open the inn? You know she can't manage it alone."

Hannah hesitated. "I know," she said at last.

Kelsey sucked in a breath. "You want her to sell it, don't you? Mom, that will break her heart. You can't do that to her."

"What choice do I have?" Hannah asked defensively.

"None, I suppose," Kelsey admitted, "but I hate this, Mom."

"I know. So do I, but I can't stay here. I just haven't figured out how I'm going to explain that to your great grandmother. You know how she is once she gets an idea into her head."

"A lot like you," Kelsey said.

"Yes, well, that is the problem, isn't it?" she said wryly. Suddenly it occurred to her that there had to be a crisis of some kind for Kelsey to be calling from college in the middle of the week. "Enough about what's going on here. I'll figure out something. Tell me what's up with you."

Kelsey hesitated. "Maybe this isn't a good time. We can talk about it when you're back in New York after you get things straightened out down there."

A sense of dread settled in the pit of Hannah's stomach. "Isn't a good time for what?" she prodded.

"You're sure you don't want to wait and talk about this another time?" Kelsey asked, sounding oddly hopeful.

"Now," Hannah commanded.

"Okay, then. Remember how I told you at Christmas that school pretty much sucks?"

"And I said you were just going through a rough patch," Hannah recalled.

"Well, it's more than a rough patch, Mom. Don't freak out, okay? I've really thought about this and it's what I need to do right now. I've decided to quit college, come home to New York and get a job."

Hannah's grip on the cell phone tightened. "In your

junior year?" she said, her voice rising despite her best attempt to remain calm. "Are you crazy?"

"I knew you wouldn't understand," Kelsey said petulantly, sounding like a spoiled child rather than the responsible young adult she normally was.

"No, I don't understand. And unless you've got an explanation that includes full-time employment several steps above flipping burgers, I'm not likely to understand. We had a deal. If I went into debt to get you into Stanford, the school of your dreams, you would stick it out and get your degree in graphic design, no matter what. Remember that?"

"I remember," Kelsey said meekly. "But, Mom—"

Hannah cut her off. "No, there is no *but, Mom*. You got into Stanford. I've paid for three years at Stanford, and you are finishing at Stanford. Period. You don't get to back out of the deal now."

"I can't stay here."

Years ago, after her divorce, Hannah had learned the value of being stern and unyielding. Otherwise, even as a toddler, her strong-willed daughter would have run roughshod over her. She called on that skill now.

"Of course, you can stay. If your courses are too hard, if that's what this is about, you can consider dropping one of them, but you're not dropping out, and that's final." She told herself all her daughter needed was a pep talk. She'd probably gotten something below an A on a pop quiz and decided she was heading for failure. "Come on, kiddo. You can do this. You're smart. You're more than halfway to getting your bachelor's degree. You just need to park your butt in the library and do whatever amount of studying it takes to get out of there next year with a degree."

"You don't understand," Kelsey said.

"Of course I do, sweetie. We all hit bumps in the road from time to time. We can't let them throw us off course."

"Mom, this isn't that kind of bump in the road. I'm pregnant," Kelsey blurted.

If Hannah hadn't already been sitting down, she would have fainted dead away and probably cracked open her skull when she hit the floor. Apparently things *could* get worse. And now she knew how.

Get 3 FREE REWARDS!

We'll send you 2 FREE Books plus a FREE Mystery Gift.

FREE
Value Over
$20

Both the **Romance** and **Suspense** collections feature compelling novels
written by many of today's bestselling authors.